MAYHEM AND MADNESS

CHRONICLES OF A TEENAGED SUPERVILLAIN

J. A. DAUBER

HOLIDAY HOUSE · NEW YORK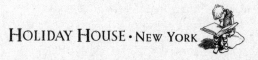

For my parents
On their fiftieth anniversary
In love and in awe

Library of Congress Cataloging-in-Publication Data

Names: Dauber, Jeremy Asher, author.
Title: Mayhem and madness : chronicles of a teenaged supervillain / by
   Jeremy Dauber.
Description: First edition. | New York : Holiday House, [2019] | Summary:
   When sixteen-year-old Bailey discovers a secret lab beneath his house,
   complete with an outdated Macintosh computer and mechanized
   supervillain armor, he believes he might be able to find his father who
   disappeared six years ago.
Identifiers: LCCN 2018040564 | ISBN 9780823442553 (hardcover)
   Subjects: | CYAC: Supervillains—Fiction. | Robots—Fiction. | Family
   life—Fiction.
Classification: LCC PZ7.1.D3358 May 2019 | DDC [Fic]—dc23
LC record available at https://lccn.loc.gov/2018040564

I did *not* expect to be spending the night of my winter formal hiding from the police.

I mean, I've never even been given a suspicious *look* before.

Yes, sure, sixteen-year-old boys can be prime targets for the neighborhood-watch list. Even skinny ones like me. But I don't do stupid stuff like vandalize mailboxes, or spray-paint walls, or even smoke.

Well, not stupid stuff like that, anyway.

And these aren't local police. These are SWAT teams. Backed by the National Guard and who knows what else. I think they may be calling in the army, even special forces. I'm not an expert, but my on-board computers are identifying highly coordinated movement. These aren't amateurs.

I hope I don't have to hurt any of them. I said I wasn't going to do that anymore.

At least, I don't want to.

I'm dictating this into my phone. There are other ways I could do it, with what I've got, but given what I've learned, simpler is better. I'm sure that if—when?—I don't make it out of this, the government will confiscate everything I've ever touched. But maybe the recording will help me at my trial, or juvenile hearing, or whatever.

Not that they'll ever let anything like that happen. At least not in public. I'll end up in some supermax prison or one of those CIA black sites being waterboarded every day to try to get me to give up information about the Bloody Front or Mr. Jones.

But at least I got a date out of it, right?

Which reminds me: Rebecca's probably sitting at home waiting for me. I'd like to think she's crying her eyes out, but who am I kidding. Hard enough to believe she agreed to go out with me in the first place.

Maybe I can make it up to her once I hit another bank vault?

No. I'm not going to do that anymore, either.

Let's be honest: all of this is pretty much beside the point. I hear a helicopter—no, helicopters—and they're definitely not reporting on weather and traffic. And if I'm reading this panel correctly, it's telling me there's stealth technology being employed in the area—I mean, aside from mine. If the government is moving F-35s into my neighborhood, how long can I really have left?

I better get this recorded while there's still time. I'm going to try to tell the whole story. From the beginning. Put it in order, with the whens and wheres laid out nice and neat. Almost like one of those outlines Mrs. Delgado keeps wanting us to make in English class.

I'll try not to leave anything out. Even if it makes me look like a monster. And I think some of it does.

No one's going to believe it, of course, even if they do get to hear it, but some of the evidence speaks for itself.

I meant well.

You have to believe that.

THREE MONTHS AGO

The thing you should know about my dad is that he was relentlessly normal. The only weird thing about him was the way he disappeared without a trace seven years ago.

He was an assistant regional service manager for one of the big chain stores. I'm not going to say which one, but we got great discounts on electronic goods right around Thanksgiving and Christmas. I'm sure he had hobbies, but I don't know what they were. He loved my mom, and used to give her a kiss or a squeeze as they maneuvered around the kitchen, enough for me to guess they still—well, you know—but not enough to be gross or embarrassing. He never raised his voice, except to remind Mom that there was no smoking inside the house. He was a fanatic about it, ever since I had had an asthma scare when I was three—or so I'd been told.

Absolutely, totally, normal.

He was good at the dad thing, too, until he vanished. We played this rhyming game when I was little where I would have to complete a rhyme with a part of my body. Like: "It's something everybody else can see, the middle of your leg it's got a—" and then he'd tickle it.

We would spend hours building those Playmobil and Lego kits together, sprawled out on the floor of our guest room. The only time I ever heard my dad curse was when he stepped on one of the Legos, hopped up in the air, and then landed right on another piece. My mom was there, and I could see that she wanted to warn him about language, but she was laughing too hard. So was he, and so was I.

Later, I got into the Beatles, which made him really happy. We made up a new game where we'd have to identify one of their songs using the fewest words. I still remember stumping him with "is not," which, believe it or not, appears only once in all their lyrics. It's in "Tomorrow Never Knows," in case you were wondering.

Like I said, he hated smoking, so I can't use the "he went out for cigarettes and never came back" line. Knowing what I know now, of course, I can't use any line at all. I just assumed he was in some terrible accident and that he'd turn up in a hospital, face wrapped in bandages, wallet missing, identifiable by a birthmark only my mom knew about. It was the only explanation for something so ... abnormal.

I was in fourth grade, but I remember the whole thing sharp and clear. Came home from school, started homework, Mom got home, asked where Dad was, I said he wasn't back yet, Mom grumbled because it was Dad's turn to start dinner, she waited, we ordered sushi, I could see Mom rehearsing what she was going to say to Dad, it got late, Dad didn't come,

Mom tried calling his phone for the fifth, tenth, fifteenth time, I couldn't go to sleep, I went to sleep.

The next day I stayed home from school, and the day after that. I don't particularly want to talk about the police, given my current circumstances. I *will* say, looking back, they seemed as caring, professional, and committed as possible given that they clearly assumed my dad had skipped out on us.

So *that* sucked.

You probably need to know a bit about my house for this next part to make sense. It's not an old house, but it's not new, either: just your average ranch on a half-acre lot surrounded by other ranches that look pretty similar. We're in this part of town that the real estate agents like to call "in transition." It was built back after World War II when the plastics plant started up and they needed workers, but then things got kind of sketchy when the plant was automated and they let a lot of those workers go. Some people moved closer to the center of town, but we didn't, so I grew up surrounded by empty houses. I used to think that was just bad luck or something, that Mom and Dad had made a mistake when they chose our house and we couldn't afford to move.

Looking back, I'm not so sure.

It's just me, no brothers or sisters, and we never did do much with the guest room. There's a couch, and a desk with an old computer, and wedged in against the wall is a treadmill my mom and dad would occasionally get on after the holidays. I was more of an outdoor runner myself, although

I tended to stick to the school track: I'd gotten shin splints once after hitting the pavement too hard, definitely not an experience I wanted to repeat.

But then there was this one rainy Sunday three months ago.

My mom was watching TV in the living room, smoking one cigarette after another, and I had a paper I was seriously putting off waiting for me in the bedroom. School had just started, junior year, and I was already drowning in homework. I had to get out of the house, but it was pouring, I mean, *pouring*. Finally I announced that I was off to use the treadmill, since my lungs were going to need all the help they could get. And before she could answer I stormed into the guest room and slammed the door shut, knocking a framed picture of my parents off the wall.

That accident: verification step one. As it turned out.

I thought I heard a *click* as the door closed behind me, but I was already on the treadmill starting to jog, then sprint, then run.

So quickly, and so angrily, that the stupidest thing in the world happened: I slipped.

I didn't fall *off* the treadmill. My reflexes were too good for that. I grabbed the window frame right next to the treadmill for support, squeezing exactly the right—or wrong—place.

Verification step two.

Immediately, the small shag rug next to the treadmill slithered under the couch as a trapdoor opened to reveal an entrance to the basement.

Here's the thing, though. We live in a ranch house. We don't *have* a basement.

But there it was: a circular opening, about the size of a manhole, leading down from our guest room into who-knows-where. It was concrete. Machine-smoothed. And, judging from the way the ladder leading down was rusted, it'd been there for a while. I tried to remember how long we'd lived in the house, and couldn't remember exactly. Since before I started elementary school. More than a decade, I was sure.

Is it weird that I didn't call my mom in? I think it's like— and I hope this never happens to you—if you discover evidence around the house of your parents engaging in, uh, adult activities, what you do *not* do is go over to one of them and tell them you've found the stuff from their drawer or on their hard drive or whatever. No, what you do, of course, is ignore the whole thing, forget about it, banish the images that have entered your consciousness, and never, ever bring it up for the rest of your natural life.

Now, this wasn't the same thing. At all. But there was a similar sense of the . . . forbidden.

Maybe that was why I didn't call Caroline right away. Which is what I would normally have done. But I had the feeling that this was something private. A secret.

Family business.

I think that was it. It's hard to remember. Only three months ago, this was. But it seems like years.

I took a deep breath and looked down into the hole. It was dark and I couldn't see much, but really, what choice did I have? Maybe you have a different opinion, maybe you think you'd do something else, but then I think you're not being honest with yourself.

I hadn't gone more than three rungs down when a set of lights switched on. I could see the rest of the ladder, now. It went down what looked like at least twenty feet to hit a plain concrete floor. Nothing else down there but the bottom of the ladder. Like some kind of deep, narrow, empty swimming pool.

But that wasn't the thing. This was the thing: someone had dug twenty feet under our house.

We did a unit on local geography in Earth Science class in sixth grade. It's all bedrock around here. Thus the ranch houses. Digging through twenty feet of solid rock: that's just nuts.

When I got to the bottom, I realized I was wrong: there *was* something else down there. You couldn't see it from up top, but there was a door set into the wall. Just a plain old gray steel door with a pull handle, the kind you see around the back of any commercial building. If it wasn't hiding under my house, I wouldn't have paid the least bit of attention to it. Or to the keypad lock next to it, one with letters and numbers like on those old push-button phones.

Considering what I've learned since, I guess the security could have been a lot worse. It could have been a retinal scanner. Even a DNA swab. The keypad must have been state of the art when it was installed and just never got upgraded. Which seems careless. Judging by the past few days, careless seems to run in the family. . . .

A locked steel door is still a locked steel door. I got up close to see if any of the numbers on the keypad looked more faded from repeated pushing—maybe it would help me guess the combination—but they all seemed the same.

And then I thought I heard my mom calling.

I got up that ladder and closed the trapdoor behind me so fast that if the JV coach had seen it he might've thought twice about cutting me during tryouts. I didn't want Mom to come in and find me down a hole that shouldn't exist.

I think even then I'd realized this had something to do with my dad's disappearance.

But as it turned out, whatever guesses I had about how it was involved were wildly off base.

Not one of them, for example, involved me dodging incoming missile fire.

⟋

The next day I skipped school, which wasn't as hard as I thought it would be.

I'd never tried it before. Like I keep telling you, I'm a good kid. Or, I guess, I was.

It just meant doubling back after my mom dropped me off on her way to work, and avoiding the other carpooling moms and dads. A lot of hiding in bushes and behind buildings. I was going to have to make up a Biology test, and turn in a paper late, and probably forge an e-mail from my mom's account, but all that seemed doable. I've known my mom's password for years. She never changes it. Out of sentiment, I think—it's Baileycutie01.

I'm Bailey, by the way. Pleased to meet you.

Now Mom's going to have to change her password.

Probably a good idea, though. There'll be a lot of people interested in her now that she's got two generations of felons in the family. . . .

My phone buzzed as I got back to my house. A text from Caroline.

Where are you? What is going on? Are you sick? I told you that fifth piece of pizza was a bad choice. And the sixth was even worse.

Caroline doesn't use abbreviations in her texts. She says it's because her mom, who is an English professor at the community college, would kill her. I think she likes being different.

I texted her back that I was at home, that I was fine, and that I would see her tomorrow.

Which led to like thirty more texts. Asking questions I didn't know how to answer.

Explain everything tomorrow promise promise, I promised, having no idea if, or how, I'd be able to.

I am going to hold you to that promise, she texted back.

To which I responded *k bye* ☺. Then I put the phone down and took the photo frame off the guest room wall.

Yeah. The photo. I'd noticed it lying on the floor when I climbed out that first time, once I realized Mom hadn't been calling for me. It wasn't until later that night that I wondered if there might be some connection: I was sure I'd touched the window frame plenty of times before, and I'd never seen any tunnel. So when I took the photo off the wall a second time and heard a faint *click* deep inside the walls, I wasn't completely shocked.

I grabbed the window—this time without the surprise

and the scrambling to keep my balance—and the hatch in the floor slid open, pushing the rug aside. I climbed down and stood in front of the door, trying to figure out the pass code. But not trying too hard, really: I got it on the third try, after my dad's birthday and my parents' anniversary. It was his name: G-E-R-R-Y. The door opened, the floodlights went on, and I saw it for the first time.

The armor.

Everyone knows about Mayhem, of course. It's impossible not to know: those pictures of a big mechanical monster landing in front of a bank, crashing through the wall, and tearing off a safe door with its bare hands (well, bare gauntlets, I guess) spread as fast as the Internet would allow back then, before I was born.

And with every robbery he pulled off over the years, the theories got crazier. He was some sort of supersoldier and the robberies were government black-ops tests before they unleashed a squadron of the things on America's enemies. He was a terrorist, trying to trash the American financial system. He was an anarchist who didn't even care about the money—a few large anonymous deposits into various orphanages' bank accounts went a long way toward supporting that theory.

The name "Mayhem" came from one of the first eye-witnesses. He said something to a reporter about how the guy was creating mayhem all over downtown, and the name made its way onto one of those CNN crawls, and it stuck. Mayhem never spoke, so who knew what he thought of it. During recess you used to be able to see kids pretending to play Cops and Mayhem. You could tell who got to be Mayhem—they always had something stuck on their head and they always got away in the end.

Nobody had seen or heard from Mayhem in years, which, of course, led to new theories about what had happened to him. I didn't have much of an opinion. There was enough crime and terrorism and corporate destruction of the environment. In the scheme of things, what was the big deal about one nut who'd managed to put a few iPhones together and make a robot suit? It felt like comic-book stuff.

That said, it became a much bigger deal when the nut in question was your father. Obviously.

I'd never seen my dad do anything more complicated than change the batteries in the smoke alarm. Even working for the big chain store whose name I'm not going to mention, he wasn't one of the guys who built or installed the electronic equipment. He just did paperwork. But given what I saw scattered around the workbenches that lined the room behind the steel door, he'd clearly been taking advantage of the employee discount.

Or—now that I'm thinking about it, trying to put the whole story together, not just live it in the moment—maybe he hadn't. I mean, if he robbed banks, he probably wasn't too worried about taking some stuff home from work without paying, right?

The room was crammed with tools I didn't even recognize, much less know how to use, and the walls had shelves packed with bottles of nasty-looking fluids and boxes heaped with rusty gears and sharp blades.

But it was the armor that was terrifying.

Not its size. Hanging there, from the hooks, it actually didn't look so imposing. More like wet laundry hung up to dry.

But its presence. And its . . . implications.

One supervillain on the planet. Turns out it was my dad.

It's getting warm in here.

The armor's working overtime to keep the shield functioning, so the internal controls aren't running the way they should.

But a little sweat is the least of my worries.

Maybe getting arrested won't be so bad. I *am* a minor, and a citizen. So maybe they won't send me to Guantanamo right away.

That's assuming no one else gets to me first.

I can hear the soldiers shouting at one another: the receptors in the Mayhem armor pick up everything. No one has made visual contact yet—I guess my cloaking device is still working—but they're monitoring energy usage, and I wouldn't be surprised if they black out the neighborhood just to find me. They're out for blood, after all.

I'm going to have to make a move soon, or else just sit here and wait for them. And maybe I'll have a convenient accident as I get taken in. . . . I'm sure nobody'll shed any tears.

Not after Clapham Junction. At least, not after the way the news will cover it.

Such cynicism in one so young, I can hear Mr. Jones saying. Well, it's his fault, isn't it? But I'm getting ahead of my story.

THREE MONTHS AGO

I couldn't spend very long down there.

Mom was at work, yeah, but I had visions of her coming back to the house for something, and—of course—I'd forgotten to close the trapdoor behind me. I just looked around long enough to notice another door and a computer workstation, glowing invitingly. On my way out, I saw a Styrofoam coffee cup, the kind you get at the gas station. I looked inside and grimaced. Judging from the mold, no one had been near it for years.

Which would make sense, of course.

I climbed back up, headed straight to my bedroom, and thought about it. A lot. My dad: Mayhem. It just didn't compute—like when you see old movies of Arnold Schwarzenegger and wonder how that bodybuilder with the oily muscles and the loincloth went on to be the governor of California. I mean, I don't think I'd ever heard my dad raise his voice, and I know I'd never seen him raise a fist. Meanwhile he'd been ripping open safes and brawling with cops? And *winning*?

But where had he gone?

According to the Internet, there hadn't been any Mayhem sightings for years. Most of the remaining online fan communities—my dad had *fans*—were going with the usual theories that he was dead, or he'd been caught, or whatever. There was one commenter who suggested that he'd retired, gotten out while the getting was good, and was sitting on a beach somewhere counting his money. *Nope*, I thought at first, and then, *Who knows?* I mean, if my dad really *was* Mayhem, who's to say he wouldn't abandon us to sit in a cabana with some new young girlfriend? That didn't seem like him at all . . . but then again, neither did using super-advanced technology to create a suit of armor and live a life of crime.

One thing I did know. School was going to be tough to handle the next day. Especially since Caroline was going to want to know exactly what was going on, and I hadn't the vaguest clue of what I was going to tell her.

Luckily, the fight made that irrelevant.

❧

No, not some sort of supervillain fight. Not yet, at least.

That Tuesday I was still just a kid with a massive secret, like half the other kids at school—although theirs are generally about having an abusive uncle or how they're sniffing glue or whatever.

The thing was, I knew Caroline was waiting for me in our usual spot, near the back door to the library, and I hadn't figured out what to say to her, and so I went another way, a different way, and if it hadn't been for that—

Getting ahead of myself again. I have to talk about Caroline first.

I'm not sure what to say about her. But I have to say something. Right? For anyone who hears this? Eventually?

She'd kill me if she heard me waffle like this. *Just spit it out, Bailey*, she'd say.

All right. I will. But I'd better backtrack a minute.

I'm sure you've read those books where the kid with a personal tragedy—say, a missing dad—becomes an outcast and walks around school with a deep sense of resentment that eventually morphs into violence against himself or others. That's not what happened to me. The kids in my town were, by and large, a decent group. So when my dad disappeared I got plenty of sympathy.

Which *sounds* nice, but it stuck to me over the years, like a bad smell. Who wants to hang out with the kid who misses his dad all the time? Mom thought high school would give me the chance to start again, find a new crowd. Right. Everyone on social media knows that starting over is impossible. The only people who think otherwise are grown-ups. Kids know better. Things were pretty much the same as in junior high, only with slightly better desks and lockers on account of the extra money the football team boosters brought in. I wasn't a loner, exactly, but not quite finding my place, either. Nothing really clicked. No one really got me.

Except Caroline. There was always Caroline.

We met back in fifth grade, when we were both miserable orphans.

Not like that—although her parents were divorced and she

lived with her mom, and my situation was . . . well, I guess it was more complicated than I thought at the time. I mean we were both *playing* miserable orphans. In a community children's theater production of *Annie*.

It had been Mom's idea. It'd be fun, she said. I'd be onstage and she'd be behind the scenes, helping with sets or something. I don't have a scrap of musical talent, but it was community theater and they didn't like to turn kids away, I guess. They invented a role for me in the chorus. The only boy.

Caroline was in the chorus, too. I recognized her from school: we were in the same grade, but different classes, so we didn't know each other well. But there were these long rehearsals where we didn't have much to do—and it turned out that Mom and I hardly saw each other, she was always backstage or running errands or something—and so somewhere between "It's the Hard Knock Life" and "You're Never Fully Dressed without a Smile," Caroline and I became friends.

Good friends. Best friends, if either of us ever used that kind of phrase. Though that implies that I have lots of other friends, which is not true. At least not friends who talk to each other about everything, or everything that doesn't include your dad being public enemy number one. Apparently.

But it wasn't just that we had some family stuff sort of in common, the poor sad kids finding each other or anything like that. She had the coolest takes on pop culture. We once spent two weeks watching unboxing videos and she asked me, "Why aren't *boxing* videos a big thing? Is it because everyone will think they're sports stuff and not click on them?" I mean . . . maybe? But who else thinks like that, right?

She played, like, three instruments, and although her singing voice wasn't anything special—part of the reason she'd ended up in the chorus—she had this musical understanding of tone, if you know what I mean, which made her an incredible impersonator. Once she imitated our principal, Mrs. Wentworth, so well it made me snort cherry Diet Pepsi through my nose. Which was both incredibly painful and awesome at the same time.

We talked about serious stuff, too. Whether she should spend Christmas with her dad this year after three years in a row with her mom, and what that might do to her relationship with both parents. How I felt about my mom, how angry I got, sometimes, because she was always at work, and how guilty I felt because I knew those double shifts were what paid for my new sneakers. Whether Caroline should learn the French horn just to put it on her college résumé. (No, we decided.) We even speculated about what we called the TGT, "The Grand Theory," meaning whatever we'd come up with as the newest possible reason for my dad's disappearance.

And she was basically cool with me going on and on about Rebecca until any normal human being would be clawing their eyes out with boredom.

I guess I should say something about Rebecca at this point, too. Rebecca. Who I'd been thinking about obsessively since the first time she showed up to school freshman year with that charm bracelet around her ankle, and I was just . . . well, just gone.

Rebecca was funny. Or at least I assumed so, since her

girlfriends laughed at things she said. I was rarely close enough to hear what they were talking about. She was a talker in class, which I liked—she was smart, and not afraid to show it. Definitely a girly girl, the kind of girl you'd expect to be a cheerleader. But she wasn't. She spent all her time producing our school podcast, interviewing the latest student movers and shakers. Grown-ups, too: she had the local state assemblyman on for a long interview about no-bid recycling contracts. But those were less popular, obviously. In fact, judging from the numbers, I might have been the only kid who listened to that one.

Yes, I listened. To every episode, sometimes more than once. It was the only time I got to hear her voice: warm, smooth, charming. I remember reading the phrase *dead sexy* in some book, and I thought of Rebecca's voice right away. Being the focus, the direct target of that voice, that attention—it would be enough to strike you dead. Me, anyway.

Not that she was all hearts and flowers as an interviewer. She was tough. If she didn't like something or someone, she was not afraid to let them know it. But that didn't bother me. I fantasized about getting the chance to talk to her, one-on-one. I mean, other than my undying feelings for her, what did I have to hide?

Before. I mean before.

At first talking about Rebecca with Caroline had been a little awkward. There had been this one time, early on, sixth grade, maybe, when I guess you could say there was a . . . moment. Once. At Caroline's place. In her mom's den, when her mom went out to the store . . . something could have happened.

But it didn't. That was the thing. We could've kissed, but we didn't. We just stood there in the middle of the room and ignored the conversational pause, and that was that.

I never forgot it, though, so I was wary of mentioning girls until one day when Caroline told me about this guy in band she thought was *Byronic*. Which I had to look up. But once I did, and realized what she was talking about, and that there was no possible world in which the word *Byronic* could apply to me, I felt totally comfortable unloading my Rebecca stuff on her.

Sometimes I think she regretted ever mentioning that guy. Turns out he was a senior so she never saw him again. But she got to hear about Rebecca *all the time*.

Her opinion on the subject of Rebecca and me—after lots and lots of discussion—boiled down to this text message: *?*

Which was, I pointed out to her, not a complete sentence.

She pointed out, in turn, that it was the name of a classic-rock band, and thus a proper noun, and I should know better than to challenge her. I checked and she was right: *?* and the Mysterians.

It was a fair point: *?* After all, Rebecca and I might not have had anything in common. I had no idea. She didn't know I existed, at least not in any meaningful way. But, as Shakespeare or somebody said, to true love there are no impediments.

Well, maybe one impediment.

I should explain about Logan. He is, as you have already guessed, Rebecca's boyfriend. It's a total cliché that he's the captain of the football team, but in both their defenses, that's because (a) it would be very hard for anyone, even Logan, to be immune to Rebecca's charms and (b) who wouldn't want Logan? He is by all accounts a great guy, and he seems to be a good boyfriend. As far as I know he doesn't hook up with anyone behind her back, despite having plenty of opportunities, and he's always looking out for her, giving her little gifts, carrying her books, and he's not afraid to look mushy doing it.

Of course, that could be because no one would dare make fun of him, since he'd pound them into the ground. I'm not big into football, but even I know a linebacker's not generally the team captain. I heard the quarterback was afraid to take him on for the position.

Part of his good boyfriending is being protective of Rebecca from things he thinks would bother her, which includes any person other than him showing any sign of romantic interest. It's not like he's heavy-handed about it or anything. But when you're his size, you don't need to be.

Everyone else has declared her off-limits as a result and they basically slink around cautious and frightened in her presence. That's just not possible for me. Much as I worship at the altar of John, Paul, George, and Ringo, I have to disagree with them: Love isn't all you need. But it's pretty much all I've got.

And so sometimes, on particularly depressing days, I felt the need to be around Rebecca. To just . . . soak in the beauty of her presence. I know I sound pathetic. It wasn't much different from the huffers out by the bleachers, except that I called it love.

Maybe you can see where this is heading.

Usually, I was subtle about it. Super-subtle. So subtle I was pretty sure that neither Logan nor Rebecca noticed my existence. But this time, to avoid Caroline and her inevitable questions, I'd taken an alternate route to Rebecca's locker, where I figured she'd be. Meaning I was approaching Rebecca's locker from a different direction than usual. Around a sharp corner rather than down a long hallway. And when I turned the corner and was suddenly full-on facing her and Logan in the middle of a hot-and-heavy kiss, I hadn't had any time to prepare myself. I didn't—couldn't—look away. I wasn't even jealous. It was more that I was almost . . . awestruck. Lost.

Of course, from Logan's perspective, I was a little perv staring at a private moment between him and his girlfriend.

And something had to be done about that.

NOW. FRIDAY. 8:23 P.M.

I'm sure most of you have tasted your own blood at one time or another. What's surprising to me—and I've had more opportunity than I'd like to sample it recently—is that it doesn't taste terrible.

You'd think evolution would have gotten on that, to make absolutely sure you don't want any of it on the outside for a quick lick or whatever. On the other hand, I guess it figured the pain would take care of that, so why bother.

Right now I'm tasting it because of that last wave of bullets. The armor stopped them, but something sproinged inside because of the impact and I got a gash across my cheek. Maybe I'll have a sexy scar for Rebecca to Instagram to all her friends. Assuming she ever sees me again.

Assuming anyone does.

To be fair to Logan, I'm sure he didn't mean to hurt me that badly. At least not consciously. Especially given what happened later, I want to be clear about this: I don't think he's the kind of guy who beats on people. At all. I think he was a little annoyed, and a little embarrassed, and he just wanted to give me a push, like, *Nothing to see here, move along, stop making this weird.*

But he doesn't know his own strength, and I'm a lot lighter than most of the football players he moves around in practice. Maybe I was light-headed and off-balance from the kiss by proxy. What I definitely was, was unlucky.

The push tripped me up and I stumbled into a locker the wrong way: face-first. I heard this *crack* as my nose moved about three inches to the right of its original location. Logan didn't even notice; he and Rebecca had already headed down the hall. Rebecca did, and I *think* she looked at me with sympathy, but the truth is I'm not sure. My hands were covering my nose and it was a little hard to see.

I wasn't going to make a thing about it. I really wasn't. But it wouldn't stop bleeding—gushing, really—so I had to go to the nurse. When she asked me what had happened, I lied and said I'd walked into a door when I wasn't looking where I was going. The truth didn't come out until Caroline—who was *absolutely furious* at Logan on my behalf when I told her what happened, and was not going to let him get away with it, and was *definitely* not going to accept any excuses or anything on his behalf, even from me—started spreading the actual story. And then it looked like I was too traumatized and scared to admit I'd been bullied. And by the school's greatest hope for a state title. . . .

Well.

Teachers got involved. Coaches got involved. The administration got involved. And thankfully for them, they managed to make sure the press did *not* get involved, which would have destroyed the season, and maybe Logan's career. Which, I have to say—especially given what happened later—he 100 percent would not have deserved. Like I said, he hadn't even noticed what he had done, and he certainly hadn't intended any real harm. When he found out, he was miserable, and genuinely apologetic. That went a long way toward things blowing over. Even with Caroline.

The administration was happy to let things lie as low as possible. I think they wanted me and any possible nose-related scandal out of the school spotlight. And my mom wasn't snooping too closely into any non-nose-related behavior. The upshot being that although I didn't exactly have a free pass to skip school any time I wanted, for the next two weeks if I held my nose and said I had a throbbing headache, my mom let me stay home and the school didn't have a problem with it. The freedom almost made the cotton balls I had to shove up my nostrils worthwhile.

And in the craziness, Caroline forgot about that first mysterious, unexplained absence of mine.

This was only the second-best thing about the incident—I've been calling it a fight, but who are we kidding. The best thing was that all of a sudden I was a big deal at school and Rebecca was drawn to attention and celebrity like a . . . well, I was going to say like a magnet, but maybe the fairer thing to say would be "like a journalist."

I mean, obviously there were, how can I put it, conflicts of interest, given the circumstances, and so she never did or said anything, but—for the first time ever—I saw *her* looking at *me* sometimes, rather than the reverse. Nothing more than that, not then, but this was a change on the order of, I don't know, the Revolutionary War or something.

I had no idea how to handle this. Any of this. Some days it seemed easiest to just stay home.

Well, about twenty feet underneath my home.

⟋

I had already started thinking about putting on the Mayhem suit, if I could figure out how to work it. I told myself it was how I could learn who Dad really was, maybe even discover what had happened to him. But now I think I know better. I think the decision to do it was just . . . aesthetic. Like it would have been weird not to. I know that sounds horrible, and I guess it is, but it's probably the truth.

As to what came after . . . I'm still figuring that out, I guess.

Anyway.

I knew—or thought I knew—what everyone knew about the Mayhem suit: it was made of tough metal, the kind bullets bounce off. But from that first close look, I could see it was actually some sort of soft material, almost cloth, that hung loosely off the hook. . . .

Maybe there were some answers on the computer down there. I mean, there are always answers on the computer, right?

Dad was full of surprises. I assumed the computer would have some sort of insane encryption and that would be the end of my life as Mayhem. But the computer—which was an old MacBook, like, at least six years old by now—just asked for a password, the kind you need to get into the user settings and profiles. This one was a lot harder to guess than the door keypad one, though, since it had more possibilities, and I was worried that if I put in the wrong thing more than two or three times it would shut down completely or activate some knockout gas or who knows what.

Except there was one thing I *knew* about Dad: he had a terrible memory. Which made me bet he'd hidden the password somewhere in the lab. Or, when a careful search didn't turn up anything passwordy there, some place in the house.

It took a while. I had to be supercareful about putting things back where they'd been—my mom had gotten more distracted since my dad disappeared, but she'd still notice if her shoes were put back in the wrong order. Eventually, tucked into a small space between the vanity and the wall in my mom's—my parents'—bathroom, I found a scrap of a printout with three long combinations of letters and numbers.

I'd been wrong: you didn't need *a* password to get into the computer. You needed three, one prompt popping up after another, after another. But once I painstakingly entered them—and you better believe I put that paper back exactly where I found it, after copying the sequences down for myself—there they were: a bunch of files arranged in neat folders on the desktop.

When you put them all together, the files added up to something like a car manual, but for a supersuit: *To activate blowtorch, press your ring finger against the palm of your right hand twice.* (That's just an example. The Mayhem suit doesn't have a blowtorch. It has something more like a microwave-based thermal amplifier . . . not the point.) There were notes about Dad's training with the suit, like: *Since you don't want to repeat that incident with the cow in New Hampshire, always be sure to refill the gas cartridges before you go out.*

Like I said, Dad had a terrible memory. I figured they were just notes to himself that also happened to make the perfect personalized instruction manual for his son.

In retrospect, it was pretty stupid to imagine he had done all this alone.

NOW. FRIDAY. 8:32 P.M.

I'm trying to keep this in some kind of order for whoever's listening, but it's hard. My cheek hurts and it's getting cold and I really have to figure out what I'm going to do next.

The scanners aren't picking up any more radio chatter. That means the military's gone dark. They know I'm listening. And the thermal scans are useless: the fire is making the signal goofy. I'm blind here.

But they've got to be going building to building by now. And once they find me, they'll let loose with everything they have. No mercy. No worries about civilians, either, since they've evacuated the area.

I can't blame them. I mean, considering what they think I did.

And when I think about what I *did* do, I'm pretty sure I deserve whatever's coming.

TWO AND A HALF MONTHS AGO

I didn't meet Mr. Jones right away.

Well, *meet* isn't the right word. I still don't know his name, or anything about him. At least nothing certain. I haven't even seen his face. And I'm pretty sure a lot of what he told me wasn't true, or, at least, was designed to be misleading.

But whatever did happen with Mr. Jones, this is how it started.

I was going to fly.

Everyone had seen Mayhem do it in the old video clips. There were detailed instructions on the computer. I knew I had to try. But first things first: I had to get the suit on.

I practiced in the lab, two, three dozen times. Slipping the bottom half on, then the top, then the helmet, constantly checking the instructions. The reference to *accidental decapitation* encouraged attention to detail. Only once everything was on, floppy but firmly secured, did I activate the electric stimulus that armorized the whole thing.

Everyone knows what the suit looks like from the outside. Inside, it looks . . . I don't know, exactly. When it's floppy, it looks like the inside of a sweat suit. When it's not, you're in it, and it's a lot like trying to look down your shirtsleeve—not as easy as it sounds. It feels smooth and metallic, though. And it adjusts to your size somehow—I mean, I'm much bigger in the suit than I am in real life, but somehow you don't feel like you're rattling around in there. There's *some* give—enough to keep a few things close to your body, like your phone—but not much. Inside the helmet looks like a giant wraparound computer screen, and it responds to voice controls and facial movement.

I have no idea how any of it works. The armorizing, the size adjustment, the screens . . . not a clue. But I don't understand how my phone works, either. Something about radio waves full of data that fly through the air? I don't know. It works just like the instructions say. That's the main thing.

Once I'd mastered putting the suit on, I moved on to checking the weapons systems, making sure they were charged, all the indicators glowing green. I couldn't do more than that without blowing the lab apart. But it looked like I had enough firepower to take on an army.

Well, maybe not, as has now become clear, but that's what I thought then.

The door at the other end of the lab led to a tunnel, which ran for about a quarter of a mile underground and ended in a hatch that opened onto a ravine. The first time I peeked out, not wearing the suit, I got a face full of thorns. Smart way to keep anyone from snooping around—and, of course, with the suit you just brush them away without thinking twice. And then there was the second layer of security: those thorns—and the hatch—were thirty-five feet up from the bottom of the ravine. Straight up. If you *were* snooping around, you would have to be rappelling down the ravine wall.

Or flying.

So one night I waited for Mom to go to sleep. She had a routine that never changed. At 11 p.m. the TV in her room would go off; then, five minutes later, the light, and that was it until 6:30 a.m. I waited another half hour after the light went out, to be sure. Then down the ladder, into the lab, into the suit, through the tunnel, and toward the hatch. The files said the suit was capable of rapid ground transport as well as flight, but I didn't want to risk it. Maybe I'd smash into a wall and cause a cave-in. There'd be a lot of fuss when someone found my Mayhem-wrapped skeleton.

The ravine was a good place to practice. Despite the temptation to rock out with the suit's weapons, the more careful side of me knew explosions and rocket fire would bring attention. I mainly focused on working with the suit: running and jumping and even—at a very low altitude, still inside the ravine—flying.

I have to admit, I thought flying would be cooler. I guess it's a lot like when you're on a plane. You're in the air, but you still feel like you're inside. The suit's the same way. Maybe if you could feel the wind on your face or something, but the suit filters all the air, and all you can see on the faceplate monitors are readouts displaying four or five different aerial views. It feels like you're flying a drone or playing a video game, except that you happen to be a few hundred, or thousand, feet above the ground.

Still, I mean, it's pretty awesome.

And after about five or six flights, every other night or so, I was beginning to get the hang of it. The suit was starting to feel like an outgrowth of my own body, just bigger, more powerful, more capable, more . . . adult, even, though that sounds silly. It made me start to think I could take on big things, like, maybe figuring out what had happened to my dad. I was smart enough to know that this was dangerous territory, but dumb enough to think I could handle it.

For a week and a half, anyway.

I don't *think* I almost died the night I met him. Mr. Jones, I mean.

But I'm not 100 percent sure.

Nothing special was going on that night. I guess that was part of it. I mean, yes, I'd been having these incredible experiences with the suit, but the rest of my life was lonely dinners with my mom who hardly looked at me between drags on her cigarette and occasional days at school moping about Rebecca and dodging Logan and Caroline.

Not literally, in Caroline's case. We were still hanging out whenever I went to school: walking to class, eating lunch, even comparing notes on the latest episode of *The Great British Bake Off*, which we were both inexplicably into. But . . . earlier that day . . .

Have you ever been talking to someone when you really had to go to the bathroom? I know, this is gross, but it's the only example that works. You don't want to tell them the reason you're only half listening, both because it's embarrassing and because you want to be nice. But since they don't know, they think you're mad at them or something.

This wasn't quite that bad—I mean, there wasn't that same *urgency*—but Caroline knew me pretty well. She knew there was something going on. And, being Caroline, she called me on it.

I told her I was having headaches from my nose, but when she wanted to take me straight to the school nurse and I said no, that led to more questions. Then I tried to say it was about things at home and could we leave it at that, but, of course, she wouldn't. And why would she? We'd always talked about that kind of stuff before.

So I told her that it was something private, and that when I was ready to tell her I would, but that she had to stop crowding me.

Yup. Pretty much a direct quote, I'm ashamed to say.

She looked at me, and told me I was being a—well, it doesn't matter what word it was. It was 100 percent accurate.

And then she said, "If you need some space, Bailey, *trust me*, I am happy to provide it for you," and then she got up from the lunch table and walked off.

Leaving me to bus her tray, I couldn't help noticing.

I felt terrible. We'd had fights before, but this was worse. It felt . . . deeper. And I didn't quite know how to fix it. I knew I needed to apologize, which was fine, but I also knew I needed to explain.

And I wasn't sure that I could, or should.

And although I knew getting into the Mayhem suit wouldn't help me figure it out, I didn't think it could hurt, either.

So that night, after making some random fragments of conversation with my mom, which ended with her mentioning my dad and trailing off into space, which tended to happen about three nights a week, I waited until I heard the television turning off, and then I went down, and out, and up.

Considering how specific the "manual" was about some stuff, it was surprisingly vague about how high you could go in the suit. But since it had some comments about how to avoid being spotted by aircraft, I figured the answer was: pretty high.

That night, I wanted to take it to the limit.

I finished my usual routine. And kept going. Higher and higher. Hit the clouds. Went through. Kept going.

And then I was flying faster. And faster. And higher and higher. I don't know how high the atmosphere goes, so maybe I wasn't that close to outer space. It sure felt like it, though. I *knew*—had absolute certainty—that if the suit somehow developed the tiniest crack, I would freeze and choke and gasp and burst all at the same time, and it would be over.

But it didn't. I just kept gaining altitude. This was the Mayhem version of riding your bike down a big hill with your feet off the brakes. Right? Kids do this sort of thing all the time.

Except I hadn't told the suit to keep going.

At first I thought I'd pushed one of the thrust buttons by mistake. Things are a little loose for me inside the fingertip control units and I was always worrying about hitting the wrong button. I hadn't done it yet, but, of course, there was going to be a first time.

No biggie, though. I waggled my right index finger in the other direction to compensate.

Nothing happened.

I waggled harder. Still nothing. I was zooming up, up, up, with no way of stopping.

And then the thrusters stopped, stopped dead, and I was falling out of the sky, and I realized that up was better.

Although that would imply that I was thinking clearly, which I was not. I was flailing, pressing buttons, trying to activate screen menus at random, hoping something—anything—would work. Nothing responded. The only thing I seemed capable of doing was going *splat*.

Well, that and screaming. Screaming I could do just fine.

After a million years of free fall that probably lasted around fifteen seconds, the thrusters cut in. I wasn't falling anymore—just flying, straight and fast, in a random direction. I didn't have any control over the suit, and whatever was running it had killed the monitors and maps. So I was helpless, blind, and in the dark—you can only see through the monitors, remember—and I had no idea how close I was to hitting the ground, a mountain, an airplane, anything.

I'm going to let you imagine how that felt.

After a long time—it was longer than ten minutes, and less than an hour, but I couldn't have told you much more precisely than that—I felt something. Or the lack of something. The boot thrusters had cut off again. I only had time for about a millisecond of panic before I felt the gentle *thump* of my feet against a floor.

And then the monitors crackled back to life, and there

was the bright light of big floodlights, blinding after being in pitch-dark for so long. I wanted to throw my hands up to cover my eyes, but I couldn't. The suit was still frozen. So I shut them tight.

When I opened them again I could see that I was standing in an office.

Not a very big office. And not a very nice one, either. Like it had seen better days, or hadn't been used in a while. I could see a beat-up wooden desk, and behind the desk was one of those ratty old swivel chairs, and sitting in that chair, looking at me, was a man with a plastic Mayhem Halloween mask covering his face.

"Hi, Bailey," he said. "A pleasure to meet you. You can call me Mr. Jones."

❧

I looked at him. Pretty much all I could do. The suit wasn't moving an inch. I tried. Believe me, I tried. It was like being inside a steel statue.

"I've been watching you," he said. "Every time you fly, any-time you're out in the suit, I'm there. Watching."

"Where are we?" I said. "Who are you?"

"There's a tracker in the suit, you see," he said, like I hadn't said anything. "I put it in when I built it. It lets me know whenever it's activated. When. For how long."

"*You* built it?" I said. "Underneath my house?"

"And that's not all I added," he said. "After all, you didn't get here voluntarily, did you?" He tapped a tablet on his desk. I couldn't see the expression on his face through the mask, but I bet he was smiling.

"You'd better—" I started, but he cut me off.

"I'd better what?" he asked. "Tell you what you want to know, or you'll blow my head off with your forearm rockets?"

I wasn't going to say that. Or, at least, I would never have done it. Back then, I didn't think using the suit had to involve hurting anyone.

Shows what I knew.

"Why don't you try it?" he said, and did something on his tablet.

My hand swung up in the air by itself, as if I had the answer to a question in History class, and the monitors informed me that rocket A was armed, target was locked, and launch was imminent. "Hey," I said, "Wait—"

And then it launched. The rocket. Tiny, yes, not much bigger than a pencil, but—at least according to the manual—powerful enough to punch through several feet of solid steel. It flew straight and true, right at him—and clunked to the ground a few feet from the desk. Deactivated. Harmless.

"Anytime I want, Bailey," he said. "I want you to remember that. I can take over."

I waited. There wasn't anything else I could do. I was rooted to the ground in a big metal suit I couldn't control.

"But I don't want to," he added. "I think it's time to give you a choice." He paused.

"You can walk away from the whole thing, if you want. That is an option. Say the word, and in less than forty-eight hours, a man in a ten-thousand-dollar suit will appear at your door with a gigantic check and a set of keys to a mansion in the next town over. You and your mom will live the rest of your days in prosperity, and Mayhem will be something to read about in the news." He paused again. "Unless you *ever* say anything about any of this, of course. In which case it would all be taken away from you as easily as it was granted."

And then he paused a third time.

"Or," he said.

Now, you know which choice I made. I want to say that Mr. Jones knew it wasn't really a choice . . . but that's just me not taking responsibility. It was me. It's on me.

But here's the thing.

I didn't make my decision because I *wanted to pursue a life of crime*, at least not consciously. I didn't even do it because I thought the bad boys get the girl, although I have to admit that did cross my mind for a fleeting second.

No, I did it because of what Mr. Jones said next.

"Or," he repeated. "If you listen to me—if you do exactly what I say, every time—then I will teach you how to use the suit. To its fullest capacity."

And then he said three more sentences. Just three more. But they were enough.

Enough to hook me in. Enough to get me started. Enough to make me even more scared than when I was falling out of the sky.

Here's what he said.

Sentence one: "Your dad is a prisoner of the Bloody Front."

Sentence two: "I need you to help me get him back, and take them down."

And sentence three: "Before it's too late for him—and for us all."

Okay. Sort of a good-news-and-bad-news situation here.

Good news: I've changed location without anyone noticing. They may be getting closer, but they don't have visual. Which matters because even the best cloaking devices don't work against a set of eyes looking directly at you. I made it into a building a few blocks away from my last known coordinates. And the thermal scans I ran were right—the building is abandoned.

The bad news: When I landed, I must have hit a structural beam and right now there's about three tons of rubble on my legs. I'm not hurt—the armor is pretty strong stuff—but at the suit's current power levels I don't have enough strength to get the rubble off me. So I'm pinned here like a bug.

None of my options are good. I could (a) let the military know I'm here and get life in prison, (b) sit here until they find me and get life in prison, or (c) starve to death . . .

Where was I? Might as well keep going, in case this turns out to be more of a last-will-and-testament thing. Sorry. Not funny, I know. But I'm afraid if I don't laugh I'm going to scream. Or cry. Or both.

TWO AND A HALF MONTHS AGO

All those radio shock jocks and ultra-right-wing talking heads were so happy when the Bloody Front made its first appearance all those years ago. Finally, they'd been proven right: Islamic fundamentalist terrorism, ISIS-style, had made its way to America. The fact that the people responsible for those first Ohio mall shootings didn't make any statements about Islam, and that there was no proof they were Muslim didn't make much of a difference. One of them, at least in the fuzzy security footage, seemed to have a beard, and another one was waving a black flag with some scribbles on it. Which, the commentators helpfully explained, were not Arabic characters, but again, that didn't seem to matter. Someone on the news called them the Bloody Front, and it stuck.

The name may have made the group sound like a bunch of old-time pirates, but they were genuinely scary. They would come out of nowhere, hit a civilian center somewhere in the United States—never a major city, always somewhere suburban or vaguely rural, and never less than a hundred miles away from a previous site—and then disappear, watching the whole place dissolve into terror and chaos. And they'd gotten a lot more active over the past year: attacking every month or so, rather than once every year or two. Which meant every town in the country was scared, not just the big cities. Maybe the FBI or the NSA or whoever had leads on who they were. If they did, they weren't saying, which didn't do much for public confidence.

The recent wave of attacks hadn't affected us that much, not at school. I was still going around pining for Rebecca, nursing my nose, avoiding Logan, and mostly back to normal with Caroline.

I had figured out a way of being honest without telling her everything. I told her that I'd found some old stuff of my dad's, hidden away, and that I'd found out some things about him that were really tough for me to process.

"Does it change TGT?" she asked.

I told her, truthfully, yeah, it did, maybe a lot. Our latest version of TGT had been that my dad was in a fire or accident that had not only killed him, but also burned him beyond recognition and destroyed his ID so no one could identify his body. He'd ended up a John Doe somewhere, buried in what, apparently, is called a *potter's field*. Caroline had even done some computer searches of newspapers and police reports from the time of his disappearance to try to see if anything "popped," as they say on those *Law & Order* reruns that Mom watches every night. We hadn't found anything, but that didn't mean it wasn't true.

"For better, or for worse?" Caroline asked.

And I said for worse. Which was half-true.

On the one hand: proof my Dad was alive.

On the other hand: he was the prisoner of a psychotic terrorist organization.

On some imaginary third hand: I was going to do something about it.

You bet I was. When they've taken your dad prisoner, it gets a whole lot more personal. I know I sound like a tag-line from some cheesy eighties movie starring, I don't know, Bruce Willis, maybe, but that doesn't mean it's not true. I wanted to rip them to shreds. I wanted to beat them to a pulp. I wanted to—

I just wanted them to go away, and I wanted to have my dad back. That's really what I wanted. To be playing Chutes and Ladders, or whatever the game-night equivalent has progressed to now that I'm not eight years old. I didn't want to have to think about terrorists as anything but somebody else's bad news.

I felt that—all of that—the second Mr. Jones told me that they had my dad as their prisoner. And then what I did was, I blinked.

Under other circumstances I might have reacted more dramatically, but I was essentially paralyzed from the neck down.

"Could you please unfreeze me?" I finally asked.

He thought about it for a second. "All right," he said, doing something to a tablet on his desk. "I'm restoring limited mobility. The weapons won't work, and if I see any sudden movements you're a statue again. Got it?"

I got it. It was nice to move my arms again. But I didn't move much more. I just stared at him. And he stared back, from behind that cheap Halloween mask.

I broke. "Are you going to tell me anything else? About my dad? And why the Bloody Front took him?"

"Maybe if you ask me nicely," Mr. Jones replied.

Ripping a piece out of the wall seemed more attractive. "Please," I said through gritted teeth. And then he started talking.

Looking back, I think his whole demeanor could have been an act. I'm not 100 percent sure of anything when it comes to Mr. Jones. . . . But if I tell it straight, the whole thing, maybe it'll make more sense. I'm sure I won't get it word for word, but I'll try to get as close as possible. Maybe something about the way the conversation went—all our conversations—will be important. We'll see.

"They made a mistake," he began. "The Bloody Front. They'd figured out that it was Gerry flying around in the Mayhem suit, but they also assumed that he'd been the one to build it." He looked down, and I could hear the sadness in his voice. "I always told him to take more precautions. Building his hideout beneath his own house?" He shook his head. "But he was willing to cut corners a little too often. He didn't want to have to drive somewhere else to get into the suit, was what he said. That was what got him."

Even though I could sense something not so nice, something patronizing in how he was saying it, I had to admit it did sound like my dad.

"I've been using every resource, tapping every network to

get him back," Mr. Jones said. "For years. Not just to return him to his family. But because the Bloody Front has something terrible in mind."

He looked up at me. He was probably looking me right in the eye, but it was hard to tell, with the mask and all.

"We used the Mayhem armor for good," he said. "Maybe our methods were illegal—robbing from the rich to give to the poor is still robbery—but with such injustice in the world, who cares if our financial institutions are forced to undergo some belt-tightening? But unlike us, the Bloody Front has no scruples."

"What—" I said, but I couldn't quite finish the sentence. I cleared my throat and tried again. "What are they trying to do? And why do they have my dad?"

"Isn't it obvious?" he said, and again, his tone was odd—like he knew it wasn't obvious and wanted me to admit I didn't get it. Showing who was in charge again. I didn't get that at the time, either, but I see it now.

I shook my head.

"They want your dad to build an army of Mayhems," he said. "To blow up the world."

❧

"Cat and mouse, cat and mouse," Mr. Jones continued.

I didn't say anything. The suit wasn't paralyzed now, but I was. This was . . . too big. Too much. Part of me was listening to what Mr. Jones had to say. Part of me was stuck on a loop repeating: *blow up the world . . . blow up the world . . . blow up the world . . .*

"They pressured your father to build them the suit. Gerry

doesn't know much more about how to build the suit than you do. But he's a smart man, your father. And brave," he said. "So he delays them. Sends them off on wild goose chases. Rare equipment from here; precious metals from there. The random-seeming attacks aren't quite as random as the news believes. Each one lays tracks. Gives me clues to plan a rescue."

"Then why haven't you *done* anything?" I practically shouted.

"And how do you suggest I go about it?" he said. "Go to the police? The government? I'm the creator of Mayhem. They'd throw me in some deep dark hole—and believe me, they wouldn't lift a finger to help your father. *Let him rot*, they would say. I've been doing it by myself, getting closer and closer, thanks to your dad, but even if I find him, how am I going to rescue him? Me and what army?"

"The Mayhem suit," I said. "You could remote-control it, like you just did. Fly it out of our house—"

The Halloween mask was shaking violently from side to side. "Oh, no, no, no," said Mr. Jones. "For an operation this sensitive, to save a cherished companion, you couldn't possibly rely on"—he tried to find the right words—"a *drone strike*. No, you need a living, thinking human being. Who can make his own decisions on the spot. Who has proven, based on my extensive observations, to be a worthy candidate for the task."

I caught my breath. I know he saw it.

"To save his father and destroy a threat to the world in one blow," said Mr. Jones. "Not a bad arrangement."

"But you—you said—" I stammered. "You said you haven't found him."

Not exactly, he admitted. But given the most recent clues Dad had left, for the first time he knew where to get that information. "I've narrowed his position down to fourteen locations within the continental United States. Employing a series of differential algorithms—well, never mind the details, you wouldn't understand them," he said, a little smugly. "I've found what must be a supply node, a central facility from which the Bloody Front sends material to its various splinter-operation sites. I'm sure your dad is being held at one of those. The computer data inside the main facility will tell us which one."

All my anger and annoyance just . . . went away. "Let's go!" I shouted, as I activated my boot thrusters.

And didn't move.

Mr. Jones was tapping away on his tablet. "I warned you," he said. "No sudden moves." And he sighed. "I want to get your dad back, too. But we need to be careful. Anything less than mastery of the suit—absolute control, which requires total obedience to my training plan—and you'll get everyone killed. It's amazing you haven't blown yourself up yet."

Whoever Mr. Jones was—that wasn't his real name, obviously—the one thing I could tell was that he was not a parent. He had no idea how to talk to teenagers.

I argued. I protested. I shouted. And eventually I gave in.

But at least I convinced him to start the training that night.

Which was *horrible*.

*

"We'll practice here," Mr. Jones declared, and I looked around, thinking, *In this little office?*

He tapped on that tablet of his, and the wall split into two sliding doors. And there, behind him, was a warehouse the size of a football field.

Actually, more like three football fields. With a roof at least two hundred feet high. And with all sorts of structures scattered around the edges. The first two floors of an apartment building—or of the outside of an apartment building, at least. It looked like one of those false fronts you see in movies about Hollywood back lots. Something that looked like a rock-climbing wall, only much higher, and with cannons sticking out here and there. And an actual stretch of highway running the length of the warehouse, with cars, trucks, and even a tank parked along it.

It kind of looked like God's toy train set.

"Welcome to our practice facility," Mr. Jones said with pride. "It's been a while since anyone's used it. Good luck."

"Um, wait, aren't you going to—" I started, but he had already disappeared through a small side door. Before I could ask him where he was going, guns opened fire on me.

I shrieked and flailed and went fetal. And then I heard Mr. Jones in my ear, telling me to keep calm, stay in control, take a breath, and *think*. Nothing in the room could hurt me, he said—in fact, very little in the whole *world* could hurt me, except my own carelessness or foolishness. *Easy for him to say*, I remember thinking. *He's not the one in the suit.*

As it turned out, although the bullets bounced off me, the hits weren't completely painless—the spunging and zinging rattled my teeth and practically gave me a migraine.

But I mean, I was *bulletproof*.

The bigger headache, though, came from the constant voice talking away in my ear. Between Mr. Jones's never-ending stream of instructions and the suit's readouts and monitors, it felt like I was playing an online video game—one I sucked at. I'd thought I'd been impressive, flying around on my own and all. Once I began trying to dodge multiple streams of cannon fire while picking up a mailbox and throwing it through a second-floor window of that abandoned building, I started to see that what I'd taught myself was deeply inadequate. Much as I hate to say it, Mr. Jones had been right: if I'd charged ahead that night, I probably would have gotten someone killed.

I have to hand it to him. Maybe he wasn't a parent. But he was a pretty decent teacher. Despite the fact that he was driving me crazy, he was good at watching. Diagnosing bad habits and mistakes. "I know you're left-handed, Bailey; that means you're overcompensating on the right-hand fingertip verniers. Ease back." Leavening legitimate frustration at my suckage with rare but earned encouragement. "Well, you're learning. Your father was a lot worse when he started out, I can tell you that." It was kind of . . . well, not nice, exactly. But valuable. And even, I have to say, appreciated.

After about forty hours of this—although according to the suit's internal clock it was more like forty-five minutes—the voice in my ear said, "All right. I think that's enough, don't you?"

I wanted to protest, but I couldn't speak, I was breathing so hard. The suit does all the real work, yes, but you're still moving around inside it. Even lifting five-pound weights for the better part of an hour can take it out of you.

"Good," he said. "Keep practicing. I'll be in touch."

And before I could object or ask questions, the darkness descended once more and then the thrusters went on. I heard the rumble of machinery—the roof opening up, maybe, I don't know for sure—and then I was moving, moving, until about five or ten minutes later everything blinked on and I found myself—according to the GPS—about a hundred miles from home.

It took me another half-hour or so to fly back to the ravine. I was smarting, frustrated, sore, but, somehow, unexpectedly, a little happy and maybe even proud of myself.

Which didn't count for much when, two weeks later, he took over the suit *again*.

Okay, I just tried shifting the rubble. It didn't work. Something moved, but I'm worried the rest of it will come down on my head. And even though I assume the suit's armor would hold, the thought about what might happen if I'm wrong is . . . gross.

I'm going to hold off. Breathe deep. Not focus on how much I am on the verge of totally freaking out right now. Think about something else. The story. Think it all through.

TWO MONTHS AGO

There I was, hurtling through midair. Once again. And once again, there was nothing I could do about it.

It was less terrifying this time, but much more infuriating. When the monitors went back on and I saw that Halloween mask again, I let him have it. I didn't care if he bashed me against a wall until I was crushed to a pulp. I didn't care if he raised my own right hand to my head, activated the missiles, and blew my head off. He was *not* going to do that to me again.

I'm realizing now that none of my threats included never getting back into the suit. I wonder what that says. . . .

After I finished shouting, Mr. Jones sat there quietly for a few seconds. Then he put his hands on his mask, and for a second I thought he was going to take it off. But he just said, "You're right. I'm sorry. It won't happen anymore. We're partners."

"Well, uh, good," I said. It was so sudden that I felt knocked off-balance.

"You need more practice, though," he added, and then

proceeded to put me through more drills, more live fire, more bizarre orders: *Somersault in the air while throwing chunks of concrete at painted targets on the wall! Burrow under the ground floor of the fake building, pop out the other side, and nail two vehicles with the flamethrowers on each hand! Cut power while in midair, drop exactly one hundred feet, then let loose with the missiles at three drones flying patterns above, below, and beside me!*

I was on the go for at least three hours. Long enough I almost didn't notice that by the end he wasn't giving much advice—just issuing the next order.

"All right, that's good," he said, finally, and walked out to where I'd landed, stinky and sweaty. "You're a natural. And you've been working hard." I sure had. Practicing every night, on my own, for hours and hours, and during the days when I told my mom and the school I was feeling "a little vulnerable." Plus I'd been reading the manuals backward and forward, learning them better than I'd ever known any Spanish vocab words or algebraic equations. Much to the distress of my GPA. I was just waiting for him to be in touch.

And whatever anger or annoyance I had about the way he took me by surprise, his next words made it all disappear.

"I think you're ready," he said. "Get some rest. We're hitting that central facility, the supply depot I told you about, tomorrow night."

I half-expected that while I was jumping for joy—about fifteen feet high, with the suit—he would take over and send me flying out into the darkness, despite what he'd promised. But he didn't.

"You've done good, Bailey," he said as he turned to go. And

then he stopped, and though I couldn't see behind his mask, I thought maybe he was struggling to keep it together. Maybe there was even a tear or two in there. "Your dad is lucky to have a son like you."

And then I was the one trying to keep it together.

Because it wasn't just his words. He'd given me proof that he really trusted me: my GPS monitor had come to life as the training area door closed behind him. I knew, for the first time, where the headquarters was. I'd be able to come back on my own.

That night I flew home, not on a cloud, but through a bunch of them.

But here's the thing. At some point later on, I wanted to talk to Mr. Jones. Face-to-face, or helmet-to-mask, I guess. So I went back to the warehouse.

It was gone. Just a big pit in the earth. I suspect he'd had the whole thing bulldozed within hours.

Mr. Jones, I've come to learn, is a very careful man.

I wondered how Mr. Jones would get in touch with me the next day. A self-disintegrating note in my locker, maybe? Or a tap on the shoulder from a janitor who'd turn out to have been a henchman under deep cover for years?

He just texted me. First thing in the morning. I came out of the shower and there it was. There was no name attached to the text, but it was obviously him. Nobody else I know has a number without an area code. Or would tell me to be in the air exactly thirteen miles south-southeast of my house at precisely 11:14 p.m.

I was so excited I almost forgot about Caroline's band auditions.

I'm not sure if it was a band, technically speaking. I don't know what you'd call it. Whatever it was, it was a cool idea. Caroline was calling it the mp3s, because it was kind of like a mix of a cover band and karaoke. Basically, she'd take classic rock songs and strip out the instrument tracks that someone wanted to play themselves. If she got a drummer, then that guy could take the Ringo part; a guitarist, Jimmy Page or whoever. Her end goal was to make a record of a bunch of classics with different kids on each track.

She'd been talking about it for a while. She was good with computers—not, like, *hacker* good, but a whole lot better than me. And this was a nice way to put it together with her love of music. I think she had come up with the idea when we were hanging out and was like, "We should do this together!" I thought it was a good idea, though with my lack of both musical talent and coding ability, I thought it was more of a good idea for *her*.

And I was hoping to back out of the auditions—especially now—but I got a text from Caroline that same morning, fifteen minutes after Mr. Jones's. It was even bossier:

Dude. I have programmed all your favorite Beatles songs. Your John Lennon is not as terrible as you believe it to be. Show up and show the world that they are better than the Rolling Stones, once and for all. If you can.

This was a joke, kind of. We had been arguing about the Beatles versus the Rolling Stones forever. Caroline claimed that "Sympathy for the Devil" was the best song in rock history, and I told her that she was wrong, it was a toss-up between "Revolution" and "Golden Slumbers." Each of us changed the particular songs every now and then, but the *lines of battle*, as my mom once put it, were the same.

So I dragged myself to the music room after last period that day. The look on Caroline's face when I showed up—she was so surprised she dropped a few notes off the chorus of "Money for Nothing," but even that couldn't erase her smile.

That's one thing I feel good about. At least there's that.

After two or three guitarists took their turns—why everyone wants to play "Stairway to Heaven" when no one but Jimmy Page can do it justice is beyond me—Caroline waved me over.

"Let me guess," she said. "You're looking for . . . something up-tempo, right? That's what you need. So . . . 'It Won't Be Long'?"

"Deep cut," I said, "but no. Something else. Not the Beatles."

She raised both eyebrows.

I told her the name of the song, and in the three or four minutes it took her to do whatever digital stuff she did, she figured out—by ear—that incredible guitar riff, that constantly repeating progression, and worked out an arrangement she could play on the piano. Her musical chops . . . they're intense.

It turns out that "Message in a Bottle" sounds really good on piano. As I sent Sting's SOS out there to the world—really, to my dad—Caroline joined in singing the chorus and . . . it was great.

Of course, I wasn't the one who needed the SOS. My dad was. I had the song totally backward. Story of my life.

Normally, the waves of applause—okay, a single freshman yelling "All RIGHT!"—for my performance would have kept me going for a day or two. But I had other things on my mind that night. Like a very particular rendezvous time.

Precisely 11:14. That's what Mr. Jones had said.

At that point, I didn't think the timing mattered so much.

I knew I was going to have to cut it close no matter what, since my mom didn't go to bed until eleven, and I was supposed to be in bed then. I stayed under the covers until I heard her door close, then quietly, very, very quietly, peeked out every few minutes to see if the light under her door had gone dark. Finally it did. At 11:08.

I was in that guest room like a bat out of you-know-where. I slipped down the ladder and into the lab—11:11—and was in the suit and out of the ravine by 11:13, kicking the thrusters and scaring a nest of warblers out of their feathers. I just hoped the humans in the area thought a jet had flown too low.

I got there at 11:16. Precisely.

"You're late," the voice in my ear said.

"Two minutes," I protested, flexing my fingers to make sure I still had control over the suit. I did. He was keeping his promise.

"These operations require *surgical precision*," he said.

"One hundred and twenty seconds are a lifetime in these matters—"

"Okay, sorry," I responded. "I promise, it won't happen again. Let's *go*. I bet I can make the time up in the air."

"You'll have to," he said.

On the way, there were all sorts of rules:

1. I had to travel fast enough to hit the supply facility at precisely 11:57, which Mr. Jones's surveillance had indicated would be right during shift change.
2. But not too fast, because even though the suit was cloaked, the sound dampeners only worked up to a certain speed, and the guards might pick me up as I arrived.
3. I was to avoid physical interaction with the guards, but to cause as much property damage as I could on my way to the central computer room.
4. At the same time, I had to make sure the electrical grid wasn't affected because sudden surges could wreck the precious hard drives.
5. But most of all, I had to get in and out within ten minutes. That was the approximate response time of the local authorities, and we wanted to keep Mayhem's reappearance a secret. And, of course, the minute the Bloody Front saw Mayhem, they would start wiping the drives left and right.

And there were even more instructions. The hard drives

will probably look like *this*. The guards will move like *that*. I knew it was important stuff, but I was only half-listening.

I was a guided missile, on a righteous mission to save my dad.

The monitor screens turned yellow. I was within radar range of the target. I activated the cloaks to avoid getting spotted by instruments, then flew higher to avoid visual detection, and then came in fast and direct, hitting the coordinates—a nondescript warehouse—at 11:56:56. A little faster and more direct than I intended . . . the suit cushioned some of the g-forces, but I felt my lips skin away from my teeth as I hit the warehouse roof hard.

Immediately, Mr. Jones groaned in my ear: "Didn't I just tell you not to make physical contact until you saw the first guard?" he said. "The pressure sensors will trigger—"

But I wasn't listening. Not to him, anyway. I was paying closer attention to the high-pitched beeping in my left ear that meant a silent alarm had been triggered inside somewhere. And then I was running for the roof door, which, I had noticed, had begun to crack open. I jammed it shut with enough force to mangle the frame, and the directional microphones picked up the sound of muffled cursing and bodies tumbling down steps. I figured I'd bought myself a few minutes.

Then the two automatic machine guns hidden in the shadows of the roof opened up on me, and the training I'd had—with Mr. Jones, by myself, in the air—all went away.

His voice was screaming in my ear, but I couldn't listen. I just acted on instinct, leaping away from the gun I was facing down and landing right against the other.

The suit protects you against most temperature changes. You don't feel cold when you're flying, and, assuming its bodily integrity hasn't been compromised, you could probably walk through a five-alarm fire without much more than a prickle of warmth. So even though a machine gun was aiming right into my back at full power, it felt like how I imagine a hot stone massage might feel: some pushing, rubbing, and a little heat. It was almost pleasant.

That made me feel better, more in control, so I turned around and ripped the still-firing gun out of the wall. And then, for good measure, I walked over to the other one and tied the two barrels together.

The resulting backfire and explosion were pretty satisfying—strike one against the Bloody Front!—until I realized something.

Mr. Jones had gone completely silent.

I tried calling his name, first softly, then louder, but he only spoke when I headed toward the door. "Don't bother," he said bitterly. "While you were playing around up there, they wiped all the data and escaped." I started to say something, but he cut me off. "And not only did you fail your mission," he continued, "but you got made. There are cameras on the roof, not just weapons. You could have disrupted them with a micro-electromagnetic pulse and preserved some anonymity. If you had listened. Now they know there's someone else out there with the Mayhem armor."

He paused. At the time, I thought it was because he was worried about me.

"I managed to break some of their encryptions and I'm

monitoring their communications traffic," he said. "They're moving your father. Tonight. And it could be anywhere. We're back to square one." I heard him take a long, raggedy breath. "You've been headstrong, and you've been stupid, and it's put your dad in greater danger."

I tried to respond, but all that came out was this kind of coughing sniff. I was not going to cry. I was not going to give him another sign that I couldn't handle the pressure. I promised myself that.

"Now get out of there," he said, cold and detached. Like he didn't even care anymore. "On top of everything else, you forgot to monitor the police bands. There are several cruisers on their way."

So I got out of there. And on the way home, I didn't keep my promise not to cry. Not even a little bit.

School was intolerable the next day. Just agony. I bet I would have given even Rebecca a nasty look if she'd come over and said hello. Of course, the odds of that were almost zero. Maybe not as infinitesimal as before the nose incident, but still really, really, really low.

But the odds of seeing Caroline? As Mrs. Rojanski in Math class said about quizzes, *The probability is approaching one.*

And there she was, right by my locker, wanting to play me one of the early auditions I'd missed. I couldn't listen for more than a minute without thinking about my dad, about how I'd screwed things up . . .

I don't know what my face looked like. It must have been pretty grim. Caroline's voice faded, like someone had turned the volume knob way, way down. "Bailey," she said. "Bailey, what is it? What happened?" And then she whispered, "Is it about your dad?"

I wanted to tell her. I wanted to shout at her to go away. I wanted to just go fetal right there at her feet.

The right choice would have been to say something like, *I'll tell you. But not right now. Let's make a plan to talk about this. Tonight or tomorrow.* I just didn't have the strength. So instead I told her that I wasn't feeling good and had to get to class and I brushed by her to the men's room, which was the one place I knew she couldn't follow me. I hid in a stall until five seconds before the bell rang.

I needed the day to end. To get back in the air. To show him he could trust me. That I was good enough.

After sixth period, my schedule overlapped with Caroline's again and I apologized. I did a good job, I guess. At least, good enough. She even smiled, and I think there was a joke or two, before she was off to French and I was off to Spanish. But it wasn't . . . whole. There wasn't time to make it whole. Even if I'd known how.

Eventually—finally—the last bell rang, and I was home. I got back in the suit, flew around, and waited. But there was no voice in my ear. Not that night, or the night after that, or the night after that. It got to the point where I almost *wanted* to see the monitors go dark, the boot jets to fire without me telling them to. There was nothing to keep me company but my own guilty conscience and the nauseating feeling that I'd done something terrible to my dad.

As it turns out, he wasn't the only collateral damage.

If you live around here, you might remember that our football team was on its way to the state championships. Thanks to Logan. Although in the local news interviews, he always gave credit to his coach and teammates. I'm telling you, even though he basically broke my nose and was hooking up with the love of my life, he was a good guy.

It was terrible, what happened to him.

I don't know why I didn't think of this earlier, but I've managed to reroute power from the weapon drives to the suit's servomotors.

I hadn't just been fooling around with flying and shooting things all those weeks. I'd learned some stuff about the suit's mechanics, too. I'm not sure it's going to be enough, but a bunch of indicator lights that were red are now yellow. Which is better than nothing.

Here goes.

Okay, shifted the rubble off one leg. And nothing else fell on my head in the meantime. So far so good.

Better wait a minute to make sure nothing else got disturbed before trying the other one.

I guess I should keep going. With the story. But it gets tougher from here. . . .

Why isn't there anyone firing machine guns at you when you need a distraction?

The thing is, you can't grow up in my part of the US and not know something about football. I'm not sure which one the nickelback is, and the difference between most of the pass plays are beyond me. But I know the basics.

And I also knew—everyone did—that that week's game was crucial. If we won, we went to the state group of eight, which would be the furthest our team had gotten in about fifteen years, longer than some of us had been alive. The school was going crazy: cheer rallies, locker decorations, random kids running through the halls dressed as charging rams. Normally, I would have found this deeply annoying, but I had other things on my mind. To put it mildly.

And then it was game night.

If you can't picture the scene, just hit the Internet. There's video everywhere. Given what happened.

It was the third quarter and we were down by three. The other team had the ball and they were making good progress downfield. In other words, it looked like they were going to score, and if they did, that might be it, since they'd been shutting down our quarterback all night.

Their defense was good. But ours had Logan.

Like I said, it's rare for a linebacker to be team captain. Logan made great, key plays—especially the blitz. Everybody knew that. And that was, I guess, the thing: *everybody* knew that. In an area like ours, where high school football gets covered obsessively on the radio, local TV news, Facebook groups, everywhere . . . everyone was just waiting for Logan to put his head down and knock the opposing quarterback into the dirt.

The coaches knew it. The other team knew it. Our team knew it. Everyone in the stands knew it—I mean, even the little kids knew it. Everyone was shouting, "Blitz! Blitz! Blitz!" and jumping up and down on the sidelines, generally going crazy. The incredible thing about Logan was that even though everyone knew he was going to blitz, nothing could stop him.

Well, nothing on the football field.

The other team's quarterback called hike, and the backfield went into action. The crowd was on their feet roaring as Logan spun and whirled and flattened an offensive lineman and charged at the quarterback, who was backpedaling, wheeling, looking for anyone to throw the ball to, but there was no one open. It was third down, and it looked like the other team was going to lose another ten or fifteen yards. Which meant they were going to have to punt the ball away, which would have pretty much ended their momentum and put us right back in the game. It was the kind of play most players hope to have once or twice a season. Logan had two or three every game.

And then his left foot exploded.

The police determined later that the charges were attached to his cleats and set off remotely. But to the people in the stands, it looked like he'd stepped on a land mine.

I've watched the videos maybe two hundred times. I haven't wanted to, but I've made myself sit down and watch. Over and over again.

Logan goes flying. His shoe—what everyone *hoped* was just his shoe—goes the other way, flipping over and over in midair. The crowd screams. Everyone is ducking for cover. The teams abandon the field—all except, of course, Logan. He's groaning and crying and puking, lying on the turf holding the place where his foot had been.

That's where it gets hard to watch. I mean, literally, my neck wants to turn itself away. Like it's under someone else's remote control.

I force myself, though. It's the least I can do.

Yeah, it's true, they were able to recover the foot, and with all the donations that came in he was able to get the best surgeons in the country to stitch him back together. Within a month, he was walking with crutches and a limp, which would have been impossible for anyone other than an athlete at the top of his game.

But he would never play football again.

In those first few crazy hours, everyone assumed it was a homegrown attack, some trenchcoat-mafia student or a Centerville booster who'd gone way too far. When the Bloody

Front made their YouTube announcement taking credit later that night . . . everything went nuts.

But that's not the full story. If it was, I'd probably have been able to shake it off.

No one knew the full story, not even me, until three days later. When Mr. Jones showed up in the lab.

I don't know how long he'd been waiting. I guess he wanted to make a dramatic reappearance after ghosting me for days. If that was his plan, he must have been a little disappointed. There'd been an unannounced assembly, a not-quite-memorial service for Logan, since he wasn't dead, but kind of one for his foot, his playing career, and the hopes for our season. And, if you want to get all poetic about it, for a kind of American innocence, too, since if the Bloody Front was attacking high school football games, what wouldn't they do?

So I was an hour or so later to the lab than usual. I'm not sure if this is nice or disturbing or just anal retentive, but he'd taken the time while he was waiting to clean up the lab a little, organize the tools and whatnot. Which meant his first words to me were something about the need for order and cleanliness, and while I was trying not to jump down his throat in return, he followed up by blaming me for Logan, too, which was kind of a surprise and not a surprise all at once.

The attack on Logan had been unusual for the Bloody Front. The journalists who had invaded our town before the YouTube video was a day old called it a troubling new direction for the group. The national security specialists had theories about why they might have changed their approach, but none of them had hit on *revenge on the community they were pretty sure their supervillain adversary belonged to, since they'd tracked the supervillain in question's flight, since the supervillain in question forgot, in his discombobulation and inexperience, to activate his cloaking device when he flew off after attacking their warehouse, leaving a chemical exhaust trail even the rankest amateur could follow.*

Which was, more or less, what Mr. Jones told me.

Which in turn sparked an argument in which I denied forgetting to turn on the cloaking devices, and he denied my denial, and we went back and forth until he held up his phone and showed me a rapid stream of data which he said were the logs of the suit, which clearly indicated they had indeed been off. He said it was lucky that I'd done enough damage to the Bloody Front's infrastructure that they were only able to narrow my return flight path down to a general region, not a specific neighborhood or house. Hitting the golden boy quarterback was their retaliatory strike.

It was all Greek to me. I was *sure* I had turned on the cloaking device. But I wasn't *positive*. And, like I said, even before Mr. Jones showed up, I'd had the sinking feeling that the attack on our local hero couldn't be a coincidence.

Yes, you could say Logan was a thorn in my side. Yes, my nose still hurt most mornings. But he didn't deserve *that*.

The thing is, while Mr. Jones was telling me this, I kept thinking about something else. This one moment at the memorial service earlier that day that I kept flashing back to. Over and over.

Rebecca standing by Logan onstage. Tears rolling down her eyes.

But. But.

But when Logan put his arm around her, having to limp over to do it, she flinched.

Just for a second. And she immediately looked terribly ashamed.

But she flinched.

And it filled me with hope.

Whatever's happened to me—whatever's *coming* to me—sometimes I think I deserve it.

Mr. Jones was in the lab and I didn't care, because I was fixated on that moment at the memorial service. Rebecca and Logan weren't going to last much longer. I could feel it.

Of course, just because she wasn't going to be with Logan didn't mean she would end up with me. I understood that. I wasn't insane.

Except I was convinced that after she flinched away from Logan she had looked directly at me.

Maybe I was kidding myself. Maybe I wasn't. Even now, with her as my date for winter formal, I'm still not sure. I'm afraid to ask her. Either she'd tell me, or she'd lie. I'm not sure which would be worse.

Meanwhile, I tried to focus on Mr. Jones, who was apparently not used to people not giving him their full attention. He demanded to know what I was thinking about, and—maybe so he'd stop lecturing me, maybe to avoid feeling guilty about everything for just a minute—I answered him.

"I'm hopelessly in love with Logan's girlfriend, Rebecca," I said.

I couldn't see Mr. Jones's expression. He was wearing another mask, of course, this one of Richard Nixon, or maybe it was Jimmy Carter. Then he leaned forward, and his whole tone changed.

"Rebecca," he said. Sounding out the name. Like it was in Latin or something.

He wasn't the teacher anymore, or the angry scolder. This was something else. Something I hadn't seen before.

"Rebecca," I agreed.

Another long pause. And then he said, "A beautiful name," like he was a judge on one of those cooking shows and had just tasted something that was going to win that week's challenge. "A name one could easily fall in love with."

And then—to my total shock and embarrassment—he started talking to me about love.

He told me that falling in love with someone was the most powerful thing in the world, and he said it in a way that made me understand he'd been there, too, and I added a mental note to my *Figure out who Mr. Jones is* file. Maybe he hadn't been a parent. He may or may not have been a teacher. But he was, or he had been, married. To someone he loved. A tremendous amount.

I couldn't believe it. For the first time, we were having a real conversation. So now that we were, you know, *talking*, I thought I might be able to try asking him something more personal. About my dad. How they met. How this all started.

And so I did. Direct. Out of the blue. Figuring he'd shut

it down. But something had changed between us and he *answered*.

They'd been college roommates, him and my dad, and although my dad wasn't the off-the-charts, Nobel Prize–worthy genius Mr. Jones was, the two of them connected. They spent hours talking about how to change the world, that sort of thing. And they kept it up, beginning to work on the suit together, until my dad met a woman—my mom—and that soured things a little. "A smoker," Mr. Jones said theatrically. "Ugh. Still, I suppose she had her charms."

Mr. Jones wanted to keep refining the suit, strengthening it, using it to save the world like they'd talked about, but my dad wanted to stop, marry my mom, raise a family. Their compromise was to keep their work low-key, make sure my mom never found out—she wouldn't have understood, especially with a kid to think about. "He showed me your picture when you were just three days old," Mr. Jones said. "Suffice it to say you're better looking now. Wrinkled monkeys and such."

They kept to victimless crimes where the proceeds went to charity, that sort of thing. But then Mr. Jones pushed harder. "There were too many problems in the world to leave unaddressed," he said. "Considering the power we had at our fingertips." And so they tried something bigger: taking on terrorism. My dad was willing to risk wearing the suit again for something that . . . consequential.

As smart as they were, they just weren't ready when they went after the Bloody Front. "I made a mistake—an enormous one—and your dad paid for it," he said, his voice muffled beneath the mask. "I . . . can't tell you the details now. I don't think I could get through it." I nodded, a lump in my throat. "I've been trying to track him down, watching out for you and your mother, making sure no harm comes to you. But I was always the partner behind the scenes, and to get him back, we need force. We need Mayhem. And that—no matter what's happened in the past—that means you."

I nodded again. The lump had gotten bigger, and I don't think I could have said anything even if I'd wanted to.

"But we have to be *careful*," he said. "We have to do this right. Can we do that? Can *you* do that? Do you understand you're still new to this, and that doing the wrong thing has . . . consequences?"

I nodded a third time.

"Good. I'll be in touch. For now, think about Rebecca." I couldn't see, but I think he even smiled. "And about how you might go about . . . attracting her attention. At least that will provide some sense of business as usual."

For someone as smart as Mr. Jones was, he was totally off base about *that*.

But I had to postpone figuring out any kind of plan. Because the most important relationship in my life was rapidly going down the toilet.

✐

Caroline's mp3s thing had come together, with a girl on drums and a girl and a guy playing guitar. They sounded good, but you never really knew what was fake and what was real. Story of high school, I guess. They were hoping to have enough songs down to put out an album by the end of the school year. In the meantime, they were booking small gigs here and there for practice. They'd even gotten a spot during winter formal. Not as the main band—that was some semi-professional wedding-type orchestra from the city—but as a warm-up, a morale-booster-for-the-home-team kind of thing.

Of course, Caroline took it obsessively seriously and was devoting all her spare time to practicing, even though winter formal was over a month away. I'd gone to rehearsal a couple of times to watch on days when I made it to school—the music teacher let them practice in the band room during free periods. They did a pretty good job on "Light My Fire," Caroline whaling away on that Ray Manzarek keyboard part.

It was keeping her busy, which was what I had thought I wanted, but here's the thing: I was missing her.

I mean, we both had our stuff, her with the band, me with a giant robot suit fighting terrorism and trying to rescue my dad, but I didn't have anyone to *talk* to about my thing. Except for Mr. Jones, and despite our recent breakthrough, I wouldn't have called him the ideal conversational partner.

Which led to the cafeteria incident.

It must have been a few days after Logan's quote-unquote memorial service.

Everyone was a little on edge. Well, more than a little. The whole campus was on high security alert. After all, the Bloody Front had attacked us, and although they'd never struck the same place twice, the federal government had covered the place in SWAT teams. FBI agents were going from classroom to classroom asking kids about their whereabouts, behaviors, and whatnots. The coach, the team's equipment manager, and the janitorial staff were all in what the principal called *administrative detention*. People were afraid.

Even I was afraid, and when I was in the suit, nothing could hurt me.

Yeah, like I believe that. I didn't even believe that *then*.

And on top of that, I was preoccupied with trying to think of a Rebecca plan. With no appreciable success. And there was Caroline, rattling on about the band, about how one of the band guitarists had a crush on her, and the drummer kept missing her sticks when she threw them up in the air but kept insisting on doing it at the end of her solos anyway, and they couldn't agree on a final set list for next week's gig. By the time she got to describing the new microphone she wanted, I had started getting annoyed.

I mean, how dare she care about this stuff? When I was clearly suffering? Why wasn't she there for me?

I understand that I sound like a jerk. There's a good reason for that. I was *being* a jerk. Yes, I was under a lot of stress. . . .

No. No excuses. I was being a jerk. But just wait. I get jerkier.

That's when it started, at the cafeteria, with my stating that it was impossible to look *good* playing drums, that everyone looked like they were suffering from a stroke. Usually that would have led to some hilarious argument, maybe with lots of drumming hand motions, and that would have been that. Not this time. I pushed and pushed, insisting I was right, insisting she tell me I was right, until she asked me what had crawled up my behind and died.

So I got up and left her sitting there. With my lunch. Let *her* bus *my* tray this time.

And then I stewed for the rest of the afternoon. During Mrs. Rojanski's Math class. During our discussion of Roman latifundia in History. I just sat there, getting madder and madder. And knowing there was nothing for me to be mad about, which made me even more self-righteous.

She was waiting for me by the school front steps at the end of the day. And she let me have it. According to Caroline:

1. I had secrets I wasn't telling her.
2. We used to tell each other everything.
3. If I wasn't letting her into my life, then it was a matter of self-defense for her to try other things.
4. She had been walking on eggshells around me for weeks.
5. She had been waiting for me to come to her.
6. She knew whatever it was, it was about my dad, and it was big, and she was trying to be sensitive.
7. But it was getting, as she said, "real old real fast."

Her words.

I should have just told her then. I could have taken her down the trapdoor that night, shown her the suit. But instead I got offended, and huffy, and defensive, and walked away, knowing I was being an idiot but feeling powerless to do anything about it.

Maybe if I had told her then, everything would have turned out differently. Maybe I'd be able to call her right now and tell her to bring me a crane. Or a can opener. Or something.

Or I could at least talk to her while I wait for my fate to meet me. Right now, I'm just talking to you. And you're not even really there.

I replayed every minute of the stupid fight that evening. Trying to find the perfect sentence, the one that would somehow get things back to normal.

But things *weren't* normal. And there wasn't a magical sentence that could fix things.

Well, that wasn't true. There was one. *Caroline, I'm going to tell you everything.*

But I couldn't do that.

Right?

And then I got a text from Mr. Jones, the only thing that could possibly have distracted me:

Get into the suit as soon as you can. Wait for instructions.

It took forever for my mom's bedroom light to go out that night, and I was in such a hurry to get to the lab that I banged into the bookcase right outside the guest room door and knocked over a shelf of books. I held my breath, but miraculously, the light didn't come back on, and I was down in the lab and suited up in under five minutes.

"Where were you?!?" Mr. Jones shouted, almost taking my head off. That warm, confidential tone from our last conversation was gone. He didn't even let me talk.

"The Golden Gate Bridge. Now." I don't live anywhere near

the Golden Gate Bridge. I mean, a-thousand-miles-away not near. I started a question and he cut me off again. "If you're not heading west at maximum speed in the next five seconds—*with the cloaking on*—"

I was.

Only then was I able to get him to tell me what was going on. And I kind of wished I hadn't.

Apparently, the Bloody Front was planning to blow up the bridge.

On the bright side, Mr. Jones told me, a little calmer now that I was on my way to save the day, my previous screwup had had a silver lining. I'd rattled the Front, and now they were acting irrationally, getting sloppy, which could yield information for us. That was how he'd been able to pick up chatter about the bridge attack. If they hadn't skimped on their standard security protocols, he'd probably never have known. And maybe they would even let something slip about my dad . . . that was the hope.

On the other hand, their panicked, sloppy behavior might have been what was *causing* them to make this grand gesture—which could get a lot of people killed.

"The Golden Gate Bridge is pretty public," I said. "Aren't people going to see me? And then everyone'll know Mayhem's back?"

Yes, he said, it was regrettable we had to go public like this, but we didn't have a choice. Lives needed saving. Which sounded pretty good to me, I have to be honest. After everything that had gone on, it would be nice to be a hero at something.

"At least it's far enough away so Mayhem won't be connected with your home state," Mr. Jones said, then barked, "Watch out for that jetliner!"

I banked sharply. Not that I was anywhere near bumping into it—I'd set the proximity alarms properly—but I was getting close enough to be spotted. People look out the window every now and then and, of course, the cloaking devices don't do anything to the eyeball or a phone camera. I didn't want the Bloody Front knowing I was coming. Or anyone else, for that matter.

And they didn't.

Which explains the hubbub when I landed at the foot of the bridge. Right in the middle of an anti-terror-solidarity midnight rally.

My first thought was that the Bloody Front was more seriously sick than I'd ever imagined, trying to kill the people who'd shown up to prove they weren't afraid. But that wasn't it.

I scoped the bridge six ways from Sunday on my way down. Explosives sniffers, radiation gauges, fourteen other types of threats identifiable via the drop-down panel. I couldn't detect a single one. Nothing. Mr. Jones was talking away in my ear, asking me if I saw anything suspicious, telling me to use my instruments and my instincts, and I was coming up with zip.

The news reports were nuts. I mean, what a story: thousands of crunchy hippie types, holding signs with flowers about peace and love and freedom to live their lives without fear, and then this gigantic metal robot flies down right into the middle of them.

I was doing my best to handle it, making peace signs left and right—there was even that one shot that's all over the Internet of the beautiful girl with the long hair putting that flower necklace around my helmet.

And then the cops who had been sent to patrol the event started shooting.

It had absolutely zero effect on me or my suit, of course. But the bullets were ricocheting off me into the crowd. When I yelled at the police to stop shooting, they just kept going, and when I picked up some sawhorses and threw them in their direction to get them to stop—not the best decision, in hindsight, but it wasn't like I had much of a plan—they thought I was assaulting police officers, and then it was a whole new ball game. They had called for backup anyway—I mean, long absence or no long absence, Mayhem *was* wanted for all those bank robberies—and by that point I think they were on the phone to the National Guard. It was time to get out of there.

I wanted to fly, but with the place so packed, I was afraid activating my boot jets might burn someone. Instead, I ran. Right through Golden Gate Park. I kept clear of as many people as possible, but I did barrel over one or two idiots who wanted to take selfies with the suit. One of them ended up in the hospital with a broken arm, I read later, but I don't feel bad about that. It was her own fault.

At least that's one thing I don't feel guilty about . . .

The point is, I had no idea where I was going. And then I heard helicopters overhead.

And the sound of Mr. Jones in my ear. He was humming this old song "Smoke on the Water" by Deep Purple. (Like I said, I'm a big classic rock fan.) I asked him—screamed at him, really—what was going on, where was the Bloody Front, how could he have gotten it so wrong, and most important, *how was he going to get me out of here.*

"Bailey, you're in no trouble whatsoever," he said, smooth as ever, ignoring my questions. "Watch your readouts. Monitor the scanners. There's nothing within ten miles of you that could make the tiniest dent in the suit. The only thing that can defeat you is your own panic."

Which happened to be spiking as one of the helicopters shone its searchlight directly on me.

"If you're going to fight the Bloody Front," Mr. Jones went on, completely worry-free, "you're going to have to learn to deal with the unexpected. To impose order on the chaos. You are in charge."

I almost lost it. This was a—to use one of the worst phrases adults have ever come up with—a *teachable moment?* Was the Front ever even supposed to be there? I started to tell him what I thought of him in no uncertain terms, and then realized that the helicopters were getting louder. Idiot that I am, I'd stopped running when I heard Mr. Jones talking. He was right, after all. I really did need to learn to focus.

"So what do I *do?*" I shouted.

"Well," he said. "That is the question." And switched off. Great. Teachable freaking moment it was.

I took a deep breath, and thought: *How do I get away?* Keeping to the ground was no good—too many people around. I'd end up hurting someone by accident. And yes, my flight skills were getting better every day, but now there was a *swarm* of helicopters up there, and some of them might try to get too close. I had a vision of a spinning, flaming chopper, rotors smashed from contact with the suit, spiraling down into the crowds . . . No.

So not by land and not by air. That left one other option.

I checked the map and changed direction, heading straight for Fisherman's Wharf.

I'm sure you've seen the news footage. There were helicopters and searchlights and news cameras covering everything, and it was all very dramatic how I battered through this one boat on this one dock and then came out the other side and disappeared into the bay.

As it turned out, the yacht belonged to one of those Internet billionaires, and when the police and Homeland Security investigated, because of course they did, they found computer files that showed the guy had been selling people's credit card data on the Dark Web.

At least I got to be the good guy once, even if it was by accident. I guess that's something.

✦

Mayhem was back, with a splash. Literally: I probably spent an hour underwater until I was pretty sure the helicopters had gone. It's amazing what the suit can do.

I'd like to say it was all anyone was talking about at school the next day, but I have no idea. I was exhausted from trying to avoid the coast guard—one of those things you never read about in the comics—and couldn't concentrate on much of anything.

There was lots of stuff on the Internet about it, but most of it was superlong and almost all the stuff I *did* read was wrong. I wasn't an *anti-corporatist* or an *ecoterrorist* or a *neo-nihilist*. I didn't even know what some of those meant. I was just trying to get my dad back. And based on last night's fiasco, I didn't think Mr. Jones was going to be sending me on any new life-or-death missions to save my dad anytime soon.

And as the next few days passed with no messages, it became clearer and clearer that he agreed. I had blown it. I didn't have the chops. I wasn't even good enough to be given a third try.

I had also irreparably ruined everything with my best and only real friend. That was lodged in there pretty tight, too.

There was so much going on inside my head, in fact, that it took something on the order of a personal thermonuclear explosion to make me sit up and notice anything else.

Which is to say, it took Rebecca coming over and talking to me.

Coming over. To *me*. And *talking*.

I *know*.

✄

Something was up with her. That was clear right away.

Part of it must have been Logan. He wasn't back at school full-time yet, but he'd been coming more and more, and for longer periods—some booster had paid for an aide who walked with him, helped him carry his backpack, that sort of thing. Under normal circumstances, this would be when all the kids he'd ever tormented would be lining up to make fun of him and take their revenge, but Logan had never been that kind of guy. Plus the way he'd been taken out was so terrible that people were doing everything they could to make his life easier.

Except Rebecca. Not that she was mean to him or anything. She wasn't a mean person. If she was, I like to think I wouldn't have been attracted to her, even from a distance. Cruelty has always felt like a turnoff . . . but honestly, who knows? Not the point. She wasn't. But she was . . . distant, I guess. I don't mean physically—she was always there for him if he needed additional help with his crutches, or navigating the stairs, that sort of thing. She was patient and she would smile and all that. But she wasn't *there*. And he could tell. And so could everyone else.

Anyway, I don't know what was going through Rebecca's head at the time. But this is what happened.

I was standing in front of my locker getting my Biology loose-leaf, and I smelled her. There was only one girl in the school who wore that perfume.

"Bailey," she said.

I hadn't been sure that she knew my name; although I guess after the thing with Logan she did.

I didn't turn to look at her right away. I was afraid I would make the wrong face, say the wrong thing, and that would be it. Forever and ever.

"Bailey, um . . . you know what? Forget it." And she turned to walk away.

I heard myself say no, and I saw my arm reach out to hers. I got the warm, soft part of her upper arm—I could feel that softness for days, replaying it at home, at night, in midair, wherever—and she didn't freeze up, she didn't pull away, she just looked at me.

And then I said the wrong thing. Probably the worst possible thing.

"How's Logan?" is what I said, and even now, with my arms pinned by rubble, trapped inside a metal suit, all I want to do is smack myself on the head again and again and again.

Because it got even worse. I figured she'd just turn and walk away, or laugh at me, but no. That would have been too easy. Instead, she started crying. My first conversation with the love of my life, and I had *made her cry*.

Of course, being Rebecca, even her crying was kind of sexy. Just these two or three tears, shimmering on her bottom eyelid. I had a sudden urge to reach over and wipe them away, but I had enough self-control not to take *that* trip into crazytown.

"Sorry," she said, digging in her bag and coming up with some tissues. "Sorry."

"No," I said, and I honestly did not know what words were coming out of my mouth. "No, I'm sorry, I'm an idiot—"

"I mean," she said, not looking at me, "he's so good, you know? So strong? Well, *you* know." She reached out in the direction of my nose, and for a second I thought she was going to touch it. I couldn't breathe.

She didn't, though. She just went back into her purse to get eyeliner. (Or mascara: I'm not really sure which is which, or if they're the same thing.) She still didn't look at me. "I don't know. I just . . . what I feel for him now, more than anything else, is . . . it's pity. The rest of it—whatever it was—I think it's been . . . driven out. You know? And . . . I just don't think that's enough." Now she looked up at me and I could see she had done a terrible job with the eyeliner. Or mascara. "It makes me think . . . I'm worried that I don't even know what was there to begin with. Was it just . . . curiosity? Because of . . . who he was?"

There was only one thing to say, and I said it. "No," I said, and was grateful it could mean pretty much anything.

"He deserves more," she said, and although I don't know a lot about girls, I don't think she was really talking to me. "Doesn't he?"

I managed to move my head slightly, very slightly, in an up and down direction. I probably would have said something else, and probably would have made it worse, or different, or *something*, but the bell rang and she practically fled toward the Bio lab. But she looked back at me, this time for sure, and as she did, I saw something in that look.

Something that told me that I might, just might, actually have a shot.

Something that told me that I had to have a plan. And soon.

Looking back, that plan should not have involved my giant robot suit. But hindsight is a killer.

Was that a *crack?* I think that was a *crack.*

Something in the walls, hopefully. Or maybe it's my suit starting to give in. I'm going to have to make another move pretty soon.

Or was it someone's voice?

Probably just my imagination. I don't think there's anyone who doesn't have a robot's worth of metal with its own internal cooling systems surrounding them who'd risk coming in here. I'm sure even the National Guard is planning to wait it out and then pick up the pieces.

Pieces of me, that is. Ha-ha.

I'm starting to ramble. *That's* not good. Gas from the building? Or the suit? Making me loopy? Come on. Focus.

A MONTH AGO

The Rebecca plan was clear, at least to me: use my newly acquired secret identity to make her fall in love with me.

It didn't fit in with Mr. Jones's whole lay-low approach—at all—but I thought maybe there was a way to do it without attracting too much attention.

I know, I know.

Caroline would have fixed the plan. Made it perfect. This was the kind of thing we would have talked over, gamed out, rehearsed a hundred times.

But the truth is, even if we had been on speaking terms, even if I had told her everything, I'm not so sure I would have run the plan by her. Probably because I wouldn't have wanted to hear what I knew she'd say. Which would have been to abandon the whole idea altogether. Rebecca and Mayhem: don't mix.

There's this line. I think it's Bob Dylan, but he may have been quoting Mark Twain, I'm not sure. It goes something like, if what you've got is a hammer, then everything looks like a nail. I had problems. And Mayhem was the answer. It was going to be the answer . . .

So. The plan.

Now, stay with me here, because this part is a little tricky.

I've given you the impression that every time I've talked about Mayhem flying, or fighting, or whatever, I've been inside the suit, at least since I discovered it. The thing is, I can operate the suit from the computer in my dad's lab via remote control or preprogrammed routine. It's not as much fun, but I can do it.

And that was my plan to get Rebecca.

Okay, so here's what it looked like. It was all going to go down in the small courtyard on campus connecting the science building to the arts building. I knew Rebecca passed through that courtyard every Wednesday at some point between 11:37 and 11:40, going from her Biology class to her English class. (Yes, I knew her schedule, okay? I'm not proud of it.) The plan was to program Mayhem to land there, at exactly that moment. And then I would "scare it off."

I had to keep it simple, since I couldn't look like I knew what the suit was going to do. But I figured even that would be enough to make Rebecca look at me differently.

Or keep looking at me differently. If I understood what had happened at my locker correctly. Which I was pretty sure that I did not, despite the number of hours I had devoted to thinking about it.

But what happened instead was that the whole thing went to hell.

One minute I was standing there, trying to look like

nothing particularly interesting was about to happen while also trying to avoid looking around too obviously for Rebecca. And then there she was, walking through the passageway, talking to one of her friends. It might have been my imagination, but I thought she looked a little desperate. A little trapped. Or maybe she was just thinking about a test she had in fifth period.

But then she—and everybody else—hears it, and everything else goes away. I'm used to it by now, and most of the time I'm inside the suit so I don't hear it, but Mayhem is loud. Not quite commercial-jet loud, but when it's landing ten feet from you, it's hard to hear anything else. Even your own voice, shouting. Or screaming.

I thought I'd calculated the drop precisely—until Mayhem crashed right through the memorial fountain established for students who had fought and died in Vietnam. On the cell phone videos it looks like he did it on purpose, which didn't hurt the theories saying Mayhem was in league with the Bloody Front . . . but I'm getting ahead of myself.

Mayhem landed in a crouch and stood up, rock and rubble sliding off the suit in a cloud of dust. Everyone was either running or frozen stiff in panic. Rebecca was somewhere in between.

Within a matter of seconds, it became clear that she was the target, as Mayhem turned and looked at her. Programming that had been easy enough—facial recognition and tracking, essentially, using a picture I'd sneaked a few weeks before. He took three steps toward her, looking for all intents and purposes like Frankenstein's monster as the suit's black, featureless helmet swiveled slowly in her direction. Rebecca dropped any remaining pretense of togetherness and started screaming her head off.

And then, all of a sudden, out of nowhere, someone jumped between Mayhem and Rebecca, shouting something inaudible at the suit and brandishing a medium-size rock.

No, not me. Jimmy Anderson.

I had been so myopically obsessed with my own feelings for Rebecca I hadn't even considered the possibility that some other person in the school might be crushing on her, too. And I had just handed him the possibility of her favor by taking a stance against a supervillain—making the same noble gesture I was planning to fake.

The problem was that Jimmy Anderson's facial features and body type had not been entered into the suit's data-banks as a non-threat. And Mayhem, acting without human reflexes or responses, dealt with Jimmy the way it would have dealt with anything else.

I knew enough to have set the suit's controls to avoid fatal harm. But non-fatal harm can be bad enough.

Mayhem reached out a hand and batted Jimmy Anderson away like he was a stray napkin left on the cafeteria table. Just a flick, and poor Jimmy went flying across the quad.

I don't need to watch the videos for this part. This part I see again and again. The bones breaking, his arm bending in a way no arm should. The scream—which gets cut off, almost in a cough, when his head bounced off the ground, a second later, like a basketball. His eyes closing.

When I dream about it, Jimmy's eyes snap open and look straight at me. One time they were crying tears of blood.

In real life, Mayhem stood there, silently, over his victim. He was waiting for his cue, which was me saying, *Go on. Get the hell out of here, you punk!* But those words never came, because I was staring, shocked and horrified, at the body of Jimmy Anderson. After a minute that lasted forever, the other fail-safes kicked in and Mayhem flew off long before the FBI and Homeland Security finally came crashing in.

Jimmy was in a coma for three days and that whole time I walked around thinking I was going to throw up any minute. *This is the worst thing,* I thought. *The worst thing possible.*

But he woke up. At least he woke up.

If the school had been overrun by outsiders before, now it was mobbed. Reporters, government officials, paparazzi, everyone looking for answers. One kid got himself famous for forty-eight hours by claiming to be Mayhem's best friend. He managed to get a sit-down interview on CNN before the whole thing unraveled.

But that wasn't what I was worried about, even as Mayhem, or the substitute Mayhem, or whatever I was. I was out of my mind with guilt, yes. And, if I'm being totally, entirely, down-to-the-bottom honest, I was upset that my plan hadn't worked out. It's true, Rebecca wasn't actively turning away when I passed her in the halls—I even thought, once or twice, there was a look that kind of maybe possibly *lingered*—but she hadn't said one word to me, and I definitely wasn't ready to try something else.

Her not talking to me wasn't the worst part. Even the gaping hole in my existence of the missing conversations I would normally have been having with Caroline—Mayhem had just attacked our school, you'd better believe we'd've been talking about that, though I have no idea how the conversation would have gone, given my, um, special circumstances—even that wasn't the worst.

The worst was the single text from Mr. Jones—*DO YOU HAVE ANY IDEA WHAT YOU'VE DONE?*—and then total silence. Nothing.

The clock was ticking on my dad's safety.

I had ruined everything, and for what?

You'd think my mom would have noticed some of the behavioral changes in her son. But something had happened in the weeks since the Bloody Front had crippled Logan. She'd been spending more time at school, volunteering with the parents' organization, and had admitted, finally, that she'd started seeing someone. Someone she'd met at one of the fund-raisers for Logan, funnily enough. He was the dad of a kid who'd graduated a few years ago, and the dad had come back to help support the school. My mom kept telling me not to prejudge and that when the time was right she hoped I would meet him and try to accept that my dad had moved on or whatever. Which, of course, made me more upset and difficult and, I'm sure to Mom's mind, obnoxious.

Because Dad hadn't just left us and moved on. He'd been *kidnapped*.

And Mom's timing didn't help, either. Sure, she didn't know what else was going on, but you know when she chose to tell me? This *news*? On the day before our dadiversary.

That's what I called it: the day that Dad—well, I can't call it what I used to—but the day Dad didn't come home. We had a ritual. It started that first year, when we were still raw and torn open. That night, after dinner, Mom sat me down and reminded me of the date. And I cried, and then we had Dad's favorite dessert—which was pistachio ice cream, which both of us hated, but whatever—and Mom popped the tape in.

I know, nobody has a VCR anymore. Some of my friends may never even have seen a videotape. But it was an old home movie, and I guess Dad had never gotten around to converting it to digital, and so they kept the VCR around just to play that one video. I'm glad they did.

Some kids love looking at their mom and dad's wedding album or video, but I never did, because I had this tape. At their wedding, they were formal, dressed up and clearly doing whatever the photographer was telling them to do. But in this video . . . well, it was really them.

The video was taken by one of their friends, and it showed them in their theater group in college. Where they met. It was this play about people putting on a play. A comedy with people running all over the place, tripping over things and slamming doors, with terrible British accents. I guess people online say it's funny, but I don't know. That's not why I watch it—why we watch it. We watch it because we can see, whenever Mom's weird half-blind actress and Dad's sort-of-stupid actor look at each other, the two of them falling in love.

There's this one moment when Dad drops a line and he looks horrified, and Mom looks over and gives him this special little smile, a smile just for him, saying: *It's okay, I love you, everything's going to be all right.* I used to rewind and watch the scene, rewind and watch, again and again, for years, when Mom wasn't around.

But now she says she's moved on. So it's up to me to make everything right. Get it back to the way it should be.

Well, me and the one man who was going to help. Who was currently giving me the silent treatment.

Okay, yes, I screwed up. Big time. I'd made it more difficult to take down the Bloody Front and save his friend—my dad. But he clearly had information that he wasn't sharing. And he shouldn't have been punishing me when we could be out there putting the suit to work.

I was just so terribly alone.

And then I got the text. Well, a series of texts:

I know that we are currently in a terrible argument, Caroline wrote. *And that we have said some hurtful things to each other. And I know that we will forgive each other, in time. But I also know it is your dadiversary. And I know that this is always a tough day for you, and this year, much more so. (Even if you will not tell me why.) So I have a modest proposal.*

And then there were those three blinking dots, the ones that said a text was coming. They lasted for a long time, much longer than they should have—Caroline typed really fast thanks to all that piano practice. I could see her, finished with the text but refusing to send, smiling—*I'm gonna forgive him, but let's let him squirm*—and that made me smile, too, and even laugh out loud.

There was a sound outside my door. My mom. I guess she'd been waiting outside, wondering whether she should come in. "Bailey? Everything . . . is everything all right in there?" Clearly the sound of laughter was not what she was expecting.

I told her it was.

"So . . . can I come in? Can we talk?"

I looked at Caroline's new message, which had finally come in: *Shall we just skip to where we forgive each other now?* it said. Like I knew it would.

"Not now," I told Mom. "I have to talk to someone else." Which was kind of cruel, but fine. She was dating someone who wasn't my dad. Let her feel sorry for herself.

I was going to tell my friend what was happening.

Well, not everything. Not yet.

But Caroline was really smart—and if she could get past the whole my-best-friend-is-a-supervillain thing and, oh, the my-best-friend-somehow-put-a-freshman-in-a-coma-because-he-wanted-to-impress-his-crush thing, maybe she could help me with these two very big problems I was having. Well, two *other* very big problems, I guess.

First I needed to be able to get into the files of, if not the smartest, most dangerous man in the world, at least the most paranoid. Someone who spent what seemed like a lot of his time and energy making sure no one could track him down. Because, like it or not, Mr. Jones was the only link to my dad. And if he wasn't going to help me, then I was going to help myself.

And second, I needed to figure out how to reverse whatever allowed Mr. Jones to take over the suit. Even if I managed to find out whatever leads he had on the Bloody Front, the minute he discovered me—I can't believe I'm using this expression, but I *am* operating a giant flying robot suit, so some drama is probably unavoidable—going rogue, his first move would be to shut the suit down. I don't want to imagine the second move.

In the comics, this is where Caroline turns out to be a computer genius. But this isn't a comic. Even on her best day, Caroline wasn't close to the level of ability you'd need to get past the defenses built into the Mayhem system, much less hack into the files of a supergenius. And as for me, I knew almost nothing about computers except how to download movies and follow Rebecca on all her social media accounts.

But superhackers don't grow on trees, and they don't show up in Google searches. I didn't even know where to start looking. And assuming I could even find one, what I was asking was clearly going to be expensive, and I understood that the $350 in my savings account was not going to cut it.

Caroline would know what to do.

And I was going to tell her then, I swear. I was about to call her. And I was going to tell her *everything*. But then my phone buzzed again.

A message telling me to fly to a particular latitude and longitude. Within the hour.

I texted Caroline: *Can't talk now something up will explain tomorrow really all of it I promise really really and thanks (for everything!!!!)*. Then I took a deep breath, and waited and waited and waited and waited for my mom to fall asleep.

I made it to Mr. Jones's rendezvous point with a few minutes to spare.

It turned out to be the top of a mountain in the middle of a forest and, I have to say, I have no idea how he got there. The woods were thick and dark and if there was an ATV parked a few hundred feet away, my sensors weren't picking up on it. It was like he'd wafted out of the ground, like a ghost. Maybe he has some way of messing with the data that comes into the suit. Who knows.

He began by yelling at me about Jimmy Anderson—which I deserved. But I got the funny feeling that the anger was like the expressions on his Halloween masks: fake emotion, trying to cover up whatever was underneath. I didn't know what that was; I'm still not sure. But I think at least part of it might have been to throw me off my guard for what came next.

He sat there, on a large flat rock, wearing a mask of either Mick Jagger or that woman British prime minister, I don't remember her name, and told me that thanks to my *continued carelessness*—those were his exact words, I'll never forget them—I'd blown contacts, ruined plans, wasted hundreds of thousands of dollars. The resources he'd dedicated to finding my dad were all up in smoke, he said, wiggling his gloves. So it was clear what we had to do.

It wasn't clear to me, I told him.

He looked me in the eye—well, in the helmet visor. "Mayhem needs to rob another bank," he said.

⟍

Right away, I didn't like it.

You know those scam e-mails old people in Florida get? Or the fake Facebook messages? The ones that pretend to come from a friend who's been traveling in some other country and they lost their passport or got pickpocketed and they just need you to send them, like, fifty bucks on PayPal or something so they can get home?

This reminded me a little too much of that.

I mean, I know my dad was in the bank-robbing business. I got that. A Robin Hood bank robber, hero to some, villain to others, but he had gone into banks and taken the money just the same. Now that people knew Mayhem was back, they might even expect it.

But he'd always taken from the rich and given to the poor—not taken from the rich and given to Mr. Jones.

"Um, what do you need the money for?" I asked him.

And he told me.

Well, he sort of told me. He said words, and they added up to sentences, and the sentences became paragraphs, but they never became an explanation. There was something about routing numbers and dead drops and mentions of signal intelligence and underwater trawling . . .

The thing was, it seemed like he was trying to explain. To let me in, introduce me to the business, so to speak. And

I wasn't getting it. I was failing my dad. I was failing him. I was failing them both.

Maybe that's why I agreed to do it. But it wasn't the only reason.

It was also a way for me to get some money of my own. Because if he wasn't being honest with me, then maybe hiring computer hackers was still the way to go. I needed to find out more about this Mr. Jones. That much was clear.

My plan—to the extent you could call what I had a plan—was simple. Mr. Jones was going to set up robberies for Mayhem to commit. I would commit the robberies. Give most of the money to Mr. Jones. Use the rest to hire hackers. Makes sense, right?

Again, I had no idea how to find these hackers. But I was on a pretty steep learning curve when it came to breaking the law.

And I was about to get a first-class seminar in the subject. From the master.

━━

Mr. Jones said that my recent activity had led to *significant suspicion* that Mayhem was based in my area, so I should try to pick my first job somewhere farther afield. I confessed to him that I hadn't realized I would get to pick, to which he responded that pretty much anyone can *commit* a crime . . . the trick was getting away with it. And that always, always depended on appropriate planning. If I wanted to learn how to stay out of jail, even with a supersuit, I had to learn how to plan.

The planning sessions took place over the next few days. In the sky.

I would practice maneuvering while Mr. Jones chatted away in my ear. Once or twice I could hear a helicopter hovering somewhere out of sight. I knew it was him, because it didn't show up on my instruments. One time a drone matched me mile for mile. It was wearing a Mayhem mask on its front, one of the few times I saw any evidence that Mr. Jones had a sense of humor.

But I learned a lot. Mr. Jones reminded me about digital footprints and search history, to make sure I wouldn't type things like *how to rob a bank* into Google. He shared operational details from some of his and my dad's greatest hits. And after a few days of extensive discussion and training, I was flying reconnaissance around the banks we'd targeted. And that was when I had my idea.

Yes, I could smash and grab my way into a bank, like my dad had. But there were easier ways to get the money. Like when it came out of the bank.

An armored-car robbery is harder than it looks in the movies. Mayhem had the hardware to get through the armor—I mean, I had *missiles*—but we would run the risk of blowing up the money and the people driving it, and I had made a commitment not to hurt anyone. Ever again.

Promises are easy to make.

I didn't tell Mr. Jones about my decision, though. We were talking more—getting more comfortable with each other, I think, or, at least, I was getting more comfortable around him. Telling him about Rebecca, about Caroline (although not about my decision to let her in on Mayhem . . . I wasn't that much of an idiot), about my mom. . . . And he was this patient, listening voice in my ear. I mean, sometimes a little preachy, but overall, patient, very patient, and even understanding. There could be a bunch of time between practice maneuvers, either setting up or getting to the next mock target destination, and so we kept talking.

Well, I talked. He said things, and they were the right things, but when you boiled them down they didn't *tell* very much. Certainly not about himself. But even about my dad.

For example, I asked him again and again, as we were going over my routes, to tell me exactly what he was going to do with the money if I was able to pull this off. How it was going to help him. How it helped us figure out where my dad was. And each time he would say the same thing, not frustrated, not angry, just with the same infuriating calm. "Let's get the money first. Then we'll talk about it."

I knew a *we'll see* when I heard it. And *we'll see* was close enough to *no* to convince me I was doing the right thing, going behind his back to find out what I needed to know.

Back to the armored car. Other downsides to the idea: It's not like banks make announcements about what time the cars are going to show up. And I didn't have the accomplices to create one of those choreographed multi-car barriers you see in the movies.

Those were the minuses. The big plus was the extremely powerful flying armored suit with world-class radar and tracking mechanisms.

Most armored-car robberies happen right around the bank, which is both good and stupid. The stupid part is that there are lots of things that can go wrong near the bank—there are pedestrians, police stopping by, your get-away car getting stuck in traffic. . . . The good reason for doing it right there, though, is that it's very hard to stop a bulletproof car once it's speeding up to eighty miles an hour on the highway. And if you somehow manage to accomplish it, it's next to impossible to get off the highway with the cash and to your hiding place without being picked up by a dozen surveillance cameras.

Again, though, flying armored suit.

And so one bright Tuesday, at approximately 1:42 in the afternoon, I became a supercriminal.

I'd been lurking at five thousand feet above the bank on and off over the past few days, watching for the armored car through the spyscopes, waiting for it to pull up to the curb. Once I spotted it, I locked on to its particular engine signature—the specific chemical composition of its exhaust since no two vehicles' exhaust is the same, another fact I learned from Mr. Jones—then put the suit on autopilot to track it out of the city so I didn't accidentally lose it in traffic or something.

I'd practiced a lot more with the autopilot feature. After Jimmy Anderson.

Later, I heard the interview with the armored car's driver. He said he was driving on the highway, thirty or forty min-utes out from the bank, when there was a sudden bump. He thought he'd run over a deer or something, but he was fin-ishing a fourteen-hour shift, so he kept driving. Next time he looked out the window, he was ten feet off the ground. And then he was jerking and twisting around, and then he knocked his head against the door and passed out. He had been sure he was going to die, but when he woke up, he was safe on the ground, and the truck had had its doors torn off and all the money was gone. The police investigated whether it was an inside job, if he'd been involved somehow, but dropped that pretty quickly. Because the security video from the highway—it was a private toll road, it turned out, with cameras stationed every few thousand feet—corroborated his story. Because it showed me.

That was his story. Here's mine.

I turned off the autopilot and swooped down toward the road, ready to do one of those Superman things where you pick the truck up from underneath. Then I was going to fly it to somewhere else, let the driver flee in terror, and ransack the truck. That's what I'd told Mr. Jones I was going to do, and he seemed fine with it.

It all went sideways as soon as I grabbed the rear bumper, which *immediately* broke off—the bump the driver felt.

I stopped dead in the middle of the highway. Just floating there, about five feet off the ground, staring at the bumper in my hands, watching the car drive away.

I ground my teeth and threw away the bumper. My plan had been to gently toss it onto the side of the road, but I guess I was frustrated and not paying attention, and so I missed. It ended up sticking out of the asphalt right in the middle of one of the opposite lanes, like a fork in a piece of pie.

And I didn't want to cause any traffic accidents or hurt anybody, so I had to go over there and dig it out. . . .

The point is, by the time I finished cleaning up that mess, the armored car was a mile away.

Of course, that wasn't much of a problem. I caught up within a minute—a minute I used to figure out how to get a better grip. It involved lifting and getting underneath.

But it turns out holding a truck which has a lot of momentum is hard. It tends to want to get away from you—especially when you didn't get the best hold to begin with. It wobbled—thankfully the driver was wearing his seat belt—and there was a terrifying moment when I thought I was going to drop it from thirty feet up. I didn't know whether the thing would squish or burst into flames or both.

It ended up okay. Because it was an armored truck, it didn't break apart, although I did a lot of nasty stuff to its underside as I tried to get a better grip. I was able to hold on until I got it about a quarter mile off to the side of the road.

And then I heard the noises coming from inside the truck.

Not from the driver's seat—that guy was out like a light. From inside the truck itself.

With a sick thud in my stomach, I realized I'd never noticed, during all my scouting runs, that there were guards inside the truck itself, right next to the money. This I could handle, though. I punched a small hole in the car and tossed in a gas grenade. Waited a few seconds, avoiding the bullet fire coming through the hole, and, when the pistol wobbled and fell back in, waited another ten seconds, then ripped off the back door. Two guards, out cold.

And then another problem I hadn't thought through: carrying the money. I'd figured the cash would be in one large container, but it was in a bunch of canvas sacks. I couldn't carry more than my armored hands could hold.

After quickly searching the armored car for something, I had an idea. I took the belts off the unconscious security guards and rigged a strap to hold a few extra bags around my waist. It wasn't a perfect solution, since one of the bags slipped in midair. I guess it got recovered, but I don't know that for sure. Maybe there's some guy living off the interstate with dye stains on his hands and a new Maserati. Who knows.

I *had* realized—that is, Mr. Jones had told me—that the armored car would be equipped with an alarm system to send a signal to the police as soon as the car left its planned path. I heard the sirens, but they weren't close enough to be anything for me to worry about. Not by a long shot.

I'd committed my first federal crime. And, although there was room for improvement, I'd pretty much gotten away with it.

⚊

Mr. Jones met me to pick up the cash himself that first time.

He'd arranged a rendezvous point; nothing flashy, nothing dramatic. The opposite, in fact. It was about a quarter mile from a landfill, one so big I imagined I could smell it through the suit. (I couldn't, really. The suit filters out everything and recirculates air through some process that—like almost everything else about the suit—I don't completely understand.)

I'd snagged an empty recycling bin in my neighborhood big enough to hold the money the day before. He looked inside it, now filled with all those fifties and hundreds, and he whistled, and he laughed, and I stood there, in my giant supervillain armor, and felt pleased and proud. He was happy. I had done a good job. At that moment, it was pure and simple.

Amazing what having a dad gone for seven years and a mom checked out for most of that time will do to you, huh?

But then, all of a sudden, his face changed. Well, not his face, which I couldn't see through the Mickey Mouse mask he was wearing, but his posture. It looked angry. Suspicious.

"This is light," he said. "You're missing sixty thousand dollars. At least."

Even then, I think, I wondered how he knew. I flushed—which, of course, he couldn't see—and launched into an explanation about the bag slipping in midair.

He listened to me, I held my breath, and then he shrugged, the ears of his mask flapping back and forth as he did. "Bailey," he said. "It's not that I'm mad. It's just that every dollar you bring in gets us that much closer to finding your dad. It's that simple."

I was beginning to think that maybe it wasn't that simple.

I'd been pretty sure Mr. Jones wasn't going to let me keep any of the money I stole. Whether he was going to scare me by saying it was for my own good, or guilt me by saying he needed it for my dad, the money was all going to go to him. And who knew what would happen to it after that.

I didn't know what Mr. Jones was after, but I was positive there was something else going on. Maybe he was doing something different with the money besides using it to find my dad. And I needed to find out what.

Like I said before, I thought I could skim some off the top without his noticing. But just in case he did notice—and if he did, it meant maybe things were skeevier than I'd thought— I'd better have a cover story.

The story I just told you. Pretty convincing, right?

Caroline had certainly thought so. When we came up with it.

Hold on. I think my foot might be on fire.

Nope. Good.

Maybe I can take my mind off things by shifting some more rubble and seeing if I die.

Still here. I got most of the rubble away from my face, which is a plus, but I did it by shifting it onto my legs, so I'm still stuck. But my head and arms are free, which is good because that's where most of the weaponry is. I can be ready when the army comes for me.

Don't think like that. This isn't a last will and testament.

Isn't it?

"I knew it!" Caroline said.

Although, of course, she hadn't had a clue.

How could she? How could *anybody*?

Pretty soon we established that it had just seemed like the right thing to say, under the circumstances. She wanted to give me the impression she was on my side, no matter what. But she hadn't had a clue about what had been making me act so strange.

Actually, she had thought—and this was close to the mark, when you think about it—that I had found out my dad was in prison. And that my mom had been lying about it to protect me.

"Well," I said, "he's a prison*er*—so I guess it's true."

I know how ridiculous this sounds. But it didn't feel that way. Especially since our conversation was taking place in the May-cave, which is what Caroline called the lab. And which was just perfect.

Of course, it took her a while to process. Especially since I started the whole thing by calling her in the middle of the night, as soon as I got back from the Mr.-Jones-told-me-I-had-to-start-committing-felonies meeting. I asked her to skip school the next day and come to my house. *Will explain everything here*, I said. *Promise.*

She texted back that she'd come as soon as school was over, which was no good—the window between her getting here and my mom coming back from work was just too tight. *Trust me*, I said. *It'll be worth it.*

Trust me. That's what I told her. To trust me. And she did.

Anyway.

She did it—skipped school—which was a big thing for her. This was not normal Caroline behavior, to put it mildly. But she showed up, and said that this had better be worth it, and I told her that I was pretty sure she would think it was.

I could have tried something else. I could have tried cutting her off, kicking her out, letting the chips fall where they may. I could have tried half a dozen other things. But I didn't. Maybe it was just the easiest way out. But maybe—I've wondered this, and I know I'll never know, not for sure—maybe I just wanted to share my secret with someone who wasn't a homicidal-genius nutcase.

By the time we got down the ladder to the May-cave she was speechless. Ironically, the thing that was the least impressive was the Mayhem suit itself: it was dearmorized, so at first she didn't realize what it was.

And then, after a minute, she did.

"That's . . . that's it?" she said. "It looks so . . . wrinkly."

I started to try to explain about the armorizing process, but she was lost in thought. And then she said, "Are you, like . . . like, his henchman, or something?"

I couldn't help myself, it was too much. I laughed. Which got her offended, and confused, and finally, I just took a deep breath and went ahead. "I'm not Mayhem's henchman," I said. "I'm *Mayhem*. And, uh, also his son."

And then I got into the suit. And bench-pressed one of the lab tables, for show.

She stood there for a minute. "Wow," she said. "I mean, wow. Mayhem. It's really, you know—it's really Mayhem." And then, small and quiet: "Why did you hurt Jimmy Anderson like that?"

And that was it, I mean, that just let something loose in me, and I started crying—not just about Jimmy Anderson, but about my dad, my life, everything. Caroline sat there for a second, and then she said, "Is there a box of tissues in your secret supervillain hideout?" and I snorted through the tears. Clearly, everything was going to be okay.

Shows what I knew. But I told her everything, from beginning to end. Explained about Jimmy Anderson—to which she responded, grim and serious, "You're an idiot, Bailey," and I couldn't disagree—and that my dad was the original Mayhem, and how his disappearance was actually a kidnapping. About trying to get him back from the Bloody Front. Even about Mr. Jones, and how he wanted me to rob banks to help him find my dad. I said that I thought something was fishy with him, to which she said, "Fishy? You think a grown-up who wears a rubber Halloween mask to meet with a kid is *fishy*? I guess that's one way of putting it," which made me feel better, too.

She walked over to the Mayhem suit and stroked it. "It's like a sweatshirt," she said. "Unbelievable." Then she came back over to me and gave me a big hug. "I'm so, so, sorry, Bailey," she said. "All of this—and no one else knows, no one to talk to."

I couldn't respond, so I just nodded.

And then she said it.

"Can I help?"

She sure could. Because I needed a plan to find out more about him, and for that, I needed money.

And so the planning sessions in the sky with Mr. Jones were matched by Caroline conversations on the ground. During free periods, in whispers, and in coded notes passed in class. Paper only, as Caroline pointed out that Mr. Jones could be monitoring my phone. Which made me realize I wasn't nearly as clever about any of this as I had thought I was.

We came up with a plan. Well, we came up with two dozen plans, but most of them were stupid, or unworkable, or would have put my dad in more danger, or had one of a thousand other problems.

The plan we came up with was straightforward. In fact, it was identical to the one I had made with Mr. Jones, with one crucial difference.

I was very, very, *very* careful to make sure not a single bag of cash slipped out of my hands. Not one.

Which was why there was $62,350 hidden under scrub brush in the ravine about ten miles from my house.

—

I don't know if Mr. Jones could tell I was holding my breath after I lied to him—I was inside the suit, after all. Had he seen through our plan? Was he going to call me on it? Yell at me for being careless?

What he did was change the subject. "Asked out Rebecca yet?"

Which, as he well knew, I had not. God knows I had talked about it enough with him. Both because I always had things to say about her, and because it helped steer the subject away from any other friends in my life. I was afraid if we talked about Caroline I'd give myself—ourselves—away.

But I still hadn't thought of the right way to get myself into Rebecca's good graces. Part of it was the spectacular, trau-matizing failure of my last attempt. But it was more than that . . . it was the knowledge that it needed to be something special. Something grand. And something fast: winter formal was a few weeks away, and I thought that was a good go-big-or-go-home moment.

It was ridiculous, of course. A fantasy. I mean, Rebecca had a boyfriend. Yes, maybe they were hitting a rough patch. Maybe she was even dreading going to winter formal with him. I mean—I know this is cruel, but it's true—he couldn't dance. But they were still *together*. And Rebecca wasn't going to dump him because of an injury. That wasn't who she was.

Maybe I wouldn't have dared to even try, before the robbery. But ripping open the doors of an armored car does tend to change your perspective.

I muttered something, and while I was looking for the right words, he turned around and started wheeling the recycling bin into the middle of the forest, looking—I swear, this is what I thought—like Mom the night before trash day.

"Ask her already. I'll be in touch," he said over his shoulder.

I was left frustrated, still in the dark about my dad, and more committed than ever to getting into his files. Somehow.

I needed time to think. I told my mom my nose was still hurting and stayed home from school the next day, hoping Caroline would come over. Caroline wanted to know everything about what had happened, of course—the news had reported the armored car robbery, that Mayhem was involved and back to his old tricks, but, of course, they didn't have the first-person details. She sent me what I guess she felt was a safe text, in case Mr. Jones was indeed spying on us:

?

Those Mysterians again.

I responded that I wasn't feeling well and was going to stay home from school, but she could come over, and she texted back: *Only one of us has a get-out-of-jail-free card.*

And then a second later: *I am so sorry. Was that insensitive? I feel like it may have been insensitive.*

I texted her back several emojis, which, when you put them all together, gave the impression of general all-goodedness.

We will talk soon, she said.

So then I spent the next eight hours staring at the lab computer.

Maybe Dad had left some sort of clue, the way he'd left the passwords upstairs. Something to give me some hint of what to do next.

And believe it or not, I found it.

And I was pretty sure Mr. Jones didn't know it existed. Even though Mr. Jones could monitor every keystroke, every command that I entered . . . I couldn't imagine him finding this. Because it wasn't on the computer; it was *on* the computer.

On top of it, that is. Another tiny piece of paper rolled up, this one wedged into that small area between the computer screen and the monitor covering. So tightly that it was almost invisible. I mean, I had missed it all this time.

On it, typed in small, neat letters, was the name of a website, together with a long password.

Now all I wanted to do was plug it into my phone immediately and see what happened. But with Mr. Jones monitoring the Internet traffic in and out of my house—by now I was positive of that—that was a bad idea. I knew I needed to wait.

And the next day provided a perfect opportunity.

It was class field trip.

⌐

All right, it wasn't officially called that, since we're not in elementary school. It was a day of community service to look good on our college applications. Not that college was the first thing on anyone's mind with what was going on. But I think the administration wanted to try to do something to get school spirit back up on the heels of the "Friday Night Fright," as people called the Bloody Front's attack on Logan.

They gave us different options for where we could go. Which was agonizing for me, because Logan was coming, and he wanted to do cleanup in the town square—there was some discussion about building a memorial there to the victims of the Front—and Rebecca was, of course, going with him. And I, of course, would usually go wherever Rebecca did. But I knew I had more important things to do, so I chose the group assigned to help reorganize the stacks in the town library.

The town library, with its public, and anonymous, Internet connections.

I figured it was possible Mr. Jones had downloaded my school schedule, patched into town security camera footage to see where I was going, and started monitoring Internet traffic in and out of all the library computers. But I hoped that level of monomania and paranoia was a bit much even for him. Wishful thinking, maybe, but I didn't have a ton of ideas, and the two things I was pretty sure of were that my dad was running out of time and that Mr. Jones's promises to save him seemed sketchier and sketchier. This whole thing had to be resolved, and soon.

As you can see from my current situation, nothing worked out the way I'd hoped.

But this was the best I could think of at the time. And maybe that website from the piece of paper would give me some good ideas, even some answers. Maybe it was a clue as to how my dad had disappeared. Whatever it was, I knew I had to check it out.

I told Caroline about it on the minibus on the way over, and she agreed. "How can I help?" she asked.

And I remember saying to her that we'd figure it out as we went along.

Honestly. That's where we were in all this. Just kids, figuring it out as we went along. Or trying to . . .

Anyway. Our job was to help the librarians cull the books. Any book that hadn't been checked out in the last seven years was going to get chucked. I avoided the librarian's hopeful look when he said we could take them home if we wanted, and his crushed expression when none of us took him up on it.

The computers were in a small room off the main entrance, but most of the shelves were downstairs, so I had to be creative.

I'd been to this library with my mom and dad a lot as a kid. They both did theater in college—I think I said that before—and they were really into volunteer storytime. Their favorite was the Frog and Toad series. I remember sitting there in a circle with the other little kids, listening to my dad speaking in a deep grumpy toad voice and my mom ribbiting all over the place and thinking: *Those are my parents. None of you have parents like that.*

Which I guess, given what I've learned, is technically true. Just not the way I expected.

I didn't stop going to the library after Dad disappeared. As a matter of fact, it became a kind of virtual babysitter. My mom never believed any of those stories about bad guys hanging around the library waiting to prey on kids, so she just dropped me off and assumed I'd spend my time in the children's section. Which I did not. Too many memories. But that meant that I got to know the rest of the library pretty well over the years. Including the old back stairs.

They were kind of dark and spooky, but they led back up to the main floor—and right to a side entrance to the computer room. Technically, the door was fire-alarmed, but I remembered from pushing it once or twice as a kid that the alarm never went off. I was hoping that was still true. It certainly didn't look like they'd spent a lot of money on renovations over the years. Worst case, I'd run back down the stairs and think up something else.

It was still true.

Meanwhile, Caroline stayed near the chaperone, keeping an eye out. We'd agreed that she'd text me if he came back upstairs. If he found me on one of the computers instead of doing my job, well, it was going to be a problem.

I'd learned a lot from Mr. Jones about keeping my line of sight open, so I needed a computer facing the main door. After an awkward conversation with an old lady that involved taking advantage of her computer ignorance—I told her my homework was saved on that computer and I couldn't get it any other way—she agreed to switch.

This wasn't the worst thing I've done as a supervillain, by far, but it's one of the things I *feel* the worst about. Isn't that nuts?

I sat down, and then my phone buzzed. Caroline:

He is on the move. I am going to try to distract him with a question about the Dewey decimal system. But you may not have much time.

Like there wasn't enough stress.

I typed the address into the browser. Twice, because the first time I was so nervous I got it wrong. I thought maybe I had the second time, too, because all that came up was a black screen and a blinking cursor. That seemed ominous. But it became clear what to do and I started to type in the password, when my phone buzzed again:

It was impossible to stop him, Caroline said. *He is heading in your direction. Get out of there.*

But I couldn't. Not now.

Because before he arrived, something happened.

When I finished typing in the password, the computer shut itself down.

Along with all the other computers.

Along with all the electricity in the building.

It was daylight and the library has a lot of windows, so it wasn't like it was frightening, at first. There were some groans and moans, like when they're showing a movie at assembly and the projector stops working. Until people remembered the Bloody Front, and it got less funny. I think that must have been when the chaperone turned back, to call for advice or something. He never showed up, that's all I know.

Which is good, because the printer next to me was chattering away. Printing. Despite the fact that every other electrical item in the library was currently shut down.

Before any of the assorted senior citizens or homeless people could react, I ran over to the printer, snatched the piece of paper it had spat out, then busted my butt to make it back downstairs with the other students and stagger around and pretend to look terrified. They were shouting about how it was another Bloody Front attack and of course I couldn't tell them not to worry without raising all sorts of questions, so I just clambered up the main steps with them, the folded piece of paper burning a hole in my clenched fist.

Caroline fell in beside me and whispered, "Was that . . . was that you?"

"I think so," I whispered back. "I'm not sure. Yes."

And then she pointed to my fist, like we were playing one of those kids' games where you had the marble in one of your hands or something. I opened my hand, and we looked at the printout, with its strange jumble of hieroglyphics or cuneiform or whatnot. And slowly—it was almost *solemn*, like it was a religious rite or something—she took out her phone, and took a picture of it

What if I hadn't let her do that? Or had tried to bluff, told her that I hadn't seen anything out of the ordinary? That it was just a glitch on the grid, nothing to do with me. She might have called BS, shouted, been angry—but I could have lived with that.

But I didn't. I didn't even consider it. We were in it together.

And I guess everything else happened after that.

So I had this piece of paper, with what was meant to be an important message.

If only I could figure out what it meant.

I spent the next day obsessively focusing on it. Nothing came to mind—nothing intelligent, anyway. Even though

I knew it was a bad idea, I started looking at the paper everywhere: in the bathroom, in the halls, even in class. It attracted attention, but I didn't care. I held it up to a mirror to see if it made more sense that way. It didn't. I held a candle up to it to see if some sort of secret message came out. No luck there, either. But it had to have *some* meaning.

Caroline was out of ideas, too. We were mostly working on it separately—we couldn't talk on the phone or text about it, and midterms were coming up fast. She had to do *some* studying: she was actually trying to keep up her GPA. Unlike me.

Nonetheless, I got an intentionally cryptic text the very next night: *I have a theory. I will tell you more anon.* (We were doing our Shakespeare unit in English at the time.) Nothing else.

I spent the night running through the wildest possibilities. I even wondered, for a minute, if it was some sort of magic spell, and typing in the password was like the final incantation, and the blackout had let a demon loose upon the world . . . but that was just fantasy. This was real life. The Bloody Front was demon enough for anyone.

Especially since it'd begun picking up steam. It was hitting softer and softer targets harder and harder. Every day for a week, a different target. The carnage was . . . well, you know. We all do. Hospital, library, shopping mall. . . . People have been calling it Bloody November.

But there won't be anything like it again. Not from *them*. But I'm getting ahead of myself again.

The one silver lining, if you could call it that, was that

the Front were limiting their targets geographically. And so the authorities were able to draw a big circle around a zone of increased interest. Or, depending on your perspective, of sheer blinding terror. We were inside the circle—and after the Friday Night Fright we were definitely under the microscope—but so were other places, since the government didn't think the Front would call down that kind of attention close to their headquarters.

High-schoolers had their own methods for dealing with Bloody November. Crying and nail-biting were popular. One freshman became famous for sleeping eighteen hours a day, just to get away from reality. Someone who was handling it pretty well, believe it or not, was Caroline. In a way that only she could have done.

Basically, she and the mp3s set up right outside the school's front steps, doing a kind of DIY karaoke concert for an hour after school every day. Anyone who wanted to play or sing whatever song would make them feel better, they could, and Caroline and her band buddies would try to follow along. They were decent musicians, so they did all right.

I know this sounds stupid. But here's the thing. Everybody feels better when they have a backing band and no judgment. And even with high school being high school, Bloody November was kind of making the whole place into a judgment-free—or, maybe more realistically, a judgment-not-so-much—zone. A lot of people played, or sang, or both. Logan, as it turned out, did a goofy and yet also strangely soulful performance of "Free Bird," and there were these three sophomores who insisted on singing "Gettin' Jiggy with It" every day.

Maybe it shouldn't have been too big a surprise, then, that Rebecca asked Caroline to be her guest on that week's podcast.

My stomach churned when I heard the news. I mean, I was happy for her in theory, but in practice there were huge, gaping dangers involved.

It's not like I was expecting her to say something along the lines of, *Oh, yes, well, I do have some interesting news to share, Rebecca—it turns out my best friend owns a gigantic supervillain robot suit!* But I wouldn't have been surprised if there had been hints or overtones. Which, if anyone from the various federal agencies that were still nosing around the school happened to be listening, could have called attention to me. Or to Dad. Unlikely, but it was the school's quasi-official podcast. So maybe?

It turned out that that wasn't what I had to worry about.

I have the podcast on my phone, of course. Let me see, here's the part where my stomach tried to bust out through the roof of my mouth. It came about twelve minutes in. I'm pretty sure almost no one else was listening. I'm grateful for that, at least. Okay, here goes. For the record.

. . . And so, Caroline, besides the mp3s helping the school get through Bloody November, you're also playing winter formal.

That's right, Rebecca. We're the opening act. We've been rehearsing a lot, and we're pretty happy with our sound.

And you still have three weeks to go.

That's right. So by the time we get onstage, we'll be totally tight.

Well, I'm sure all our listeners are looking forward to it. Tell me, how do you pick your set list?

Some of the songs, actually, came from the school-steps concerts. And I think we're going to have some guest stars onstage, from the sophomore and junior classes—

That sounds like fun—

And of course Laraine and Melissa had some suggestions.

Your bandmates.

My bandmates, right. But the ones I like the most—

Here there's a little pause. Like she's wondering if she should go ahead. And then she does.

—the ones I like the most, some of them were songs Bailey introduced me to.

I've played this podcast at least forty times. But of course there's no video, so I have no idea what the expression was on Rebecca's face when she said:

Bailey?

Caroline is in full attack mode, zero to sixty.

Yes. Bailey. Maybe you remember his name. Your boyfriend broke his nose for looking at you the wrong way.

Why Rebecca didn't edit this part out, this whole part, I still don't know. She could have. Easily.

Or maybe she couldn't. Maybe it would have felt like . . . chickening out. Not facing up to the feelings of guilt she had. Maybe she wanted to put it on the record.

Which is something I can relate to.

That's not—Logan—

He still *gets* headaches, you know? He still stays home from school. Two months later, his nose still hurts. Every day. All because he cares about someone who *doesn't know his name.*

There's another long pause. And then there's no mistaking Rebecca's tone. Cold. Icy cold. The tone of someone putting an end to something that had never actually begun.

I know his name.

There's more after that, but that's all that mattered.

I've been here too long already. I'm going to have to move.

Here we go.

Well, that went better than I'd feared. I'm standing up, which means the power's working. I'd never be able to get the suit off the ground using my own muscles.

So let's see. Three-step plan.

Step one: Set the delayed-action grenades for fifteen seconds.

Step two: Wait fourteen and a half seconds.

Step three: Jump straight up right in the middle of the *boom*.

The idea is that it'll confuse them. Make them think the building collapsed on itself because of the gas and flames. Get them to waste their time combing through the wreckage while I'm miles away.

I'm not saying it's the world's *best* plan. But it's definitely a lot better than staying here and waiting for them to come in and get me.

Okay, grenades armed and countdown started.

I'll be back. Right after this boom.

Or, I guess, I won't.

Did it. Still alive. And in the air.

My ears are ringing. Well, no, not really. The suit's acoustic sensors modulate and dampen, like very fancy noise-canceling headphones. But I definitely have the impression of LOUD.

It worked. At least for the moment I'm clear. So I can get back to figuring all this out. . . .

THREE WEEKS AGO

I was mad. Steam-out-of-the-ears mad. Absolute-silent-treatment mad. You-ruined-whatever-slim-shot-I-had-with-the-love-of-my-life mad. So mad that there was nothing Caroline could possibly do to make it up to me. Which she knew, because when she texted me: *What can I possibly do to make it up to you?* I wrote back: *Nothing*, with about five hundred o's. To make the point even stronger.

But there was one very obvious, dangling thing. Involving a mysterious message.

And this is what happened. After about sixteen hours of radio silence from Caroline, the part of me still furious with her was beginning to listen to the part of me that said that I'd done my share of stupid stuff in our friendship, too. And her admittedly boneheaded move had come out of caring too much, rather than the other way around. . . . I was pretty miffed, though.

But then she sent me another text, just as school was getting out. And this one I didn't understand at all.

Not because she was making some deep emotional point or anything. I literally didn't understand it. Because it wasn't in English. It was made up of those same weird symbols— well, not exactly the same, but the same *kind* of symbols— that had been in the library message.

My first thought was that someone had hacked Caroline's phone. The same someone who'd created the original message. They'd hacked Caroline's phone, and were trying to mess with me, or put a curse on me, or something.

And then another text popped up: *Like I told you. I always text in complete sentences.*

Before I had time to respond, she wrote: *Come find me. I have answers.*

No, I didn't know her schedule down to the minute like Rebecca's, but I had a pretty good idea of where she was. It was her free period, which meant she was probably hanging around the music room.

When I got there, she looked at me and smiled.

And then she started speaking in tongues.

I mean, this flow of absolute . . . gibberish was coming out of her mouth. Seeing the look of utter incomprehension on my face, she laughed out loud.

"Doesn't ring any bells?" she said.

I just stared at her.

And then she laughed again and said, "Come with me. You're not the only one who has a dark family secret."

⟓

I'd never been to Caroline's house before.

I mean, I'd been to her *mom's* house, where she lived with her mom and her mom's new husband. I'd been there dozens of times. Maybe even hundreds.

But I'd never been to her *original* house before. The one she lived in before her parents split up, where her dad still lived.

We took an Uber over there, on the account her parents set up for moving between houses until she got her unsupervised driver's license. It was only about twenty minutes away from my house. Close enough to the ravine that if her dad had looked the right way at just the right time of day, he might have seen Mayhem flying around.

Caroline's dad had just gotten home from work. He was so happy to see her. It wasn't her day to visit, I guess. And then he asked if she was staying for dinner, and she said she had to get back to her mom's, but that she needed something from downstairs, and . . .

I mean, it wasn't much of anything. A normal interaction. And she definitely hadn't intended to hurt him. But she had. I could see it.

And I was jealous of her. To have a dad. Right there. To ignore.

She took me past him and opened the door to the basement and said, "Down here."

So we went down.

Into what had become Caroline's dad's man-cave. A big TV hooked up to an Xbox, old eighties and nineties action-movie posters on the walls, and long wooden shelves running across the walls. On which were standing rows and rows of action figures in their original packaging.

All—and I mean every single one—from one movie franchise.

The truth is, I was never much of a *Star Trek* fan. I'd watched a few of the movies a long time ago, but that was about it, so it didn't mean much to me. I certainly hadn't recognized that the writing on the piece of paper I'd been obsessively poring over was written in Klingon.

But Caroline had. Well, not at first. It had been one of those things that's on the tip of your tongue, like when you remember one line of a song's chorus, but you can't remember anything else about it, like the tune or who sang it. She waited and waited around for inspiration to strike, and finally it did.

"I tried a reverse Google image search, of course," she said, while I nodded like I had any idea what she was talking about. "First thing. But it didn't work. You know why?"

"I can honestly say that I do not," I said.

"Because," she said, "the message isn't classic Klingon."

"It's not?" I said.

"It's composed in an obscure Klingon dialect that only appeared in one episode," she said triumphantly.

"Oh," I said.

"Do you want to know which episode?" she asked.

I'm not proud of this. But this is when I lost it a little bit. "*No, I don't want to know which episode it was!*" I shouted. "*I just want to know what it says!*"

And then she got defensive, saying she was sorry she was drawing this out, but she'd been spending hours online with various Klingon-to-English dictionaries, in *Trek* chat rooms, other fan stuff I can't remember.

She blurted out the message at last, and I didn't believe her. I made her say it twice.

Apparently the message was just two words. That was it. Two words. Well, the Klingon was longer, for Klingon-related reasons I don't really understand, but it boiled down to two words in English.

"*Trap-door spider*," she said, and her face got this weird expression between a grimace and a grin. I guess it was a ridiculous joke. I mean, what else could it be, right? "I checked it over and over, and that's what it says. *Trap-door spider*."

⟋

Google told us that the trap-door spider was a run-of-the-mill spider, except for the way it hunts its prey. It makes a hiding cave out of silk web and holds the "door" to it shut; then, when a bug gets close enough to set off the "trip wires," it jumps out of the cave and munches away. Which was gross, and fascinating, and didn't seem to have any connection to me whatsoever.

Then we fell down a Google black hole scrolling through pictures of spiders—insect Internet is *weird*—and somewhere in the middle of all those mandibles we realized we had totally forgiven each other. So that was good.

But we had no idea what the message meant, or who could possibly have sent it, or what they were trying to tell us. Which was bad. I couldn't stop thinking that this super-hacker who'd crashed the library's power grid just to send me a message would find out about Caroline's browsing history. And would do something stupid-slash-terrible to her.

So we decided to try Caroline's technique—go home, go about our business, and hope that our unconscious minds would make a connection—and also, study for midterms.

I was going to. Really, I was. I had the unit on the Donation of Pepin and Charlemagne out and everything.

But I think you can guess what happened next.

My phone buzzed. And there was no area code.

For a minute, I thought Mr. Jones was watching me and knew about the spider, and my heart started hammering. Turned out he just wanted me on another job. Or a number of other jobs. More cash in hand.

I told him it wasn't going to be easy. The governor had deployed the National Guard throughout the Zone. Helicopters and jets were flying overhead, kids at school said they saw drones patrolling our neighborhood. They were wrong—as I knew from the research I'd done before taking up flying around in a big metal suit, serious drones fly too high to be seen by the naked eye—but you get the point. It was going to be a lot harder to go out, commit a massive robbery, and return to home base without anyone noticing.

Plus, although the National Guard and Homeland Security weren't doing house-to-house searches in the Zone yet, the Bloody Front could commit another series of massacres next week, or tomorrow, and locals would be begging the military to trample all over the Constitution. I didn't know how intensive those searches would be, and how good they were at finding underground spaces, but I didn't like the risk.

Of course, he knew all that. He also didn't care. "I'm *trying* to save your dad," he snapped. "I'm doing everything I can.

But my resources are stretched beyond capacity, and the money from one armored-car job just isn't going to cut it."

I remember thinking he seemed distracted. Maybe Bloody November was getting to him, too. Although that seemed—seems—unlikely. But when I tried to use his distraction to get more information—I asked him about the Zone, since if the Front was around here didn't that mean my dad was, too?—he lost it. "You want to save your dad?" he practically shouted. "You want to help? Money. That's what we need. Money."

And he hung up on me.

So *that* sucked.

I guess there was some good news that day, though.

I mean, sort of: Rebecca and Logan broke up.

Or I think they did. Or had. But I definitely walked past a fight between them in the hall. A big one. There was no screaming, and there definitely wasn't anything physical. Like I said, Logan wasn't that kind of guy, my nasal trauma notwithstanding. But I was a longtime Rebecca watcher, and I could see the way they were talking and using their hands. It didn't take a lip-reader to tell it was not a pleasant conversation. And then Logan just . . . walked away.

Well, limped away. Slowly. Rebecca didn't move. She just stood there, head pressed against her locker. Not crying, not doing anything, just standing there.

Maybe someone better or braver would have walked over to her. Even taken her in his arms, or, since this is real life, at least asked if she needed a tissue or something. But I'm not that person, so I just stood there, at the edge of her vision, afraid to come close and afraid to move away. Until she looked up and saw me.

I thought she was going to be furious. To scream at me, or tell me to go to hell, or call me a creepy spy or something. But instead, she smiled—I mean, it was a kind-of smile, like there was something she thought was funny, but only kind of—and she said, "Sorry about the podcast."

I remember giving some sort of vague gesture that tried to suggest that it was no big deal and I didn't trouble myself with those sorts of things, that, in fact, I wasn't sure I had actually listened to it, but that didn't mean I wasn't also a big fan of her journalism.

I don't think I pulled it off very well.

She looked at me. Closely. I was absolutely sure I had something between my teeth.

And then she said, "Both of us, Bailey."

I honestly had no idea in what possible world there was something she thought we had in common.

"Logan," she said, like I had said what I was thinking out loud. "He's hurt both of us. It's not his fault in either case. Which makes it worse. But still . . ." She laughed. "It's kind of like we're in a club. A very exclusive club."

There have been a lot of times, these last couple of months, where I've had the feeling I was in over my head. When I was little, my dad—who loved to play dress-up . . . I guess it was from his theater days in college—pretended to be a pirate. He would take a page of newspaper, fold it up, and put it on his head while he was *yarring* and *yo-ho-hoing* around the kitchen. This was top-notch entertainment for a five-year-old, you have to realize.

Did his whole dress-up-in-costume thing lead to his decision to become Mayhem? To suit up like a comic-book character, rather than, I don't know, become an arms dealer?

Not the point. The point is that one of my dad's favorite pirate phrases was *Yarr, landlubber, here be uncharted waters!* And that was where I had been since finding the suit, and definitely where I was right then. In uncharted waters.

This rammed through my head at, like, light speed, and for once, I came up with a good thing to say, an actual clever comment. "Maybe the club should have meetings," is what I said. The second it came out of my mouth I wanted to stab myself repeatedly in the tongue because it was not clever at all. It was stupid, stupid, stupid.

But I guess it wasn't so stupid, because Rebecca smiled at me—a no-doubt-about-it, genuine, actual smile, even if it was a little quivery around the edges—and said, "Maybe."

And then she walked off, leaving me standing there confused and—at the same time—deliriously happy and excited.

For all of about fifteen seconds. And then I remembered how much everything else in my life, and I mean *everything* else, sucked.

I was totally stuck.

Whatever this *trap-door spider* thing was, it wasn't helping me get any closer to my dad. Which meant I had to keep trying to get information out of Mr. Jones—at least until I figured out something better. Which meant doing what he wanted, for now. And trying to figure out how to get him to trust me more, so maybe—maybe—he'd open up a little.

As far as I could tell, there was only one thing I had on him. One crack in his armor, so to speak.

It was that he seemed oddly over-invested in my love life.

So I used that.

When he called me back the next night, he was snapping and grumbling again, but as soon as I told him I wanted to get him the money he needed and make a grand gesture to ask out Rebecca, you could practically hear him rubbing his hands over the phone. "I know your father would want you to have *some* happiness," he said, which made me want to vomit, cry, and strangle him all at once. What would *really* have given me happiness would have been for him to just tell me what he knew about the Bloody Front. But I had to play by his rules. Follow his timetable. At least for now.

I told him about my idea for Rebecca, and he rejected it right away. I couldn't just hit a big jewelry store, he said. Oh, no. Could I even imagine how difficult it would be for him to turn the diamonds into the cash he needed on short notice? I had to go back to the banks. Plus that way I could blend the jewel theft in with the rest, making the heist one dot in a pattern of misdirection.

Which meant a crime spree. During midterms.

You remember when Mayhem was everywhere, all over the country, causing havoc? Yeah. Sorry. I really threw myself into it because, I guess, I was beginning to get the sinking feeling that college wasn't going to be an option.

Thanks to my grades, but also . . . because there wasn't going to be a normal way out of this.

At that point, that was just background thought. Now it's definite.

And then, this one Friday. Another day, another federal offense. This one was going to be what Mr. Jones called a *shock and awe* operation, where the job wasn't just to get the cash, but to make a big noise and mess in the process. I never understood why some jobs were supposed to be quick and relatively quiet and some the opposite—at least, *then* I didn't; now I have my suspicions—but the thing was, Mr. Jones said meaningfully as we were planning the day's criminal activity, the bank he was sending me to was located in New York City. Right on Fifth Avenue.

"So what?" I said.

"You'll see," he said. "Just make sure you budget a little extra time toward the end for . . . sightseeing. You'll thank me. I promise." Fine. Whatever.

I'd never been to New York before. It looked terribly ugly from the air flying in, gigantic buildings and narrow streets with no sense of harmony or personality. Maybe it was different down below. I wasn't going to have time to find out, though—I had about an hour to do this, turn around, and get home. Otherwise I'd miss my History midterm, which would lead to a serious message home and almost certainly a serious interrogation from my mom. And in my current state of mind, I wasn't sure I was going to be able to handle that.

I landed right in front of the bank. It was always fun to watch the tar and concrete of the street crack when my boots hit the ground. It was like an announcement: *Here cometh a badass.* I liked it a lot less when people ran screaming out of the way. But increasingly they didn't. I guess the word had gotten out that Mayhem wasn't in the business of attacking civilians as long as they stayed out of the way, so it was more of a *move hurriedly to the side* than a *run screaming.*

And just before I tore the doors off their hinges—classic old-school Dad move, sort of an homage—I looked around and realized, for the first time, that I was just a few steps away from Tiffany's.

Home, as I'm sure I don't need to tell you, to lots and lots of diamond jewelry.

🖋

I was in and out of the bank's safe in ten minutes. Being New York, and Fifth Avenue, it was a bigger safe and a heavier door, but that just meant a slightly larger drain on the power cells as I ripped it off. I prided myself generally on not causing too much property damage—no reason for everyone to suffer more than they needed—but given the *shock and awe* instructions, I made more of a mess than usual. Punched some holes that would probably cost a lot to clean up, and rearranged some heavy and valuable furniture in very surprising and, if I do say so myself, creative positions.

Then I walked down the street to Tiffany's. I was briefly thrown by the fact that the Mayhem suit didn't fit through the surprisingly narrow revolving front door. Instead, I jumped three stories straight up and crashed through one of the windows.

There were a lot of shoppers crowded around the display

cases. I flipped on the internal megaphone, complete with the voice distorter, and said, "EVERYONE, PLEASE MOVE AWAY FROM THE CASES. I DON'T WANT YOU TO GET HURT BY THE GLASS. ALSO IF I COULD SPEAK TO A SENIOR MANAGER I WOULD BE GREATLY APPRECIATIVE."

Within seconds, the crowds seemed to part around an elegantly dressed middle-aged woman, who looked at the suit without any trace of fear.

I'm not going to go through the whole conversation I had with her. I'm sure Tiffany's has video surveillance anyway. It was a long, somewhat awkward discussion about what kind of jewelry would be nicest for a young woman, expensive but understated, that sort of thing, interrupted only when I had to pick up two overzealous security guards and gently deposit them in a heap in a corner.

She made a suggestion, somewhat grudgingly, and I asked her to wrap it up. While she did that, I smashed through some other display cases and gathered up those diamonds, too. And when the little blue box was ready, I flew out the third-floor window.

To find—with no advance notice from Mr. Jones, I should add—three NYPD SWAT helicopters hovering overhead, along with what must have been two dozen Hercules counterterrorism units on the ground.

Now, you're thinking, *That's not so surprising, Bailey. When a giant robot breaks into Tiffany's, they're going to come out with everything they've got.*

The thing is, though: I hadn't taken *that* long in the bank and at Tiffany's. Even if they had leaped into action the minute I landed, there's no way that many police and military vehicles would have been able to get to the neighborhood in that amount of time. Which meant they'd gotten word in advance.

Which made no sense . . . until I heard the screaming.

I assumed it was because of me, even though, like I said before, it was usually more grumbling than screaming. But then I activated the scopes and realized what everyone was pointing at.

A car, rammed into the storefront, with the Bloody Front's flag tied to the side, and wires and machinery sticking out the back. Oh, and three men next to it firing off machine guns every which way.

I didn't take the time to wonder about the extraordinary coincidence of my arrival in New York City right as the Front made their latest strike. I didn't take the time to think about much of anything. I just *moved*.

I could feel the diamond jewelry stuffed inside the suit dribbling down my arms and legs as I headed for the car. I'd learned from the first gig to briefly deactivate part of the suit, stuff valuables in wherever possible, then firm it up again. It caused some scratching and scuffing, but no danger of spillage.

My readouts were reporting traces of high explosives without any indication of when they would go off. Just my luck: the Front must have been using mechanical timers, rather than electronic ones that I might have been able to jam or short-circuit somehow. Still, the car was the biggest problem, so I went for it first.

The Bloody Front members looked up in surprise as I swooped down toward them. Two of them, dumb, slack-jawed, even stopped shooting. The third looked confused for only a second, then angry. I recognized the twin scars along his cheeks and the slash of red paint on those steel dog tag–like things hanging around his neck. Anyone would, from the Internet videos and news coverage. He was the Front's leader, the one they called Assassin. I didn't think he ever went out on missions himself.

There was no time to stop and consider it, though. The clock, or whatever was attached to the bomb, was ticking. I was afraid if I messed with it, it might go off right away. I wasn't worried about myself, but I knew one of the Front's favorite techniques was to pack a lot of shrapnel into their bombs—nails and spikes and pieces of rusty metal that would be thrown in all directions by the force of the explosion. There were too many people crowded around to risk that.

I remembered reading an old comic where the good guy threw a bomb into outer space so it could "explode harm-lessly." The armor wasn't strong enough to throw anything nearly that far up, but it gave me an idea.

So I picked up the bomb—well, not so much the bomb as the car that was wrapped around it—and did my best imita-tion of a trash compactor. I was betting that if I didn't give the shrapnel anywhere to go the chances of civilian spikage would go way down.

It was too big for me to get my arms around at first. So I started with the back—not grabbing it by the bumper this time, I'd learned my lesson, although, of course, this one wasn't moving—and kind of rolled it up, like it was a wet towel at summer camp. It wanted to break apart, go in every which direction. I didn't let it.

Glass shattered and burst outward when I got to the car windows. Most of it just bounced off my chest: maybe a little bit got away, but nothing much. And then, when it was a nice comfortable size, bear-hug ready, I pushed the suit up to full power and squeezed.

I knew the suit was strong. I'm not sure I really understood just how strong it was.

The car popped, I guess is the best way of putting it. *Pockitah*ed and *squinch*ed and popped and then crumpled into something that looked like a scrap paper ball you'd try to shoot into a garbage-can basket from your desk chair, only made out of metal and weighing a ton or two.

Assassin was shouting something. An order. And the other two Bloody Front goons started emptying their guns directly at me. The bullets bounced off, of course. One of the shooters got hit by a ricocheted bullet and dropped to the ground screaming and bleeding. I couldn't say I felt terrible about it, but I wasn't paying much attention. I was still squeezing.

By the time the bomb went off three minutes later, it was lodged in the center of a large sphere about the size of a coffee table. I heard a muffled *ping* or two as the few nails that hadn't been crushed together traveled an inch or so, but it was mostly *phlumph*.

Once that was over, I turned my attention to the Bloody Front members left standing. But there was just one, it turned out. The leader—Assassin—had slipped off some-where while I was trash-compacting.

The goon kept shooting at me. I didn't like that. I grabbed the gun out of his hand, and from the way he howled I might have broken a finger or two in the process. Again, the guy'd been shooting at civilians and trying to detonate a car bomb. I didn't feel for him. Then I treated his gun to a miniversion of what I'd done to his vehicle. He was suitably impressed.

"TELL ME WHERE MY FATHER IS," I shouted.

He looked . . . befuddled.

"What—what are you talking about?" he said. His teeth were chattering. Probably because, I guess I forgot to men-tion, I had grabbed him by his sweatshirt and flown him about three hundred feet in the air. He looked down at his dangling feet. One of them had lost a shoe.

"I WON'T ASK AGAIN," I said.

Which was when the helicopter buzzed me.

"NYPD," they shouted, as if I didn't know. They ordered me to land on the nearest roof, release the suspect, then power down and remove the suit.

Call me crazy, but I didn't think I was going to do that.

The first helicopter was joined by a second. And the sec-ond by a third.

"LOOK," I told the terrorist. "TELL ME WHAT I WANT TO KNOW OR I GIVE YOU TO THEM."

This—as I know now, all too well—is not an appealing prospect. Maybe that was why he did what he did.

Or I wonder, was he scared of something even worse than the police?

Whatever the truth was, what happened was crazy. I don't know if you're going to believe me.

He started wriggling and jerking around. For a second, I thought he was trying to attack me, which seemed totally pointless. And then, just as I realized that he was trying to get out of his sweatshirt, the one thing I was holding on to, he succeeded.

I tried to grab at him, to catch him. I did. But when I did, I swiped his head, which knocked him farther away, and as I grabbed for him again, I think I broke one of his legs.

I can still hear him screaming. All the way down.

I can't focus on that now. I have to keep powering through.

Anyway, the police helicopters opened fire on me, and I said more than a few bad words. I'd had this hope that maybe, *maybe* I'd've been able to skip all this trying to figure out some way of getting information out of reluctant supergenius Mr. Jones and just shake the information out of the Bloody Front.

Nope.

I gave the police helicopters a very rude gesture. And then got out of there as quickly as I could, blowing past them in seconds.

Of course, the way the news footage and the Internet put it together, everyone immediately insisted Mayhem was in league with the Bloody Front. Which makes no sense—I mean, why would I have destroyed my own partners' bomb?—but a picture's worth a thousand words, and that shot of me and the terrorist in midair . . . it kind of looks like I rescued him, then disposed of him when the police got near in order to save myself.

So *that* was great.

I got the shakes on the way back, once the adrenaline wore off. I even let myself cry a little bit. Not for the terrorist, at least, I don't think so, but for . . . well, for whatever it all meant. I was sure that the Bloody Front were going to take it out on my dad. And the only person I could talk to about any of this was Mr. Jones, and there was definitely something weird going on there.

I kept going over and over it, long after I'd landed, gotten to the May-cave, caught my breath. I knew the attack couldn't have been a coincidence. Mr. Jones must have been monitoring the Front's communications and knew they were planning something in the area. But why send me there? And not tell me about it?

There'd been warning signs: he was keeping other things from me, he wanted more money, he still hadn't shown me his face. . . . But this was a different level. Someone had died. It was a terrorist who had been totally fine with murdering innocent people, but still. I wasn't a *soldier*. I wasn't a *killer*. Not intentionally, anyway. Never.

I finally managed to get ahold of him. I said a lot of things, but I wasn't sure exactly what they were. And then he was talking, totally calm. "It was a final test," he said. "You see? I couldn't tell you they were going to be there. If I had, I wouldn't be able to observe your reaction to unforeseen conditions. And when you go on your rescue mission, those are the only conditions there are going to be."

I have to be honest: I wanted to believe this. It *did* seem like a pattern of his. First the Golden Gate Bridge thing, where I'd—he'd—blown Mayhem's cover wide open, now this.

"But that guy—what happened to him—"

"He did it to himself," Mr. Jones said, and his voice was calm, sympathetic. "You have nothing—*nothing*—to feel bad about. I'm proud of you. You've come a long way."

Maybe I should have stayed skeptical. Maybe I should have gotten *more* skeptical. I mean, it seems like Emotional Manipulation 101, right? *You've come a long way.* It sounds like the end of one of those sports movies where the kids from the wrong side of town get revved up by the coach. But I was caught up in the moment.

Mr. Jones was patient, and he listened to me sniff and snuffle, and made the right soothing noises. And then he said, "Let's change the subject. What did you get for Rebecca?"

I hadn't had a chance to check while flying back, but I was safe in the May-cave. The Mayhem suit's gauntlets are more suited to big, rough work like smashing concrete than to opening tiny blue boxes, but I managed. It was a thin silver bracelet, maybe platinum, I wasn't sure, supporting a tasteful, but not what you would call small, diamond, set off by tiny blue stones—sapphires, I think, but I wasn't sure about that, either. Jewelry isn't really my thing. My guess is it cost more money than my mom made in a year. Maybe in five.

"Beautiful," Mr. Jones said. "Hold it up to the light, so I can get a better look." I did, and I heard a whistle through the speakers.

And then we talked strategy. Although I disagreed with about half of what he said, we both felt I shouldn't give it to Rebecca right away. Not tomorrow, anyway. But it was going to be burning a hole in my pocket until I did, that was for sure.

The glow only wore off when I had some time to think the episode over, especially Mr. Jones's part in it. But whatever else was going on, there was one thing Mr. Jones was telling the truth about. Whatever he'd meant the encounter to be, it *had* been a test. Could I take on the Bloody Front? Could I deliver a you-know-what whupping?

And you know what? Yes. Yes, I really could.

I was just so freaking naive.

And also, grounded. Not a flight metaphor. Like, *grounded* grounded.

⟋

I'd been missing more classes than I'd thought. And averaging worse on my tests and papers than I'd calculated. And even though I thought I was bulletproof, between the nose thing and the national security crisis taking place nearby, including in and around our school, leave it to the guidance counselors to suddenly determine enough was enough. I guess report cards were maybe being compiled, and it's all automatic or an algorithm or something.

The point is, someone called my mom. Delicately, given the circumstances. And so she sat me right down that night and started the interrogation.

I had told Caroline it was about to begin, and that I was in real trouble. She texted me back: *I believe I have a solution. Stall her. I will be there in twenty minutes.*

I had no idea what that meant. But I trusted her. I really trusted her. So I did what she said.

Mom was serious. She even let her cigarette burn down to her fingers, she was staring at me so intently. Asking questions about where I'd been and what I was doing, and she could tell right away I was being *evasive*, and, on occasion, *full-fledged deceptive*. Her words. Not that she was going to come up with the real reason, of course. First I assumed she thought I'd started drinking or drugging. But then she kept asking me in roundabout ways if it was Bloody Front–related stress.

I couldn't go there. I was afraid that she'd insist on having a conversation about the Front, and something Dad-related would let loose inside me. Something I wouldn't be able to hide.

The situation was getting desperate. So I went to Defcon 1.

I told Mom her tuna noodle casserole had disagreed with me and that I had to spend a few minutes in the bathroom.

Which, Mom, if you ever listen to this, I'm really, really sorry. For all the things I've done to you and for all you're going to have to suffer for this, I should make one thing perfectly clear. You're a great cook, and your tuna noodle casserole *rocks*. I just want to say that. On the record.

I knew her well enough, and she knew me well enough, to know she was extremely skeptical. But I did look flushed and sweaty and pale—being on the verge of getting unmasked as a superfelon and losing the chance to save your dad forever can do that to you—and so she chose to believe, I guess.

I hid out in the bathroom, texting back and forth with

Caroline to get updates on her ETA, and emerged, drying my hands, about thirty seconds before the doorbell rang.

I bounced out of the chair that I had just slooowly sat down in and raced to fling open the door, Mom right behind me.

Which is why she was there to see Caroline throw her arms around me and kiss me straight on the mouth.

*

This is the point, where, if this were a teenage love story, I would say that it was the kind of kiss that made me forget about everything and everyone but her. But here's the truth. It was awful.

I don't think this was her fault. I wasn't expecting it, obviously, and I had a lot of spit in my mouth from being nervous, and I think mostly she got the side of my chin with a little bit of drool thrown in. But whoever's fault it was, it wasn't very good. And so after the first moment of utter shock, along with the immediate worry that Caroline had gone out of her mind, all it did was make me think about how wonderful it could be with the right person. The right person being Rebecca. And how maybe, if my plan worked, I'd have a chance to find that out at winter formal.

But then I couldn't think about that anymore, because Caroline *kept doing it*. Pushing me back, kind of awkward-walking down the hall, holding on to me, leaning in to nuzzle my neck, which was mostly ticklish. Paying absolutely no attention to my mom, standing there, openmouthed.

And then she *licked my ear*.

I was trying to figure out what to do—pushing her away seemed, well, unchivalrous, I guess, but I had to do something before she swallowed my face—and then she whispered, "Just follow my lead."

Which was fine with me, although I had a whole bunch of questions.

But for my mom, apparently, this was supplying a whole bunch of answers.

"Why didn't you *tell* me?" she asked a little gleefully.

I think we did okay after that. Okay enough for me to get away with just a *provisional* grounding, in no small part because my mom didn't want to discourage my "relation-ship" with Caroline.

It helped that over the past few weeks my mom and I had already had a bunch of talks about my relationship with Caroline. Not a *relationship* relationship, of course, but since our friendship had had some twists and turns lately, it had come up.

Usually the conversations had gone something like this:

Mom: "Bailey, you're moping. Why are you moping?"

Me, not really knowing where to begin: "Well, Caroline—"

Mom, moving on: "Oh, Caroline. Well, I'm sure everything will be fine, then."

Me, letting it drop: "Yeah. Sure. Good."

Or:

Mom: "Bailey, you look happy."

Me: "Yeah, well, Caroline and I—"

Mom, once more moving on: "Oh, Caroline. Well, I told you it would work out, right?"

Me, once more letting it drop: "Sure, Mom. Exactly. It's all good."

And that would be that, because Mom was, as I've said before, kind of perma-distracted and preoccupied. Sorry, Mom. You know it's true.

But I suppose you could say that some sort of seed had been planted.

So we got away with it, I think. My mom did say she was going to watch me *like a hawk*, but she—how can I put this?—didn't. Which was a relief, but not too much of a surprise.

I mean, yeah, she checked in every day, or two, but it was kind of . . . preprogrammed, you know? Like she had set an alert on her phone to ask me about Caroline. Or my grades. And once I had satisfied the conditions of her formula or whatever—*Things are okay, Mom, much better* or *Studying hard, I really think I'm going to turn it around*—she would go dark until the next time Siri reminded her. Part of it might have been that she was spending more time with this boyfriend. I don't know. I changed the subject whenever she brought him up.

And in terms of changing the subject, aside from a few brief conversations about getting our cover story straight in case my mom asked, Caroline changed the subject pretty quickly whenever that evening came up. It was never to be spoken of again, which was fine with me.

Well, no. That's not true. It came up once more. But we're not there yet.

Caroline's clear desire never to repeat the kissing meant I could annoy her with a thousand different drafts of the three sentences I was going to write on the note to give to Rebecca along with the necklace. Could? Did. And did and did and did.

I knew I'd get Rebecca's attention. Kids were doing all sorts of stuff to ask girls out for winter formal, like arranging flash mobs to sing their favorite songs and cramming their lockers full of stuffed animals, but I was pretty sure no one else was getting a necklace worth more than a car. A really nice car.

Did I think that she was going to go to winter formal with someone she'd hardly spoken to—our weird moments in the halls notwithstanding—because of jewelry?

I mean, she said yes, right? So that's the answer, isn't it?

But I think . . . in fact, I'm sure now . . . that it's not. It wasn't the jewelry. She's not that kind of person.

I have another theory.

I think everyone's attracted to mystery in their lives, particularly when those lives seem dull and humdrum. I mean, I was—am—a case in point. I think maybe if I'd been one of those guys whose parents owned a mansion up in the hills, she wouldn't have given me the time of day, even with jewelry ten times as expensive. Instead, I was this sort of weird, mysterious, against-my-will public figure, and if I could make myself even *more* mysterious . . .

And she was—is—a journalist, after all.

But also, I don't know if she felt she had other options. Everyone else assumed she was going with Logan. I mean, how could she not? And so no one had asked, not even poor Jimmy Anderson with his neck brace. I think she'd probably been thinking about what her winter formal was going to look like: sitting on the side with a guy who couldn't dance, trying not to be pitied. Instead, she could be striding out with a guy who'd put diamonds on her arm. More than a little bit different. Definitely out of the ordinary. And at least worth exploring.

I finally settled on a message the next day. I ran it by Caroline, who thought my theory was stupid, but also had a pretty low opinion of Rebecca since the podcast incident, so she figured it might work anyway. Well, what she texted me was: *If your theory, which is stupid, is correct, then this may be the least stupid way to go about it.* Which I decided to take as a thumbs-up.

I wrote it on the small card the elegant store manager at Tiffany's had provided for me. Slipped it into the soft blue pouch. Jammed it in my pocket for the next day. I was ready.

I had a few hours left before Mom came home, so I spent them looking through my dad's files on the lab computer.

I thought I'd seen everything, but I guess I hadn't, because a little icon popped up on the bottom right after I opened this blank file I'd never bothered with before. I clicked on it and a photo album opened. Pictures of my dad and my mom, and then of the three of us, when we were much younger. Mom and Dad looked happy, and young, and beautiful, and even though we had family albums upstairs, I'd never seen any of these pictures before. I thought about printing them out, but if Mom found them it would raise more questions, and anyway there was no printer in the May-cave.

I turned a picture of the three of us, where I'm in a stroller, into a screensaver, and went back upstairs. Mom would be coming home soon, and I had to start making dinner.

Friday. My heart was pounding. I was going to do it.

Approach Rebecca.

I was sweating. I thought I might throw up. Or pass out. Or both.

I guess they weren't broken up, or, if they were, they were telling everyone and themselves that they were still good friends, because they were together. Logan was limping down the hall about five feet behind her, though. I'd noticed Rebecca had picked up the habit of moving quickly, to get a little ahead of him. I think some people thought she was embarrassed by him, but I knew—or, at least, I thought I knew—it was more complicated than that. It was like she was trying to . . . escape, I guess. To fly free.

That was what I was hoping for, anyway. That all she needed was an excuse.

I walked over to Rebecca, almost passing her by, then leaned in like I'd spotted something on her shirt. She looked startled, and then—I thought—I saw the hint of a smile. Which gave me courage.

Just like I'd rehearsed it a hundred times, I said, "I think you dropped this," pressed the bag into her hand, and walked away. Smooth as I could make it. I think my voice cracked a bit, but overall it went well. Clearly it went well enough.

I can guess how the next part went. Rebecca, heading around the corner, opening her hand, seeing that distinctive blue color that says Tiffany's, peeking in, seeing something bright and glinting. Maybe going into the girls' room, sitting in the stall, opening it up. Other girls might wonder if it was real, but Rebecca knows her way around jewelry. And she recognizes the Tiffany stationery along with the bag. So she thinks maybe it's real. And then she reads the note:

There's more where this came from. You'll find out what—and how—at winter formal. On my arm.

Your mystery man

And then my cell number.

I wish I could say it made me feel bad, or disappointed, when I got the text forty-five minutes later. The first contact I'd ever had from Rebecca. But when I read it—*Intrigued. Meet me after school*, and then a time and classroom number—I jumped and shouted out loud in the middle of the hallway, which led to a bunch of smirky looks, and (in one case) the finger.

I will spare you the embarrassment of the various fantasies occupying my brain for the rest of the day. Suffice it to say I'm not sure I thought about Mr. Jones or Mayhem once. Not even my dad.

School ended, and I think I set a new land-speed record running for the classroom.

Except when I got there, it wasn't a classroom. It was the school recording studio, where Rebecca recorded her podcast.

It was actually a former double-size janitor's closet that the administration had redone, which meant that it was tight. There was enough room for two chairs and some sound equipment, and not much else. When Rebecca came in and closed the door behind her, maneuvering herself into the other chair, our knees practically touched.

My entire body had gone dry and nervous and flushed. I had this odd thought that it would be great to get into the Mayhem suit, which was cool and metallic and polished, and never showed any flaw or break.

Well, back then it was polished. Now it's a different story.

But I had to handle this one by myself. No suit. Just me.

I started to say something, but Rebecca put her finger to her lips, and put on her headphones. Then she motioned for me to do the same thing, hooked up her phone to the soundboard, and pressed the Record button.

"We have a new, surprise guest for this week's podcast," she said into the microphone. "A man of mystery. Bailey, tell us about yourself."

I took a long time to answer. Finally I managed to say that there wasn't much to tell.

"Oh, I don't think that's going to satisfy our listeners," Rebecca said. "I've heard, for example, that you belong to a very exclusive club."

I remember nodding in absolute confusion, and the frustrated look on Rebecca's face as she pointed to the microphone. The school budget for the arts being what it was, there was only one mike, hanging from the ceiling, so I leaned in and said that I guessed that was true.

"A man of few words," Rebecca said into the microphone. "I suppose that's a part of the mystery."

I leaned forward again, getting the hang of it. The microphone, I mean, but also the conversation. "Yes," I said, and leaned back again.

"Well," Rebecca said, and she leaned in, not into the

microphone, but past it, so that she was close to my face and I could smell her perfume, stronger than ever. I felt dizzy; I mean, it was hot and the room was slightly but definitely spinning. "Maybe I'll need to do some more reporting. To figure you out."

I think I might have managed an *uh-huh* at that point.

"At the dance," she whispered into my ear, soft and warm, and then leaned back, and said, "That concludes our show for this week," and pressed Delete on the board. Then she looked at me and said, "Now, go. I have an actual taping in ten minutes. I'll text you later."

I staggered out of the booth and went home, my head whirling.

To find Caroline waiting at my doorstep.

"I have an idea," she said. "Is your mom around?"

"What do you think?" I said.

"Good," she said. "Then let's go down to the May-cave. There's something I need to do there."

She told me to turn it on.

The suit, she meant, which was lying there on the lab bench. It looked wrinkled and sloppy, a lot like my dirty gym clothes. The only difference was it wasn't on the floor.

"Wait," I said. "Hold up. What's going on?"

And she looked at me. "Bailey," she said. "Do you trust me?"

"Of course I trust you," I said. "You're down here, aren't you? Obviously I trust you."

"Then trust me," she said. "I've been thinking about this.

For days. While you've been out robbing Tiffany's and stopping terrorists."

That's what she said, those exact words. And they sounded . . . well, glamorous. Like I was some kind of superhero or something.

Or whatever you call a superhero who robs jewelry stores.

So I nodded and started to suit up, and she stopped me. "Keep it on the bench," she said.

"Caroline—" I started.

"It's simple, don't you see?" she interrupted. "If Mr. Jones is taking control of the suit, there's only one way he can do that: by transmitting signals to it. And those signals have to come from a computer somewhere. *His* computer. If we find the computer, we find him."

That made sense to me. It made a lot of sense, in fact.

But she was still talking. This part I didn't follow as much. Like I said earlier, I don't know anything about computers. And remember what I said before about how in comics there ends up being a genius somewhere in the school? Well, this wasn't that. Like I said, Caroline was no superhacker, no computer genius.

But—if I understood what she was saying correctly—this wouldn't be the same as hacking into the computers. It was much easier to find where the messages were coming from than to find out what the messages said.

Before I could ask her how exactly she was planning to get the location without Mr. Jones finding out, she plugged her phone into one of the ports in the leg of the Mayhem suit.

I remember shouting at her not to do it. I remember saying something about Mr. Jones, how he was paranoid, how I was sure he was watching. I did. I swear I warned her. She just kept swiping and tapping and scrolling and saying that she would be in and out before he noticed. . . .

I knew I had to tell her she was wrong. She didn't know him. I was sure—absolutely *positive*—that Mr. Jones had taken precautions. But this was a lead, maybe, the only lead, since that trap-door-spider thing seemed to be a dead end.

Still, I was going to say something. Really I was. Except that by the time I managed to start getting the words out she was already disconnecting the phone.

"Here we go," she said, and after some more typing and tapping, she looked up at me. "Have you ever heard of Clapham Junction?"

Still a long time until dawn.

Eight hours and twenty-one minutes, according to the suit.

That's when the built-in solar mesh can start recharging, maybe even get the autorepair going. I won't be up for a full-scale firefight anytime soon, but at least I should be able to run away more effectively. The army has to get clearance to attack, after all. At least I think they do.

In the meantime, I need a place I can go to ground. Recover. That national park a few miles outside of the city looks good.

Maybe I could even get out of the suit. Then I'd be just another camper. Only without a tent or any other kind of gear. Including food or water—for all the cool features the suit has, a place to store food and water isn't one of them.

And it'll be hot when the sun rises. That park is desert territory—mesa and scrub brush. Beautiful empty landscapes that go on forever without changing much, but the temperature's not like that. It'll go from freezing to dehydrating in an hour or two. I don't know much about this stuff, but everyone who grows up around here knows enough not to get caught unprepared. Like I am now.

I'll worry about that when the time comes. Hopefully I'll be out of there by rocket boot long before I get really thirsty.

Heading over there now.

In the meantime . . .

Okay.

This next part is going to be hard.

Okay.

THIS WEEK

Caroline's phone came up with two Clapham Junctions: a British transportation interchange near London or, much more likely, a small town about a hundred miles away from where we lived, just a smidge inside the outer limits of the Zone.

"Huh. That's odd," she said.

"What?" I asked.

"There's nothing special about it," she said.

I asked her what she meant, and she pointed out something that reminded me just how brilliant she was.

Almost every place has *something* about it that stands out on the Internet. A hot dog stand, the local lacrosse team, something. But here there wasn't anything. It was like someone had taken special care to make sure no one would ever want to drive by the place to check it out.

I had a feeling I knew who that somebody was.

It wasn't so far away. A few hours by car, maybe a little longer with skirting around the borders of the Zone. I suggested Caroline go home, we both get some sleep, and then we'd figure out the next step. Which would have been—I swear—for me to go there on my own and check it out. It's easy to say now, but that's what I would have done. Drones, overflights, military presence: none of that mattered. I had a next step, and I was going to take it. Yeah, Caroline would be upset that I did it without her, of course, but for all her intelligence, I didn't think she understood how dangerous this was. She had never seen Mr. Jones up close. I mean, neither had I, with his mask and everything, but you know what I mean. So I was going to do it. That was my plan.

And I think Caroline could sense it. And she was *not* down with it.

For her, this was the adventure of a lifetime . . .

She insisted we go right away. Even when I reminded her about her rehearsal—winter formal was the next day, and she was supposed to spend the night with the mp3s—she came back with, "Isn't finding your dad more important than a gig?"

What was I going to say to that?

But I tried. I said, "Look, we can't go now. It's six o'clock. Clapham Junction's at least two hours away. We'd be out all night."

And she said—with a crooked smile—that one way to really convince my mom that we were together was to slip out and spend the night together.

"After all," she said. "She's seen how hot we are for each other."

That was the other time she brought up the kiss.

And it was a joke. It really was. But it was discombobulating.

And maybe—I don't know—maybe that was part of the reason I stopped objecting. I was too thrown. Or maybe I didn't want anything to get in the way of moving forward on my rescue mission. I don't know. Really. I don't.

I did convince her, though, to wait until the next day. She stayed that evening until Mom got home and we told her that Caroline was going to show up at 7:30 a.m. to whisk me away for corsage selection and final tuxedo fittings. And that I had better be ready because it might take a while, maybe even all day.

This was a better excuse than it sounds. Given everything that had happened over the past few months, the administration had decided to give us a break. Being the administration, of course, they had done it in the most backward way possible. First they had floated the idea of canceling winter formal altogether because of "security concerns." That obviously caused a riot. Then, and only then, did they consult the school psychologist and the FBI, who said the same thing: That's a terrible idea.

And so they went the other way and made it a big, dorky thing, with the theme "We Are Strong and United," which had absolutely no effect except that it covered over some of the posters from the original theme, "Mars by Moonlight."

But they *did* announce that they were giving everyone a cut day on the day of winter formal, so everything was forgiven after that.

Admittedly, my plan with Caroline would have been more complicated if my mom had asked questions—like, when had I had my *first* tuxedo fitting?—but she didn't. And she certainly didn't suspect that I was taking someone else to winter formal.

But I guess the idea that Caroline and I were dating made her happy, so I got a full-on explosion of classic Momitude that night. There was the *I always knew you would see she was good for you* routine. There was the *Sometimes you have to be friends before you discover there's something more there* routine. And there was the whole *Your dad and I went down the same road* routine, which I just. . . . Could. Not. Hear. It was a little bit rich, coming from someone who'd given up on that road.

Before she launched into another story about how the two of them first realized there was a spark there—something about practicing their lines in a furniture store during a rainstorm, where they acted out the scenes in the fake living room and realized they were meant to be or whatever by the time the storm was over—I tried to change the subject.

But she started talking about how much I looked like my dad, and that I wasn't much younger than my dad when she met him. I was angry at myself for not shouting at her, for not saying anything about her lack of faith, because I knew getting into that might somehow derail our plan.

Okay. Yeah. That's all true. But fair is fair. I also didn't say anything because I thought, maybe, *maybe*, I could see her eyes getting wet. And some part of me realized that even if she had said she was moving on, she really hadn't.

I hope that's the truth.

Caroline and I spent most of the time on the way to Clapham Junction talking to each other. You'd think it would have been about the big things—what this town could be, my history of robbing banks, Jimmy Anderson. But it wasn't. It was a little bit about movies, and a little bit of what we were thinking about for college, and some about our teachers, and there was this game where we tried to replace everyone in the Rolling Stones with their minidog equivalent. Like, Mick Jagger was an Aussiepom, for example. Caroline was particularly proud of coming up with the title "(I Can't Get No) Satisfaction (Because I Need to Go Walkies and My Owner's at Work)." Which was pretty good.

We used Caroline's Uber account, the one her parents had set up after the divorce. I thought it was crazy—I couldn't even imagine what it was going to cost—but Caroline insisted and said we'd figure out some way to explain it, like we had to go a hundred miles to get a specific paisley cummerbund or something. "I mean," she said, "the worst that'll happen is I get grounded, right?"

I should have turned around right then. I should have refused to get in the car. I should have snuck into the Mayhem suit and *blown up* the car.

Well, no, that's not fair. It wasn't the driver's fault.

I know who's to blame.

So.

We were about fifteen minutes out when we realized something even weirder about Clapham Junction than its virtual absence from the Internet. Actually, the Uber driver pointed it out, and then Caroline confirmed it on her phone. The GPS wasn't working.

Not that Clapham Junction wasn't on the map. Or, not

exactly. It was more that when you tried to get there, the GPS rerouted you away from it. Over and over. You really had to want to get there. This made me worry that the GPS was reporting the data to someone. . . . I think we can assume it was.

There were no highway signs and no turnoff routes. If it weren't for the fact that we had our eyes peeled, we wouldn't even have noticed the off-road, and we still didn't see it until we were already past it. The way it was sharply banked, and kind of hiding behind a gas station, didn't suggest the kind of place where people would ever want to get out and explore. Which, again, was part of the point.

I thought I saw cameras swerve and track our car as we had the driver turn around, but I'm sure that was a figment of my imagination. Any cameras would have been hidden, impossible to see from the road.

One thing I'm thankful for in this whole mess: I made the driver, who was already getting freaked out, drop us off before we walked into town. At least he got away. That's something.

Not much, but it's something.

The truth is, we didn't have a plan. I mean, we weren't naive enough to think there'd be a big building with SECRET HIDEOUT painted on it in giant letters. But I think neither of us had expected the place to be as . . . normal as it was. It was a small community, one of those planned exurbs, with just one or two circular roads around a series of houses that all looked exactly the same. Same low-to-the-ground fake adobe buildings, same small windows, same fences blocking alleys to the backyards, same flat roofs—no difference in age or weathering, at least none that I could see. Then I noticed the cars in the driveways were all the same, too. Chrysler Jeeps. That was creepy.

We walked around and around the circular streets. There was no one outside, though, and no indication of anyone coming in and out of the houses. I had this increasingly terrible feeling that we were sitting ducks, that there were missiles or something trained on us. I even considered slipping into the Mayhem suit and getting ready to armorize it right there.

But before I did, on our third trip around, I noticed something. A little thing, but everything else had been so routinely the *same* that it stuck out like a sore thumb.

One of the Chrysler Jeeps looked different from the others.

It was parked a foot off-center in the driveway, with two of its wheels resting on the grass of the front yard. The house looked exactly like every other house in the neighborhood. But that car's position made the whole thing look creepy. I mean, creepy in a different way.

We snuck up to it and looked inside the car. It was much less . . . sterile, I guess, than anything else we'd seen. Maybe because its owner had little kids. You could tell from the car seat and the cracker crumbs all over everything, and from the toy bulldozer wedged into the back seat.

I didn't know what was going on. This didn't seem like the kind of place where Mr. Jones would fit in. Not that I really knew his tastes in real estate, or cars, or, well, much of anything, but still . . . it didn't give off that Mr. Jones *vibe*. But something was clearly up. Something that needed exploring.

We snuck up to the house and tried to peek through the windows. The shades were down, so you couldn't see a thing. There wasn't even a mail slot to peek through.

"You should armor up," Caroline said. Clearly she was as creeped out as I was.

I told her I wasn't sure if that was such a good idea. It made the odds of Mr. Jones knowing we were there that much higher. Maybe he *hadn't* noticed that Caroline had downloaded his computer's location. Maybe he *wasn't* monitoring my every move when I was out of the suit. And maybe, *maybe* he couldn't track the armor when it wasn't turned on. But once it was . . .

She thought about it for a second. "Look at it this way," she said finally. "No one's going to spill their beans to two *teenagers*." And she was right, of course. "You knew you were going to have to get in the suit when we came here," she said. And she was right about that, too. "So just hurry up and do it."

And so I did.

Standing next to Caroline then, I realized, maybe for the first time, just how impressive it looked. It added several feet to my height. At least. The voice scramblers made me sound like an adult. And the contours of the armor made it look like I had these muscles. . . . The point is, I looked badass. And I felt badass.

That feeling would be gone in a few minutes. But, of course, I didn't know that then.

I had broken into half a dozen banks and trashed at least one world-class jewelry store. But I still felt weirdly uncomfortable knocking down the door of this house. After all, it felt different. *Civilian* was the word that came to mind. But there was something very weird going on here, and maybe the house would provide some answers. I had to start somewhere, and this seemed like the best option.

I told Caroline to stand behind me while I smashed the door. And I felt a stab of happiness, not in causing destruction, not in the way Caroline looked at me as I did it, but in the sweetest thing ever: being proven right.

Since the house's front room did not contain a couch or a TV or a dining set or even any furniture at all, but instead what looked to my inexperienced eye like several million dollars' worth of guns.

Not just guns. Rocket launchers, bazookas, a stack of what I think might have been antipersonnel mines, and crates of what I was pretty sure was plastic explosive. I seemed to remember the stencil on one of the crates—C-4—from an old television show my dad liked, *The A-Team*.

At first I didn't get it. This felt even less like Mr. Jones, if that was possible. He'd never even used the Mayhem suit himself—he certainly wasn't the kind of guy to run around holding a bazooka. And how many rocket launchers does one man need? Something this size, it was much more than Mr. Jones could possibly use. This was enough for a small army.

And then Caroline gasped and pointed, and I realized which small army these weapons belonged to.

The black-and-white banner of the Bloody Front was hanging on the wall. Right where a TV set would have been.

"Wait a minute," Caroline said. I turned to her, speechless.

"Look." She pointed through the living room, toward the back of the house. There was what I think the real estate shows call an *open kitchen*—lots of space and no interior walls. It was clear no one had used it to cook for a while, since the countertops were covered with more crates of explosives.

But beyond that, through the kitchen windows, was the backyard.

Or what would have been the backyard, if this were a normal house in a normal town. Instead it was some crazy arrangement of tents and tunnels—almost like a . . . gigantic hamster cage, I guess. And they all looked like they linked up with the other houses. At least all the ones I could see.

I remember reading about the Secret Service, and how they protect the president. If he has to leave his armored car and go someplace where there could be a sharpshooter, they put up a big tent so that no one can see exactly when he leaves the car. There's no shot to take.

Whoever—or whatever—was passing between these houses, you wouldn't be able see them from the street—the high fences took care of that—and you couldn't see them from the sky, thanks to the tents. The tents must have looked pretty suspicious, of course, but I was betting that they were hidden by some version of the GPS trick, or cloaking, or old-fashioned camouflage. A terrorist group would know all about that stuff.

"This town is the Bloody Front's headquarters," Caroline said. "It's gotta be. Right?"

I nodded. It couldn't be anything else. And if it was, that meant *my dad was here*. And I would tear down everything and everyone in order to find him.

But Caroline continued. "So why is it where Mr. Jones's messages were coming from?"

And that stopped me cold.

Because suddenly I had another theory for why Mr. Jones had known when the Front were going to strike in New York.

And I didn't like it one bit.

It didn't make sense, though. If Mr. Jones was working with the Bloody Front, why did he have me stop them? And if they had kidnapped my dad, why would he tell me about it? And if *that* was a lie—who knew what else was—then why did he send me on those missions? Just to get money? To do what?

And where was my dad?

The reasonable thing to do, under the circumstances, would have been to back away slowly and place an anonymous call to the police or Homeland Security. But we were far past reasonable.

I was going to get some answers.

But of course—saying this is like choking on knives now—I didn't want Caroline to get hurt, so we tried to be careful.

We searched the house, creeping along as subtly as an over-eight-foot-tall armored man can, Caroline trying to slip ahead of me, me trying to cut her off when she did. We looked like the Frankenstein monster playing with that little girl in the movie. Looking for clues. To where my dad was, to anything. If there was nothing there, we'd hit the tunnels and try another house. And another. And another, until we found what we were looking for. That was the plan.

And it looked like that was what we were going to have to do. Because everything else in the house itself looked normal. I mean, aside from all that firepower, which was admittedly a big exception. But not only was there no sign of my dad, there was no sign of anyone living there, of any personality. It was more like a show house, the kind you'd look at if you were going to buy real estate in the community. Not that anyone would be able to find the place on a map.

I'd kept Caroline behind me the whole time. That Jeep hadn't moved itself, after all, and I was worried someone would jump out of a closet or a shower firing a gun. If they aimed at me, all they'd get would be a ricochet back into their own head.

Which would not, of course, be optimal. I was hoping I'd be able to frighten them into telling us where my dad was kept. And then I'd save him, and get him back to my mom in time for winter formal night, and they could both stand there in the front hall with the camera and make embarrassing *oohing* and *aahing* noises about how wonderful I looked in my tux before I met Rebecca and then we'd slow-dance, maybe even to the music of the mp3s.

This was a ridiculous fantasy of course, but it was attractive. And, notwithstanding everything, a little distracting. So despite theoretically being on high alert, I was caught off guard when the suit's monitors flashed a proximity motion warning. I looked out the upstairs window and saw someone walking out of the house across the way, heading for the Jeep, the one with the cracker crumbs.

I didn't bother with the backyards, or the tunnels. I used the window, rocketing out like a flash and shouting at Caroline to avoid the shattering glass.

The person—a woman, I could see—heard the noise but didn't seem to panic. She just turned on her heel without looking up and went back into the house before I could intercept her, closing the door. And, presumably, locking it.

I didn't bother to find out. I just ripped the door off its hinges, taking most of the frame with it, and then I stomped after the woman, who was already disappearing up a staircase. Looking up, I could see high heels, followed by a long white coat.

Which made sense, because the inside of this house didn't look like a show house at all. It looked more like a lab. Glass walls, steel lab tables, lots of workstations with those uncomfortable-looking metal stools.

None of that mattered. What was important was that I had found someone I could talk to. Or at.

"GET DOWN HERE," I rumbled, and the woman turned around. No trace of surprise at seeing Mayhem in front of her.

"Oh, it's you," she said. "Haven't seen you in a while."

While I was trying to process this, Caroline arrived, panting heavily, and the woman looked at her. "And who is this? Your daughter or something?"

"OH," I said, "SHE'S NOT—I MEAN, IT ISN'T—"

The woman just looked at us, shrugged, and headed back up the stairs. I heard a door slam behind her.

Caroline looked at me, said, "Your daughter?" and started laughing. Hard. So hard she almost choked.

And then she was choking more, and turning red, and there was blood coming out of her mouth, and she collapsed, shaking and foaming.

This is the worst part.

NOW. FRIDAY. 10:34 P.M.

You know, it's beautiful out here, in the desert. Beautiful and lonely.

I should just get out of the suit and . . . walk away. Just leave. Forget about food, water . . . everything. For a while.

I think maybe that's what I should do.

But I have to get through the next part.

It's almost finished. I can't stop now.

THIS MORNING

I had never done CPR training. Plus I was in the suit. I had no idea what to do.

So I smashed through the ceiling, battering down the closed door upstairs.

The woman was sitting at a long desk covered with computer monitors, test tubes, bottles, gadgets, and lab equipment. She looked up at me and frowned. "What's with all the—" she said, or something like that. But whatever she said, she didn't finish, because I had slammed her into the wall—not hard enough to knock her out, but hard enough to let her know I was *serious*.

She sat down on the floor heavily. Her head sort of rolled to the side, and I thought for a second of Jimmy Anderson, but she'd just had her bell rung, as our gym teacher used to say.

The weird thing was, she didn't seem surprised. By any of this.

"THE GIRL I'M WITH," I shouted. I could hear my voice bouncing off the walls. "SHE'S BLEEDING. AND CHOKING. DO SOMETHING. NOW."

And she looked at me, not scared, not surprised, just focused, and asked me—I'll never forget these words, as long as I live—"You brought her into a level-seven hot zone without giving her the vaccine first?"

"WHAT ARE YOU TALKING ABOUT?" I demanded.

"I know you do your own thing, that's how it's set up, but weren't you briefed about this? This whole house is a biohazard," she said. "The girl's already dead."

Then she looked alarmed and said, "Wait—" but I didn't waste time listening and I didn't pay attention—then—to the first thing she said. I just grabbed her arm—carefully—and told her to get me the antidote right away. "It's not an antidote," she said. "It's a *vaccine*. It's too late now."

I must have said something about getting Caroline to a hospital, and for the first time the woman showed some emotion. She started shaking her head wildly.

"It's insanely infectious," she said. "It's aerosolized. And *viral*." She started speaking more quickly. "This house—it looks like a regular house, but it's sealed. You didn't notice the hiss when you came in? Negative pressure. It's got its own atmosphere. You bring her out of here, to a hospital . . . we could lose the entire state if the wind patterns are wrong." And then she said something even scarier. "And that's not the plan," she said.

"DON'T TRY TO FREAK ME OUT," I said, though she was doing a pretty good job of it. "I'M HERE, AND I'M FINE."

"Well, of course, in the Mayhem suit," she said. "It has its own filtering systems. But she's been breathing virus since she got inside."

I didn't wait to hear more.

The scientist had been wrong. Caroline wasn't dead yet. But it would have been better if she had been.

She had convulsed hard enough to break bones in her body, and she was greenish gray with big zits, *pustules* I think they call them, all over her skin. I was hoping that she was unconscious since her eyes were closed, but then I realized, with a jolt in my stomach, that they were swollen shut. I punched a wall in frustration, and my fist went through it.

She tilted her head, just a little, toward the sound of me and said, "Doctor . . . hospital . . ."

And I hated myself and hated myself, but I shook my head. "I CAN'T," I said. "I CAN'T. IT'S—" and I stopped. I didn't know what to say next. How to tell her.

But she was nodding. No, not nodding, she wasn't strong enough, but she moved her head up and down just the tiniest bit. She understood. Then she let out a rattling breath. And then she laughed, a little.

"CAROLINE," I said.

"I get it," she said.

You can't touch your face when you're inside the suit. Which is terrible if your nose itches, or something. Or you want to wipe away the tears streaming down your face.

I should have told her I loved her. I mean, I did, of course. Not romantically, but I loved her so much.

I think she knew, though. I do. At least, that's what I need to tell myself.

She didn't say anything else before she died.

I want to say that that was the worst part. The worst of all this. But you know what? I'm not even sure that's true.

Because when I looked down at Caroline's face, which was now yellow and black and bubbling, a new thought clawed through my pain. Something terrible. And terrifying.

I shot back upstairs to the scientist. She was at her computer, typing quickly, concentrating. "I've wiped almost everything already, a hard-terminal wipe," she said. "I don't know who you're working for now and I don't care. You can't take it with you."

I told her I didn't know what she was talking about and I didn't care, either. What I did care about was that I'd broken down the door when I came in. Leaving a wide open space for whatever was there in the house to slither out into the world.

I thought the scientist had been upset before. But now she looked furious. And then . . . resigned. She looked resigned. "I have a kid," she said, and I remembered the car seat, the small toy bulldozer.

"I'M NOT THREATENING YOU," I said. "I JUST—"

"No, you don't get it," she said. She turned to the computer and typed in a few keystrokes, then a few more. "I know she loves me. I just wish I had the chance to see her one more time."

"WHAT ARE YOU—"

"I just checked the weather conditions," she said, as if she hadn't heard me. "Totally calm. No wind, thank God. We still have time."

"I SAID, WHAT ARE YOU—"

"Mr. Jones always thought this was a possibility," she said, and her voice was quiet, calm, without emotion. Like she was a robot. "That's why he let the Bloody Front set up head-quarters here. Off the grid. Far away from you and your missions. Far from other towns. I don't know much about your end, but here a lot of us are just working for a paycheck. But preparations were made. There's a protocol. In case the Front ever decided to go off the rails, there were . . . precautions taken."

"PRECAUTIONS? WHAT PRECAUTIONS? I DON'T KNOW WHAT YOU'RE—" Some part of me realized this was import-ant, the smoking gun, but my head was full of Caroline and panic.

"In about fifteen or twenty minutes, based on when you made your idiotic entrance, the airborne virus that killed that girl will float past city limits. At that point, once it gets out, it could infect anyone. It *will* infect *everyone*. The only way to stop it is to burn it out."

"WHAT—" I started. But she kept going.

"I ordered an airstrike," she said. "The drones are on their way from our private hangars. Omega Protocol. We've gamed this over and over again, and the scientists don't think nuclear weapons are necessary. Intensive firebombing should do just as well. This virus doesn't do well in heat." She closed her eyes. "There won't be much left, but enough to identify this as the Bloody Front's stronghold. He saw to that, with those steel dog tags he gave those idiots to wear. They won't burn. Everyone will assume they were trying to test some weapon and blew themselves up in the process."

I felt like I was going to throw up. I couldn't get my

bearings. If I'd been standing on my own legs, not inside the suit, I might have fallen down.

"He won't care," she went on, no longer really talking to me. "He'll find some other way to do what he wants, to finish the plan. But we won't be there to see it. It's mostly Front members here, but there are others, too. Workers. Support staff. Janitorial. There should be"—she paused, and when she spoke again, her voice shook—"about two, three hundred people in these houses at this time of day. You've killed them all. Congratulations. You were a jewel thief with pretensions. Now you're a mass murderer."

I just don't understand. I don't understand any of this. I haven't from the beginning, it turns out.

Was my dad working with the Bloody Front? How else would that woman have known about him? I mean, she talked to me like I was an old coworker . . .

Maybe he'd been trying to fight them from within. Like a double agent. And then they found out, and that's why they took him prisoner.

Or . . . maybe he's not a prisoner at all. I only have Mr. Jones's word for that, after all, and he's a liar.

And my dad wouldn't have been working from within the Front. At least, not exactly. From what the scientist said, Mayhem and the Front weren't exactly working *together*. They were part of something bigger.

Something headed by Mr. Jones.

So Mr. Jones and the Bloody Front are . . . partners? And they're willing to kill people. Millions of them.

Maybe they've already killed my dad.

Oh, God. Maybe *I* did.

Maybe he was there. Hidden somewhere.

No. Mr. Jones wouldn't have kept my dad there. Not with other people. People who might have asked my dad questions about Mr. Jones's past, questions he had answers to. Not with Mr. Jones's obsession with keeping everything about himself supersecret.

I'm going to believe that. I *have* to believe that.

And why would Mr. Jones spend all this time with me in the first place? Why wouldn't he just kill *me*?

Here's the thing. If by some miracle he didn't know I was trying to figure out his secrets before—if he didn't know about the money I kept from him, the secret message from the library—he must know by now.

I have to stop him. Somehow. I'll never be safe if I don't. And even if I *could* vanish without a trace, what would that do to my mom? She's already had to go through that once, with my dad . . . a second time would kill her.

If Mr. Jones doesn't kill her first.

I'm getting too comfortable with talking about death and murder.

All right.

Let me finish this.

Then maybe I can sleep. For a little while.

THIS AFTERNOON

My main thought at the time was: *Get out.*

Get out and find Mr. Jones and tear him into tiny pieces for what he'd done. To Caroline. To my dad. To the Bloody Front's victims, however he was involved with that. Get out and make sure my mom was okay. And, of course, get out before the drones with missiles leveled the place and scorched me to a cinder along with it.

But there was an . . . ethical question, I guess I had to call it. If I escaped, I'd bring the virus with me. Wouldn't I kill more people? Wasn't the right thing to do, well—to go up in smoke? As I looked down and saw Caroline's body on the monitors, there was a part of me that knew that was exactly what I deserved.

The scientist saw me thinking—or, at least, she saw the armor stand there, unmoving—and said, "I should just let you die here with me. But I'm not a murderer." She paused. "Here's the thing. The virus only incubates in, and on, living things. Even if your vaccination's out of date, you're not exposed. The suit's filters are clearly working because otherwise you'd be dead. So you're safe. Hurrah."

I wish I'd said something comforting to her. Or something philosophical. Or anything at all. But all I could think about was getting out of there—getting out, and getting revenge.

And that was when I realized that the answers were right in front of me. To everything. To what Mr. Jones was doing. To what his plan was. Maybe even to what had happened to my dad. But there was no way I was going to be able to understand the answers, not without some supercharged version of a tech support guy; but there they were. Right on the scientist's computer.

I snatched the computer off her desk, ripped it apart, and yanked out its hard drive. Wires sparked as the screen flickered and died. Maybe that stopped the wipe. I'd read somewhere that data never truly disappears. I didn't know if that was true, but the way the scientist tried to jump for the drive and grab it out of my hands made it seem like she thought there might still be something valuable on it, too.

Then I blew a hole in the roof—I mean at this point, who cared, right?—and headed west as quick as I possibly could.

But not so quickly that I couldn't see the people venturing out of the houses, those identical houses with who-knew-how-many secrets hidden inside, to watch me go. And then I was too high up to see them, but I could imagine.

They would follow my trajectory to see where I'd come from. See the holes in the lab house's front entrance and roof. Then turn, surprised at the sound of the drones, and put two and two together. By the time I reached cloud level I was pretty sure that everyone in Clapham Junction knew the score, or at least part of it.

Which wasn't to say they deserved it. Not by a long shot.

The suit got me a little over half a mile away before the blasts hit.

They were not messing around. It was like one of those video games where the target goes up in light and flame and then just isn't there anymore. I don't mean that to be cavalier—it's the only image I can think of. I got sent tumbling head over heels by the shock wave, and the readouts showed the air temperature around me going up, up, up. Below me, the trees were catching on fire.

I guess this was the gift that came with all the hours in the suit: I didn't panic. I didn't flail. I took deep breaths, tried to ignore the fact that I was crying so hard I could barely see, and tried to get out of there.

It was only when I spotted the fighter jets heading in my direction that I started hyperventilating.

It made sense. I mean, when a good chunk of the US military is packed into a fairly small geographical area looking for terrorists, and there's a gigantic explosion nearby, they're going to check it out. And they're going to come heavy. And then when they see Mayhem flying away from it . . .

I'd done a lot of stuff with the suit over the past few weeks. But going head-to-head with the air force was taking it to a new level.

I cricked my head and eavesdropped on their chatter. It

wasn't difficult—I think Mr. Jones had bribed defense contractors to build a back door into the communications system of every aircraft in use in America. When I heard them ask their commanders whether they were cleared to shoot missiles over civilian areas, I got nervous. I set the navigation system to make sure I wouldn't fly over any highly populated areas. Not so hard to do in this part of the country, where there's a lot of ranching. Maybe if I got caught there would be some hamburgers charbroiled before their time, but that's all.

It was probably right around then that the first missile caught me in the small of my back.

It wasn't that I wasn't paying attention. I'd been counting on the radar to sound the alarm and on the automatic pilot to keep me safe—both of which I'd activated precisely according to the instructions in the manuals and files.

And neither of which came online.

I imagined Mr. Jones somewhere, smiling under the mask.

Watching the ruins of Clapham Junction and looking for revenge. And deciding to take it slowly: playing with me, cat and mouse, through his control over the suit. Until he got bored and decided to totally take over and drop me right out of the sky.

It wasn't like I had much choice other than to play along, though. I'd be dead sooner—blown right out of the air—if I didn't get it together.

The suit held together, but even with the internal dampers, the shock wave from the missile was intense. I could feel bruises forming all over my body, and I heard some funny tones. I think I might have perforated an eardrum. It gave me some sense of what that scientist must have felt like when I lifted her up. And then I thought about what had just happened to her, what she probably looked like now, and I *concentrated*.

Until this point, I'd only scratched the surface of the suit's offensive capabilities. What was the use of swatting flies with a bazooka? But now I was mad. At the Bloody Front. At Mr. Jones. At myself.

I locked on to the first jet and kicked in the afterburners. Matched velocities, then exceeded them. Headed straight for it—and then straight through one of its engines—before it had a chance to take evasive action. I knew the pilot would be able to parachute out. One down.

The second pilot was better, though, and he'd had more warning. He started twisting and turning all over the sky, firing at me with everything he had. The machine-gun bullets simply pinged off the suit. I was going fast enough that they didn't even knock me off my course. But those missiles were something else. I wasn't sure how many more of those I could take.

Mr. Jones hadn't frozen the suit yet. I guess he was enjoying this, seeing how it played out. Well, if he wanted a show, I'd give him a show. And if somehow I survived, I'd cram it down his throat.

I shot off two smaller missiles of my own. Not that he couldn't avoid them, but they'd be a distraction while I got up close, with a bit of cloud cover for assistance. Then I took the subtle route.

You know those pulses that fry all communication and electrical activity and whatnot? EMPs, they're called? Guess who can generate them from inside his suit.

Zap.

The plane started dropping out of the sky like a rock. Perfect.

The only problem, I realized, as I saw absolutely no indication of the pilot parachuting out, was that I had fried the cockpit release along with the rest of the plane.

The pilot was still in his seat, banging at the top of the window. As I flew in really close, he stopped banging and put his head in his hands. Clearly he assumed I was going to make things even worse.

Well, screw that. I'd made myself a promise—no more killing—and even if it meant my joining him inside a crater, so be it. But I hoped it wouldn't come to that.

I grabbed the plane's fuselage with one hand, the cockpit top with another, and separated the two. Quite violently. The pilot looked at me, confused, but didn't activate his parachute. He was pointing to the chair, then to his seat belt, then back again. I guess there was fried electronic stuff in that, too. Oh, and by this point, I had noticed, we were a lot closer to the ground.

Fine. I activated the torch on my right index finger—thermal amplifier, whatever—and burned away the restraints and the chair, making sure I had a firm hold on his uniform with my left hand.

Seeing the whole plane drop away from us was really something.

I rolled over as the plane hit the ground, to put my back between him and the gigantic explosion. Through the monitors, I could see the pilot was shouting at me, but the sound dampeners filtering out the explosion muted him, too. Was he saying thank you? Was he telling me to go to hell? I couldn't tell, but both were definitely appropriate.

I dropped the pilot off next to the smoking wreckage of his plane, double-checked the hard drive—still safe inside the armor, nestled against my chest—and kept flying. Home.

I kept wondering if I should fly at all. I mean, Mr. Jones had seen what I'd done to the fighter jets. Maybe he'd get tired of whatever cat-and-mouse game he was playing. Or even see me as a threat. With all the camera footage he had to tap into, he must have seen me grab the hard drive, and put two and two together. And he wasn't a man who liked to take risks. Just drop me from ten thousand feet, and that would be that.

Or maybe it wouldn't. Maybe he was worried someone would find the suit before he did, call in the FBI, and they'd discover the hard drive. A hard drive that must have something pretty incriminating on it, otherwise I'd be pavement pizza already.

So Mr. Jones was waiting to try to get it back some other way.

That was a narrow hope to hang my life on, but with each mile I didn't die, it seemed more and more plausible.

And I needed to get back home fast. I needed to get out of the suit, to try to figure out if the hard drive worked, not to mention to find someone to decrypt it and tell me what was on it.

But I had other things to worry about. Downing two military fighter jets does not go unnoticed.

The sky started filling up. I don't know how many planes are in a squadron. At least that many. Maybe it was two squadrons. Maybe six. It was a lot of planes.

By this time, I figured, someone in the government had talked to a bunch of someone elses in the government and they'd come to the conclusion that Mayhem had wiped a small American city off the map. Who could blame them? Maybe, given what had happened in Manhattan, they thought I had done it together with the Bloody Front. I'm sure that Mr. Jones is using his government contacts to push that story forward. And I know how rumors can spread and become the truth. I'm in high school.

Time for a change of plans.

I swerved and headed straight toward the largest tangle of buildings the suit could find for me within fifty miles. Medium-size city; population . . . maybe a hundred thousand or so. I didn't have time to look at all the data I was getting.

Big enough to give me a place to hide. That was what I was going for.

I could hear the pilots' response. It wasn't very nice, but at least it confirmed that they weren't authorized to attack near big civilian populations. I did hear them talking about calling in the National Guard. Going house to house, or something like that.

Well, I figured I could handle that. Bunch of weekend warriors.

I guess the National Guard had been trusted with some serious military gear when I wasn't paying attention, though. And after the Bloody Front attacks, they were not afraid to use it. I had landed in an alley and was about to dearmorize my suit when I heard the word *tanks*.

Looking back, I probably could have pulled it off. Slipped out of the suit and gotten away, just another kid looking shifty and scared. I mean, with tanks in the streets, that wouldn't have been such a stretch. But I wasn't thinking straight, and besides, I was pretty sure I'd been spotted landing in the alley. Maybe staying suited was smarter.

Only it wasn't. Because when I turned on the scanner to search local police and military bandwidths for broadcasts using the word *Mayhem*, all I heard was a loud staticky sound, then silence. And I had that image of Mr. Jones again. Like a cat batting around a ball of yarn. With its teeth showing.

I made a note to myself about yet another unpleasant thing I'd do to him when I saw him, and started running.

I headed south-southeast, in the direction of home, and then—all right!—a river. I was sure the armories of the local police departments and the National Guard here didn't extend to submarines or battleships. Pretty sure, anyway. Just get to the water, and I would be on my way, if not quite home free.

And all of a sudden I was flying.

This was not by choice. An imaginary giant's hand had lifted me by the scruff of my neck and was dangling me about twenty feet in the air, spinning me around right above a pocket park in the middle of the downtown business district. To the National Guard, I guess it looked like I was taunting them, telling them to come and get me. But the truth was that I was Mr. Jones's puppet. And it looked like he wanted me to go out in a blaze of "glory." I'm putting glory in quotation marks, since you can't see me doing air quotes.

He hadn't been worried about the hard drive, I guess. Maybe he knew about it, maybe he didn't. He just wanted to have his revenge up close and personal.

And it started arriving, in the form of heavy gunfire.

It's not like any of these attacks individually could have done much to the suit. Like I said before, the suit shrugs off small-arms fire. Even a tank shell or two wouldn't do that much to it. But it had already taken a lot of damage from the missile, and to sit there and absorb more and more . . . I wasn't sure how long it could hold out. Besides, if the military decided I was just going to be a sitting target for whatever reason—and, of course, that was what it looked like, and they weren't going to spend a whole lot of time asking me about my motivations—then even though it was an occupied area they might try to evacuate it and bring in the big guns.

And that's exactly what they did.

I could hear the megaphone blare of military instructions, and I saw people running through the street, some of them passing right underneath me, parents carrying kids wrapped up in blankets, everyone crying, probably as scared of the soldiers as they were of me. There were a few people hold-ing precious things close, like stuffed animals and photo albums. I saw one small boy drop his album and a bunch of pictures spilled out. He stooped to pick them up, but his dad almost yanked his arm out of his socket to keep him moving.

I looked through my scopes at those pictures, lying there on the ground, and I had to do something. But I was para-lyzed, hanging there, scaring the snot out of little kids and getting my butt blown off in the process. Suit integrity was holding, though based on the blinking, blinding damage alerts, who knew for how long.

Ironically, not being able to do anything gave me time to think.

I tried to go through the suit's instruction manuals in my mind. Useless. Every conversation about the suit I'd had with Mr. Jones was even less helpful. There was only one glimmer of hope, one thing that might help: that Klingon message, *Trap-door spider*. I hadn't been able to make any sense of those words, but they must have meant something—and right now they were my only lead.

Was Mr. Jones the trap-door spider? That fit, for sure: he was a secret, scuttling thing, hiding in his space until some-one disturbed him, and now he was jumping in for the kill. But somehow I didn't think that was what the note meant. But if it wasn't, then who was the spider? Was it me? That made even less sense.

But then my brain, working at speeds previously unknown, came up with another possibility. *Maybe it was the suit.* Maybe the Mayhem suit itself had some mechanism to chomp down on things that were coming in and attacking it.

Like Mr. Jones's control override.

Which, as I'd learned from Caroline—I couldn't think about Caroline now . . . I'd go to pieces, metaphorically, then literally—had to result from some sort of transmission signal, for him to turn it on and off the way he did.

And transmissions could be blocked.

Of course, Mr. Jones would have programmed the suit to make it impossible to block any outside transmissions, or at least his. He's careful.

But what if there *was* a way of blocking Mr. Jones's power. But it was something physical—like a spider's web, but a mechanical version? There'd be no way for Mr. Jones to override *that*. Like how you can't hack a dead bolt with a virus program. It just doesn't work that way.

Okay. But even if there was some kind of blocking switch, how was I going to find it? In all my time with the Mayhem suit, I hadn't come across it yet. And it wasn't like I could take the suit off to give it a thorough investigation. I couldn't even lift my arms to activate the shutoff panel, since Mr. Jones had taken control of the limbs. I thought for a second about trying to wriggle my arm out of the suit's sleeve, like a little kid getting out of a sweater, but the inside of the suit was too tight for that.

On the other hand, if my line of thinking was right, none of this mattered. Because it would *have* to be something—be some*where*—I could reach when my whole body was paralyzed. It wouldn't make any sense to put it anywhere else.

Which left my head. It was frozen—I couldn't turn, nod, shake the helmet, anything. But there was one moving part that Mr. Jones couldn't lock into place. . . .

I moved my head forward. Slowly. There was just enough give for me to touch my forehead against the monitor panels.

And then I stuck out my tongue and licked.

I felt ridiculous, and a little gross, but I stopped caring when my tongue swept across a strange, rough protrusion about an inch to the left of the center of my mouth. Strange because the rest of the suit—both inside and out, at least before the diamonds had scuffed it and the missiles had hit—was as smooth as the lines of a new Porsche.

But this was rough, and felt almost like . . . a tiny, tiny, lever.

Mentally crossing my fingers, which I couldn't do since they were frozen in a splayed position, I jabbed at the lever with my tongue.

I knew I was getting traction the minute I fell out of the sky.

I landed hard, and badly. Thank God for whatever crazy material Mr. Jones had used to make the suit. It cushioned the blow enough that I didn't break anything. Or break anything of mine, anyway, because something glitched inside the suit. The screens wavered for a minute and went black, and my heart climbed back down from near the top of my throat as they fuzzed on again.

Like I said before, I've never played football myself, but I know enough to describe what I did next as a kind of championship broken-field run: down the grand avenue leading away from the park, and out toward the highway. If the opposing team were actual, literal tanks. Like the ones ahead of me.

I considered trying to go full superpower and shove them into the buildings on either side, but the consequences to the buildings would have been . . . severe. Not to mention to anyone who hadn't been evacuated.

I have to remember to think about that kind of thing. *Always.*

There was another factor, too. I didn't want to waste the suit's power. Considering what the autorepair functions had to handle. And who knew what I might still have to deal with? Mr. Jones must have realized—from remote video footage he was tapping into, soldiers' chatter he was monitoring, whatever—that somehow I'd managed to shrug off his control. I shuddered to think of what he might come up with next.

But he wasn't all-powerful. That much was clear. Dad had monkeyed with the suit, installed the tongue switch, gotten some independence. That meant he'd been questioning Mr. Jones, too, right? It must. Maybe Dad *hadn't* been partners with the Front, after all. And that's why he ended up getting kidnapped.

Did this mean I was following in my dad's footsteps?

I was almost feeling cheerful when the tanks started shooting at me.

I guess they were less concerned about civilians than I was. Or maybe they were just confident in their evacuation protocols. I figured I could spin and weave around two or three of them, and was feeling good about my prospects of getting out of there when there was a sudden *rumble* and a *crash* and I realized they hadn't been aiming for me.

Knocking a building down on me wasn't the worst way to stop Mayhem, after all.

And that takes us full circle. To where I started from.

It's quiet here, and it's dark, and I'm so very tired. I've got to get some sleep.

I can't do anything until the sun comes out, anyway, when the suit will be able to recharge.

I think I'll stop here. For now. Thanks for listening.

Good night. Whoever you are.

It's almost sunrise. I can't believe the night is finally over.

I know it should be very symbolic—it's dawn, I'm refreshed, ready to start anew—but I don't feel any of that. I feel exhausted and drained and guilty and terrible. About Caroline. And Clapham Junction.

So to recap. I might as well do it out loud. I mean, I've recorded everything up till now, it would be a shame not to finish it. And I've kind of gotten into the habit, over the last half day or so . . .

Here's where we are. The suit is wrecked. I'm here, in the desert, bruised and banged up, can't hear out of my right ear, my only possession a battered and possibly useless, possibly priceless, hard drive.

Got to keep moving. I'm hoping that when I blocked Mr. Jones from controlling the suit I also blocked him from tracking it. But I'm not sure, and even if that's true, it doesn't mean he isn't keeping tabs on me some other way. I'm sure he has access to satellite data. Or to who knows what else.

But the sun's up. The suit can start repairing itself. It'll be good as new in a couple of hours. I can get back home. Fence the diamonds somehow. Take the cash and restock the weapons—or steal some from an armory, that should be simple enough—and find a superhacker to unlock the hard drive. Hopefully there'll be information about my dad on it.

And if not, or even if so, take the fight directly to Mr. Jones and make him pay.

For my dad. And for our family, and all these years together we've lost. For those people in Clapham Junction. And for *their* families, who didn't know, and probably never will.

For Caroline. . . .

Oh, God. There's no body. There's nothing left. . . .

What am I going to tell Mom? What am I going to tell *her* mom?

I can't think about this now. There's work to be done.

Because I have to figure out what that plan of Mr. Jones's was, the one the scientist was talking about. Because I've been wrong, and wrong, and wrong again. First I thought Mr. Jones had been hacking into the Bloody Front's computers and not sharing the information with me. And then, at Clapham Junction, I thought he and the Front were partners.

But I think that was wrong, too. Or at least, not totally right. After what the scientist alluded to. I think they might be an actual, real-life bloody front: people doing horrible evil on the outside as a front, a cover-up, so that no one pays attention to the even worse action going on behind the scenes. Was that an intentional pun? It must have been, right?

But what's going on, really? What is Mr. Jones's plan?

And how could it be worse than everything the Bloody Front has done? How is that *possible?*

No idea. Not a clue. Maybe there'll be some clues on the hard drive. For the moment I'm stuck out here. Suit's almost entirely depowered.

Clouds of dust up ahead. Something's coming over the horizon.

I'll suck a little more out of these almost-dry power cells, set the viewfinders to maximum . . .

Jeeps. Three of them. And that's the Bloody Front logo spray-painted on the sides.

I guess I was right about Mr. Jones still being able to find me after all.

I'm imagining him on the phone to whatever members of the Front happened to be outside Clapham Junction when the explosives dropped. Here's this Mayhem, he says. He killed all your—our—comrades. Yes, he and I have worked together in the past, as I don't need to tell you, but he's gone rogue. You remember Manhattan. I gave him one last chance after that, and here we are. I'm cutting him loose, and I'm offering you the chance to be the tip of the spear. Here's the latest GPS data, courtesy of my private weather satellite. He's weak. On the ropes. Vulnerable. Take out the suit and whatever you find, hand it over to me, and not only will you get revenge for your buddies, but I promise I'll toss some meaty chunks of Mayhem technology your way so the next time you blow up a Foot Locker or terrorize some little old ladies playing bingo, you can make sure you'll be able to cause maximum damage without getting a teensy-tiny scratch.

He probably didn't say that last part. But I bet I'm pretty close on the first half . . .

I'm really starting to think like him now. What does that say?

I guess I was right about one thing. He's a good teacher.

I can see a few rocket launchers perched over the struts of one of the Jeeps. And I recognize one of them through the suit's viewscreen. The leader. Assassin. He's going to want to cause a lot of pain to get back at me for New York.

I know, I sound totally calm. Right? I think I'm in shock.

What do I do? Head for the hills? With power levels where they are now, there's no way I'll outrun the Jeeps, much less fly out of here. And the directional microphones are picking up faint shouting, so I think they've spotted me, too. No escape, no surrender.

Stand and fight it is.

I'm checking the weaponry rosters one last time . . . yup, pretty much gone. Maybe a few bursts left in the flamethrower. The suit's defensive mechanisms are almost drained, too. It could probably handle small-arms fire, but a direct hit from something more serious, like one of those rocket launchers, and I'll be in real trouble.

Okay. Frontal assault is out, and so is evasive action. It's just open space between me and them. There's a hill behind me I can try to take cover behind, but they'll just drive up it and cut me down from the high ground.

Wait a minute. *Wait a minute.* I just thought of something. I mean, there's no way it's going to work. But I am out of options. . . .

Okay, here goes nothing.

I can't believe that worked. I mean, I really can't believe it.

It *almost* didn't . . . well, no need to dwell on that.

Here's what happened, though. For the record.

I directed a large chunk of the suit's remaining power to the flamethrowers and blazed off a warning shot in the direction of the Jeeps. Not to actually hurt them, although I didn't mind if that's what they thought. Just to blind them for a second.

I took advantage of that second to scoot around the hill.

I wasn't looking to escape. They clearly knew where I'd gone, since other than the hill, it was open land and sky for miles around.

But there was one other route, as long as Mr. Jones wasn't giving them real-time 3-D GPS updates.

I took a deep breath, pointed my head downward, and started tunneling. I was going underground.

My light-bulb inspiration had consisted of digging under the hill and coming up right beneath the bad guys. I actually owed the idea to Mr. Jones, I'm sure he'd be happy to know. It was a variation on one of the training routines he'd had me run.

It was different than in Mr. Jones's warehouse, though, where I'd been tunneling through the bottom of one of those fake buildings. And a lot trickier than it seemed to be in Bugs Bunny cartoons. For one thing, it was really difficult to displace the dirt. Between kicking the motors into overdrive and operating the flamethrowers at full blast I was able to blast out a tunnel, but even with all that effort I was barely able to make the hole big enough for me.

Which meant it was very dark—I was almost instantly blind, the monitors showing pure black. I had to switch to radar, which I wasn't sure was operating perfectly—and since I didn't have any time to pack the ground, the tunnel was filling up behind me as I went. Not fully—I mean, the oxygen monitors never dipped into the yellow, so I must have been getting plenty of air—but enough to be completely terrifying.

And it took a while, because I had to tunnel under the hill, and then wait there—and believe me, it was no fun hanging out there *buried alive*—while I tracked the thermal signatures of the three trucks and figured out when they were close enough for me to burst out from under them.

It was probably ninety seconds. But it lasted forever.

I spent the time thinking about my dad, and my mom, and Caroline, and Logan, and even Jimmy Anderson. So many people I'd hurt, in one way or another, whether they knew it or not. They were inside the suit and under the ground with me, telling me things. Things I didn't want to hear. They weren't real sentences, exactly, but I got the gist: *Your fault, Bailey. Your failures. You're no good. You deserve to rot there in the ground.*

And there was a part of me that didn't disagree.

But then I thought about my dad, maybe in a cell somewhere, and my mom, crying alone, and some dark, cloudy plan with Mr. Jones and the Bloody Front in the center of it all, and I was like: *Screw that noise. I can't do everything. But I can save something.*

And I pushed, and clawed, and went up.

The dirt sapped my momentum, so instead of doing one of those superhero things where I smashed through an entire truck, I sort of pushed it to the side. The move wasn't as dramatic as I had hoped, and sadly not as effective, either. By dumb good luck, though, that first Jeep crashed into the second one, which put a few of the terrorists out of commission.

The ones who were left were clever, figuring out what was going on and jumping out of their trucks right away.

And, of course, they took cover behind the Jeeps and started shooting.

I used the last of my flamethrower capability to blow up the trucks—which took the terrorists' heaviest weaponry, the rocket launchers, with them—but I got caught in the backdraft and the emergency defense mechanisms that kept me from getting boiled like a lobster inside the suit lowered my power close to zero.

So I was a sitting duck.

I stood there, looking as menacing as I could, waiting

for them to realize I was no longer a threat, and then come closer and peel me out of my shell.

Obviously, that's not what happened. Since I'm here to tell you about it. Spoiler alert. I guess.

What *did* happen was that Assassin turned around and shouted at the rest of the remaining guys to hop into the last truck. The ones who couldn't, the groaning and wounded ones, they left behind.

Maybe they'd gotten spooked by my threatening stance. But I didn't think so. I could see Assassin as he sped off, ripping a Bluetooth device out of his ear. He looked like a man who'd gotten orders he really didn't like.

Why was Mr. Jones leaving me alive after going to so much trouble to try to kill me?

Unless that wasn't what he was doing.

Unless he wanted to make sure I didn't somehow capture *them*, or Assassin, at least. Mr. Jones didn't have access to the suit anymore. He didn't know precisely how low my power levels were. And he couldn't take the risk. Because Assassin knew something Mr. Jones didn't want me—or the world—to know.

Like the plan.

There wasn't much juice left in the suit, but there was more than enough to scare a few bad guys. I wasn't going to kill anyone else. I'd made that promise, and I was going to stick to it. But that didn't mean I wasn't willing to pretend.

Dangling a grown man by the feet over a burning truck tends to encourage honesty. At least I think it does. At any rate, I believed all three panicky variations of "I'm just a grunt, nobody tells me anything!" When I asked them about a prisoner, they looked blank. When I asked them about their grand plan, they looked blanker. And when I asked them about Mr. Jones, they looked blankest of all. That made me think Assassin was very smart about only giving people the information they needed to know.

But it left me pretty much where I'd been before.

I made one of the terrorists call 911 on his cell phone and tell them three members of the Bloody Front were waiting to be collected by the authorities out in the national park. Then I twisted a few panels from the truck into makeshift restraints, pounded them down into the sand around the bad guys, and then—because it had been a long morning, and why not—made the same guy take a selfie of all of us on the same phone, me sitting next to them giving a thumbs-up. Then I left it for the National Security Agency to puzzle over. Maybe they'll rethink their assumption that I'm a terrorist.

Probably not, though.

So here I am. Walking through the desert in a gigantic robotic outfit.

Which is not recommended, by the way. The remaining power, which isn't much, is being channeled directly into the servomotors, so it's like driving a very slow car. With no extra juice for air-conditioning. I'm sweating like a mother in here. Leaving me alone with my thoughts, and with this recording for you, whoever you turn out to be.

But hey, at least the homicidal criminal genius who knows I'm gunning for him will take his defeat out on my dad. When he's not sending my name and address to a crew of homicidal maniacs, putting my mom in terrible danger. Or maybe he'll just give that same information to law enforcement and leave me facing God knows how many criminal charges, including but not limited to the destruction of tens or hundreds of millions of dollars in government and commercial property. And murder. And murder, too . . .

And oh, by the way, although this is totally trivial, I'm pretty sure I'm going to have to go to summer school.

Social death. To be followed by very real death.

So that's something to look forward to.

Yes, I know I'm giggling. It's hysterical. I'm in hysterics.

I'm going to shut up now for a while.

Okay, I'm back.

In both senses. I'm almost home, too. After a few hours of sucking up some desert sun, the suit recharged enough for me to fly the rest of the way. And I made it to the ravine without running into any fighter jets, terrorist rockets, world-ending bioweapons, or even selfie takers who'd do their civic duty by calling the police.

Man, I can't wait to get out of this thing. Take a shower. Put it behind me. At least for a few hours. I'll do the postflight checks later.

Okay. Through the hatch and heading down the passageway.

Wait a minute. The lights are on in the lab. I can see it coming out from under the door.

I *always* turn them off. Always. Someone's been here.

Maybe it's Mr. Jones. Maybe this was his plan—to make me think it was over for a while, and then kill me right when I think I can finally relax. That *would* be his kind of thing, the psycho. He probably has a death ray or something that'll eat right through the suit.

I think I'll put up a fight. Better to die with your boots on.

Opening the door.

Okay, in the lab now. Don't see anyone here, and the thermal gauges aren't registering any bodies. Just one heat source, a small pinpoint, on the counter next to the computer.

It's a cigarette. Still burning.

But Mr. Jones hates smokers, I remember. And Dad wouldn't allow smoking in the house.

. . . Mom?

Bailey.

Mom.

Bailey, I think you should come upstairs now. I think we're long overdue for a talk.

Oh, man.

Mom.

Okay. Wow. I'm back again.

In my room. Mom down the hall.

Mayhem down the hall, I guess I should say. Because it was her, all along. Not my dad. I had the story backward from the beginning.

I mean, not that it was entirely my fault. Dad disappears, Mayhem disappears, and then Mr. Jones tells me this whole story . . .

Which, it turns out, was a pack of lies. And which, like all the best lies, worked by appealing to my biased assumptions about how the world works. I figured the man would be in the robot suit. That's how Mom put it, anyway, and I can't argue with that.

The conversation went something like this. This isn't exact, but it's as close as I can remember . . .

Why am I telling you? Well, I've got to tell *somebody*. And it occurs to me, that in the whole world, I have absolutely no one else to talk to.

So here goes. While it's still fresh.

TWENTY-EIGHT MINUTES AGO

First she hugged me. "Thank God you're safe," she said. "Thank God you're safe." Over and over again.

But I couldn't deal with it for long. Not the smushed uncomfortable feeling of being up against her chest, but the . . . emotion, so much of it pouring out of her after so long. So I pushed her away.

I tried to cover it, a little, with a stupid joke. "I guess I'm not out of danger yet, I mean, I don't want to get suffocated in my own home . . ."

I hated it as soon as I said it. It was stupid and—and then she burst into tears, and as bad as I'd felt before, now I felt a whole lot worse.

I'm not sure I'd ever seen my mom cry before. Not once. Not during the dadiversaries, not when we talked about him . . . sometimes she'd be warm and glowing remembering their history, sometimes she'd be withdrawn, detached, like she was somewhere else. But she hadn't cried. Until now.

I stood there, awkwardly, wondering if I should get her a tissue or something. But then I realized we were out of them in the kitchen, and I didn't know if we had any more. So I said, "Uh, Mom? Where are the tissues again?"

And she looked up, her eyes red, her nose snuffly, and she said, "You don't know where the tissues are? You just battled tanks and you can't find the *tissues*?" And then she was laughing and crying at the same time, and then she kissed the top of my head, which even in the midst of all this I found a little annoying, quite frankly, since she hadn't blown her nose.

And then she found a tissue, and wiped her nose, and said, "I'm not sure I can tell you what you need to know."

And that's when I said that I was pretty sure I already knew most of the backstory. From Mr. Jones. That he and Dad were roommates in college, that they'd worked together to build the suit . . .

But she was laughing out loud again. This was the most laughter I'd heard from her in years. "Leonard told you *that*?" she said. She was almost wheezing.

"Wait," I said. "Wait a minute. Mr. Jones's real name is Leonard?"

She couldn't answer—laughing too hard—but she managed to nod her head. Confirmed. Mr. Jones's real name was Leonard.

This made me feel very slightly better, as you can imagine.

Mom finally managed to stop laughing, and looked at me.

"The roommates. The college roommates. Who grow up to be hero and villain. Doesn't this remind you of anything?"

"Maybe?" I said.

"Think about those old *Fantastic Fours* we used to read together when you were small," she said. "Don't you remember them?"

Kind of yes, kind of no. But when she pointed out the story he'd told me was *this close* to the story of Doctor Doom, I almost literally slapped my forehead.

I should have figured an adult with a genius-level intellect who decided to make money by building a robot suit probably liked comic books.

"I don't know how I believed that," I said.

"Well," my mom said, "the truth isn't entirely different. Just with some changes."

And I just sat there, openmouthed, as I discovered that it was my *mom* who was the scientific genius.

"But—" I said. "But—Mr. Jones said *he'd* built the suit."

She looked at me.

"Oh," I said.

"Trust a man to take credit for a woman's work," she said.

Truth was, she'd been the prime designer and architect, although he'd helped, and when they'd finished, the two of *them* were the ones who'd started using it.

"It wasn't to help people, though," she said. And I noticed that she wasn't looking me right in the eye. "Just to have fun. Make some money. After all—"

And she *blushed*. Then looked me straight in the eye.

"I was young," she said. "And in love."

I felt a little like a website that was trying to play one of those annoying video ads. I kept trying to process, but it didn't start. And then, finally, it did, all at once, at maximum volume. "*You were in love with Mr. Jones?*" I screeched.

"Or I thought I was," she said. "I know, you wouldn't understand that."

Which wasn't true. I mean, I understood loving—or at least being totally obsessed with—a person who you really didn't know. I didn't go into that, though.

So then there was the rest.

"I met your dad exactly the way I told you," she said. "And we fell in love exactly the way you've always heard. I was just . . . seeing someone else at the time."

"Leonard," I said. (Ugh!)

"Yes," she said. "Leonard. I told him that I wanted to see someone else, but I hoped we could still . . . work together. He was a perfect gentleman about it. On the surface, at least." She looked at me as she continued. "He's a planner. He takes his time." And then her mouth twisted, like someone had given one side of it a sharp pull. But her tone didn't change. "He agreed to try, and we kept . . . working. My guess is he was hoping I would break up with your father and run back to him. It had happened before—although not with anyone I was nearly as serious about as your father. Obviously."

This was more information about my mom's romantic life than I'd ever, ever wanted to know. But if hearing it was how I could find out the truth. . . . Still, I wanted to fast-forward past anything more intimate. So I interrupted. "Then you and Dad got married and had me," I said, and thankfully she took the hint.

"Yes, Bailey, we had you," she said. "After I gave birth, I wasn't supposed to"—she looked for the right words— "engage in any rigorous exercise for a few months. And then I . . . well, I just got out of the habit. So there was no Mayhem for a while. For years."

"Mr. Jones—uh—Leonard said he never got in the suit," I said. "That's why he made me do it."

"That much is true," my mom said. "I was always the one out there. Leonard was back at base, providing strategy and support. I'm afraid he used the time I was out of commission to plan . . . other things."

"But you went back," I said. "To it. To *him*."

"I didn't know what he was up to," she said carefully. "By this time, you were in school full-time, and my job wasn't satisfying. And the suit . . . I missed it," she added. "It gets addictive. You can understand that."

And I guess I could.

But by the time she finally came back from—uh—Mayhem maternity leave, Mr. Jones had changed. He was pushing her to do bigger jobs. Grab more cash. And he was being skeevy about where the money was going.

"I was beginning to get the sense there was stuff going on I wasn't aware of," she said. "But I was willing to trust him. For longer than I should have. We had a history, after all—"

And I was like, *Mom, warning, don't go there.*

"The point is," she said, "it took years of these obfuscations for me to follow him one day, from the air. To Clapham Junction."

He spotted her, of course—he could track the suit even then, as part of his support role—and, when she confronted him, he showed her around. At least, he started to.

"I don't know what he had going on there, exactly," she said. "But it was big—probably not as big as it was when you saw it, it's been years, but big enough—and it was trouble, and, as far as I was concerned, it needed to be shut down. And that is what I told him."

"So what happened?" I asked.

Mom was making a face again, but I could see it wasn't a smile. It was more like someone was stretching the skin back so you could see all her teeth.

"What happened was, the next day your dad disappeared," she said.

Obviously, she suspected Mr. Jones immediately. She wasn't an idiot—after all, she'd designed the Mayhem suit. But he had disappeared as thoroughly as my dad . . . none of her usual ways of contacting him worked.

And then after about forty-eight hours—right before she was going to take "decisive action"—he got back in touch.

With a picture of my dad. Alive. Unharmed. But clearly his prisoner.

And that's when the real cat-and-mouse game began.

On his part: Dropping hints about Dad. How Dad was doing. What he was doing to Dad. Tantalizing her, torturing her, making her pay. But also—in his own weird, emotionally manipulative way—trying to court her.

On her part: Giving him hope that it was working.

She saw my face, and said quickly, "Not that it *would*. Ever. But I had to make him think it would. That his alpha-male behavior was attractive. That it proved I'd chosen the wrong guy."

And it had worked. Enough to keep my dad alive, which was the main thing, the only thing. "I had proof of life as of a month ago," she said. "On our dadiversary. He always makes sure I get a picture of your dad then. Every year."

And I could see, in her face, maybe for the first time, the sheer weight of what she'd been dealing with.

I had had no idea.

No idea at all.

"And when the Bloody Front started up, it was even worse," she said. "It was so clearly Leonard—it had that Clapham Junction setup written all over it—but there was nothing I could do. Not without putting your father at terrible risk. Those victims are on my conscience as well."

I thought about telling her that I understood. But I couldn't say the words. I couldn't tell her about Caroline. Not yet. It would have turned the whole conversation upside down, and I needed to hear the rest.

And also, the weight of that was mine to carry around. Mom would have made me feel better. Or tried to, anyway. And I didn't want to feel better. I wanted—needed—to ache.

Mom was still talking. "I don't know," she said. "Did I do

the right thing? Sitting on my hands for years? All those people the Front hurt, killed . . . they were strangers. And it was your *father*—" She stopped, covered her face for a second. Then kept going. "But the scales were tipping. I couldn't stand by anymore. And I was getting ready to act, regardless of the cost, when a new element entered the picture."

Me.

She had known almost immediately. Long before the Golden Gate Bridge.

"You have motion sensors downstairs?" I said.

She looked at me. "You didn't straighten the picture in the guest room properly," she said, "when you put it back. And then since you never put anything away in the lab, it was easy enough to spot—"

"Okay, okay," I said.

She lit a cigarette and went on.

"I'd made it clear you were off-limits right away," she said. "From the very beginning." And for whatever reason—maybe because he understood it would be a deal breaker, that there'd be no way for him to ever come back into her good graces if I got hurt—he went with that. But once I started with the suit, it was a new ball game. Mr. Jones made it clear that if my mom told me the true story, he'd kill Dad right away. My mom made it clear that if Mr. Jones put me in real danger, all bets were off.

"Of course, as it turned out," my mom said, "we were both lying."

"What do you mean?" I said. "You didn't tell me *anything!*"

"Who do you think sent you the message in the library?" she said.

"Wait," I said. "That was you?"

"I couldn't sit you down and tell you the whole story, could I?" she said. "Leonard was watching us. But I had to do something about the control override. In case he went back on his deal. I knew you'd figure it out, even though I couldn't write anything explicit," she explained. "What if one of those federal agents crawling all over the school spotted you with instructions for operating the Mayhem suit?"

I didn't figure it out on my own, though. I had help, I thought, *a lot of help.* I saw Caroline, smiling in triumph, the code-cracker, and the hurt and anger rose up in my throat and it wanted to spill out, but I shoved it back down. "Why did you use Klingon?" I asked.

She looked at me like I was crazy. "Honey, it's because you love *Star Trek*!" she said. "You've always loved *Star Trek*, ever since you were a little boy!"

I was tempted to reply that I did *not* love *Star Trek*, and that I hadn't even thought about *Star Trek* for years, how she really had not been paying attention, but I didn't want to get off track.

"In the meantime, I was working my contacts," she said. "That's why I've been so distant lately."

Lately? I wanted to say, but didn't.

"You didn't think I was actually dating someone else, did you?" she said.

"I, um, didn't know," I said. And that led to an awkward moment.

I think it was probably around this point, by the way, that I realized why he'd introduced himself to me as Mr. Jones. I'd always assumed it was his way of indicating it was an obvious alias. Like, don't even bother to think I'm trusting you with anything close to my real identity. But now . . . well, like I said, I'm a classic rock fan, and he knew that. He knew tons about me, long before that first meeting, long before I started talking to him about anything personal.

I think it was an inside joke to me, without my knowledge. An inside joke *at* me, I guess, is a better way to put it. I think it was taken from that Dylan song. The one where someone's being told there's something happening, but that he doesn't have a clue what it is.

Three guesses what that guy's name is.

Anyway, I could see my mom working herself up into a soliloquy about how Dad was the only man for her. I deflected by going back and telling my side of the story. How I discovered the suit. How Mr. Jones discovered me. How he had me commit a bunch of crimes so I could—and now I realized I had to put this in air quotes—"train to save my dad from the Bloody Front." I saw Mom nodding along. "How much of this do you already know?"

"Some," Mom said. "And some more of it, I guessed. But not all. So keep going." She paused. "Remember. Everything he does—everything he has you do—has a purpose. Some reason behind the reason. Maybe some of the banks he had you rob were business competitors. Maybe he was helping out a rogue state whose assets were frozen. Whatever it was, it was about him. Not you. But he was keeping his side of the deal—you weren't in any danger. Then. Keep going." So I kept talking, about Logan and the Bloody Front attacking him at the football game. About the midair talks about my love life, although I kept that vague.

My mom nodded and said she'd expected he'd try something like that. He knew, after all, that my mom, best-case scenario, came as a package deal—with me—and he was trying, in his own twisted way, to set himself up as my new dad. That was why she'd sneaked down and left those photos on the computer: to remind me of my real family. Although she was sure, she added, that Mr. Jones's tactics wouldn't have worked.

I was sure, too. Pretty sure. I mean, some of those discussions . . . they were real. Or they seemed that way. I could imagine Mr. Jones's plan playing out. Somehow, tragically, Dad doesn't make it. At the hands of the Bloody Front? Too simple. Maybe in the course of a rescue. Mr. Jones puts himself across as another victim of the tragedy, someone who's lost a friend. We bond, in our shared grief. And then who knows? Maybe he confesses, one day, that he's finally ready to see my mom again. Face-to-face. Only with my blessing, of course.

Of course.

And that's when I realized, with all this talk about romance, that Mr. Jones must have told the Front to go after Logan. Of course he did. So I'd have a shot with Rebecca, and he could give me romantic advice.

And he did it before I ever told him about Rebecca. Learned about her from reading my texts to Caroline, I guess.

I feel sick. He'd been lying to me and manipulating me all along. Every single step of the way.

But Mom was saying something. "So that means you talked to him about Caroline?" she asked. "Before me." And I gulped and said that I didn't want to talk about that right now. She didn't press me.

I did tell her I'd found out about Mr. Jones's link to Clapham Junction, but not exactly how. And then I told her about what happened in Clapham Junction, but not that Caroline had been there. Or what had happened to her. I just . . . I just couldn't. Not yet.

But I did tell her about my mistake—my horrible mistake—in blowing open the door and being responsible for those deaths. I did tell her that. And she hugged me. "It's not your fault," she told me. "They brought it down on themselves." Which I didn't believe, not entirely, but it helped. Maybe.

"I knew you were there, from the news reports," she said. "By that time, though, you'd been spotted elsewhere, so I was sure you'd gotten out."

Then she stopped, for a second, and said, "So it's gone. They're all dead." And I nodded. Her face didn't look sad, or upset, or even bothered by that. It was like . . . a general's face. Some soldier pieces had been taken off the board. Nothing more.

I could have imagined that face on Mr. Jones.

But then her expression changed, and she was asking about the scientist. "The plan she mentioned. Did she say anything else? About the details?" I said all I could remember her saying was that if Mr. Jones didn't carry out the plan this way—whatever that meant—he would do it some other way.

And my mom agreed with that, 100 percent.

I kept going with my side of the story. She had known I was still alive thanks to the constant news updates, although once they'd dug through the building rubble, all she knew was that I'd escaped.

"Mr. Jones had gone to Plan B," my mom said. "Once you'd discovered his secret. He knew it would get back to me." The minute she found out that he was still involved with the Front, it was game over for sure. He knew her well enough to know that. So that meant cutting his losses.

Which meant trying to tie up loose ends, one teenage loose end in particular.

But in a way that gave him plausible deniability. Hence the terrorists hunting me in Jeeps. If they were able to get me before I got back to my mom, then he could deny everything, including his Bloody Front connection.

"But why he had Assassin turn around . . . that's what I don't get," my mom finished.

I told her my theory that he was worried that if I captured Assassin he'd reveal Mr. Jones's plan. She looked doubtful. "Maybe," she said. "But people like that don't crack so easily."

"Well, maybe it had to do with the hard drive after all," I said.

"The *what?*"

And I realized I hadn't mentioned it. I told her about the scientist's computer, that I thought it might tell me—us—where Dad was, maybe even have actual evidence connecting Mr. Jones to the Front, and she gave me another gigantic bone-crushing hug and told me that I might have done it!

"But it's in pretty bad shape," I said. "Maybe we should turn it over to Homeland Security or something like that."

Mom was already shaking her head. "Leonard has moles and double agents everywhere in the government," she said. "He'd find out what we knew as soon as we did, maybe even before, and he'd move to neutralize it. We'd lose our leverage. And then he'd have no reason to keep your dad alive.

"Besides," she continued, and she got that expression on her face again, "this is something we have to do."

But by *we*, it turned out, Mom meant *her*. And her alone. I was supposed to spend the rest of whatever-this-was being baby-sat by one of her friends while she took care of business.

Nope. No way. Not happening. I cut her off in the middle of a sentence about how this was for my own good or something—I don't know, I was so mad about the idea I wasn't listening.

"First of all," I said, "this is my fight, too. It has been for months. You can't just leave me out of it. And second of all, I've done a decent job taking care of myself up to now. Besides, there's no way your PTA friend or whoever it is will be able to handle it if Mr. Jones or Assassin comes calling."

"First of all," she said, "you have *not* done a pretty good job taking care of yourself. Yes, by some miracle, you've managed not to get yourself killed. But that doesn't mean you haven't made mistakes. *Rookie* mistakes. And we can't afford more of them."

I guess given everything that was going on, she didn't feel like she had a lot of time to be gentle with me.

Or maybe that *was* her being gentle.

I don't know everything Mom does. Like Mr. Jones, she knows a lot more than she lets on. But either way, she was right that I'd made mistakes. Clapham Junction and Caroline came back to me like a punch in the stomach and I couldn't speak.

She could tell she had me on the ropes. So she went on. "Do you really think so little of me that you think I'd put you with the neighbors? These are not friends from the subdivision. These are not friends from work. These are friends from the *old days*."

There was a pause before those last two words that said . . . a lot. "You mean other criminals," I said.

For a second—just a second, but it was there—I was a little afraid. It wasn't that I didn't recognize my mom. That would have been ridiculous. It was that I didn't recognize the look my mom was giving me. Hard. Blank. I had never seen it before. It was almost like a body snatcher had taken over her face. "I've never been into labels," she said.

She explained that there were people out there, people she'd come across over the years, who shared some of her ideas. Her . . . philosophies. And a few of them had certain skills and qualities that would come in handy. Like tremendous computer expertise. A fanatical devotion to being off the grid. And a few of them owed her the kinds of favors that needed repayment. A no-matter-what, no-matter-when kind of repayment.

"Mom, who *are* you?"

I just blurted it out, standing there, listening to her, looking at her. This woman I'd known all my life. Who I'd seen practically every single day.

And she said something funny to me. "All parents are strangers to their kids," she said. "Our only hope is that when our children grow up they'll get the chance to see us, really see us, as the people that we are."

And then she told me I had thirty minutes to pack.

Which I've spent dictating this into my phone.

Which if my mom knew about, I'm sure she'd freak out. After all, Mr. Jones—sorry, I'm never going to call him Leonard—might be hacking into this thing as we speak. I should probably be writing it longhand or something.

But I mean, come on.

Okay.

Of all the places I expected to begin our journey of revenge, the bathroom of a comic book shop was not in the top ten. Or even the top fifty.

But here I am.

Not to use it or anything. Just hiding out from my mom and Kaz while I catch this up.

So.

TWO AND A HALF HOURS AGO

While I packed, I came up with my plan.

Or "plan," in quotes. I was coming up with it on the spot, so cut me some slack.

The "plan" was that while we were on the road to Mom's friend—she wouldn't tell me much, but this person was apparently a superhacker—I would annoy her until she changed her mind about letting me help. This was a strategy that had worked in the Great Xbox Christmas Coup of Two Years Past, so I was hoping lightning would strike twice. On the other hand, I still don't have a dog.

I knew that this was serious. I knew she wouldn't agree to anything that would put me in danger, for example. I'd never be able to talk her out of that. I mean, part of the reason she never agreed to the dog was because she was afraid I'd get mugged walking it around the subdivision late at night . . . although, just saying it out loud now, I guess there were other reasons she didn't want me out and alone, rather than worrying about petty crime in a safe neighborhood. Huh.

But that didn't mean I couldn't do something to help.

Maybe remotely guiding the suit—I'd gotten a lot of practice with that over the past month or so. Or, if she was committed to flying off and bringing Dad back herself, I could be working on the files on the hard drive back at the lab. I don't know. *Something.*

I launched into my opening speech—family and taking responsibility and so on. But before I got more than a sentence in, I noticed that my mom was holding, not a backpack or a small duffel, but the large red suitcase from the storage closet. She must have gotten it before I even made it home.

"Here," she said. "Pack for a few weeks."

And I realized we had been having two very different discussions.

I mean, on the one hand, I got it. Tremendous danger, Mr. Jones, Bloody Front. My dad. But . . . I don't know . . . I hadn't thought it meant leaving for good.

And yet, somehow, my mom did see it that way.

I was about to object. Strenuously. Vocally. But then my mom made a mistake.

It was an understandable one, given the circumstances. A reasonable assumption.

She said, "Look, I'm sure you'll miss Caroline. And she'll be upset, too. But we'll figure out a way for you to tell her you're okay."

And at that point all I could do was shut up, run back to my room, and load up the suitcase. Call it . . . I don't know. Penance.

As I was repacking, Mom walked in—without knocking, I should add. I showed her the three-quarters-full suitcase to say, *See, I'm not arguing anymore,* but that wasn't what she was there for. She was heading for my closet.

I started to ask her what she was doing. She didn't answer.

And then she reemerged, holding up a few hundred thousand dollars' worth of sparkling, shimmering diamond stones.

Yes, I'd kept some. Mr. Jones's routine of *It was a test, and we'll get to your dad any day now* had always smelled. I didn't know why, but I knew it did. So I gave him everything except the stash I'd "dropped" on my way back over the Midwest as I'd "swerved to avoid a flock of geese." It was a routine that had seemed to work, so why mess with it? And he'd bought it without a murmur—I think he was already weighing the diamonds in his head, figuring how much he'd made, and blocking out everything else. I hadn't known if or when I'd need them, but it was better to have and not need than to need and not have.

That was another one of my dad's old phrases, I remembered.

Before I could say anything, she'd grabbed up the diamonds and dumped them straight into her purse. She hardly looked at them. It was like they were popcorn.

"Wait," I said. "You knew about the diamonds?"

She just shook her head, like her son was an even bigger idiot than she'd imagined. "You robbed Tiffany's," she said. "On national television. You didn't think I was going to search your room?"

I considered whether this was the time to make an issue about her not respecting my privacy. It wasn't.

"Car," she said, and walked out.

I guess there's no obvious day job for a *techno-anarchist*—my mom's term, not mine. . . . I still don't really know what that is. But if there was one, comic book shop owner and operator would not have been my first guess.

And yet we were headed to a comic book shop, in a mid-size city about three hours out of the Zone.

I was worried about security at the Zone border, but Mom zipped us right through. She handed over her license and registration to the soldiers and looked kind of . . . Mom-ish. You know, bored and hassled, like she had to get me to soccer practice and then had a million errands to run before she picked me up, and was devoting all her mental energy to putting them all in the right order.

Not that she said any of that to the border guard. That was just the impression she gave.

I knew my mom had acted in college. But I was in awe of her performance.

We didn't talk much on the way there. Not that we didn't have . . . well, everything to say to each other. But I think neither of us knew where to start.

I tried to ask her a bit about Dad, about their life together. *Their life of crime*, I guess I should say now. And when I did, Mom got weird. I mean, weird in a new way.

First she said she didn't want to talk about it. And then she started telling me stories about Dad that had nothing to do with their secret life—funny little harmless stories, like the one where the two of them, back before I was born, went to New York City to try to see Shakespeare in the Park and ended up in the wrong park because they were staying in Brooklyn. I guess New York has a lot of big parks. So they ate street hot dogs and acted out the play they were supposed to be watching from the books they had brought to follow along.

Eventually I was like, "What about Mayhem?"

Mom leaned over in her seat and put a finger across my lips as she said in a bright and cheery voice, "Yes, wasn't it *terrible* about that criminal, a thief and probably a terrorist, but I'm sure he'll get caught eventually."

I was confused—I mean, I got what she was saying, *the car was probably bugged*, but Mr. Jones already knew about Mom and me being Mayhem. But then I figured it out. If Mr. Jones was taping this, somehow, and he was mad at us . . . who knew who he could turn it over to.

Maybe that was it. Or maybe not. I bet Mom could have figured out some way of scrambling transmissions, or wiping the audio, or whatever. Maybe—I'm thinking this now, a little later—maybe Mom had her own ideas about what was going to happen next, and she didn't want to share them with me. And this someone's-listening thing was a convenient excuse.

Not that I think she saw me as the enemy. But as an obstacle? Something to be dealt with? I don't know. Either way, she didn't say anything informative, and I stopped asking.

I tried to be helpful, and offered to be the navigator. When she agreed and took an actual paper map out of the glove compartment, I kind of panicked. "Um, what about GPS?" I asked.

She shook her head and pointed up—*eyes in the sky, eyes everywhere,* I guess—and I shut up again.

She even made me take my phone's SIM card and throw it out the window. Thankfully this thing records directly to the phone, otherwise my whole story would be gone.

Of course, Mom knew exactly where we were going. The comic bookshop was called Masks 'n' Mags, which was a pretty bad name, in my opinion, and the store wasn't much better. Dark, dingy rows of Mylar-bagged comics in cartons and a few people pawing through them.

I figured that Mom would have a prearranged signal to tell her friend she was here and needed to see him, like picking up an X-Men graphic novel and putting it in the Justice League section, or something. It didn't look like it, though. She stood in the middle of the new-releases section looking lost, like it had taken a lot to get here and she didn't know what to do. Or maybe she was just doing a good imitation of a suburban mom whose teenage son had made her drive him to the comic shop. I wasn't sure.

I didn't know what to do, either. After a while, I gave up and started paging through one of the Batman graphic novels. It wasn't so much about Batman as it was about the bad guys. He has some crazy ones. This was the one who was half-normal, half-nuts, and decided which he was going to be from day to day. It wasn't bad and despite everything, I got absorbed.

After a while, the store owner tapped me on the shoulder. He was thin and had a full head of hair, even though he must have been forty, at least. He asked me—and not very politely, either—if I was going to read the whole thing in the store. I muttered something and looked over at my mom. And then he did, too.

He looked at my mom for a long time. She looked back at him. Then he said, more to my mom than me, "You know, there's a limited edition version of that, deluxe, that you might want to take a look at. But it's pricey."

"It won't be a problem, Kaz," my mom said. Quietly. Kaz—I guess that was his name—didn't look surprised. He didn't react at all. He just turned around and walked toward the back of the store. We followed.

I'd expected a high-tech security system, maybe one of those clean white rooms with tons of expensive high-end computers. But we ended up in a dingy storage area with five or six old Macs and a bunch of Dell monitors that had to have been ten years old at least. He saw my face. "The insides of things don't always match their outsides," he said. "Take you two, for example."

And then he launched into this long speech about running biometric scans on everyone who walked into the store. He had next-generation facial-recognition algorithms, but with kinetic profiling, too—movement matching or something like that.

"So?" my mom said, but in a tone of voice I knew well. The one that meant *I'm going to let you keep talking because I'm supposed to, but I know all this, and you're wasting my time. I mostly—before—had heard her use it when she was on the phone to the cable company.

He looked, not at my mom, but at me. "So you like Batman," he said.

I shrugged.

"Well, here's a riddle for you," he said. "How does two become one?"

I had no idea where he was going with that, and I guess it showed on my face. Meanwhile, my mom had reached the end of her rope. "Kaz, you're no Penguin," she said. "Let's just finish up with the little show and move on."

"It's the Riddler, not the—fine," he said. "I'm not the one running around in some supervillain robot suit. You are." He pointed to my mom. "And you are, too."

Neither of us said anything in response, which I think took the wind out of his sails. So he sat down at one of the keyboards, pressed a few buttons, and there we were on one of the monitors: split-screen images, side by side, walking through the aisles of the comic store. "And ta-da," Kaz said, but without much enthusiasm, pressing a few more buttons. And now there were two pictures of Mayhem on the screen: one of them old CNN footage of a bank robbery from before my time, the other of me in Golden Gate Park.

It was true. We didn't move the same way. And Mayhem moved like both of us.

It hadn't been a great riddle, but it was a fair one.

"Family business, I guess?" said Kaz.

"That's right," my mom said, and handed over the hard drive.

Kaz looked it over. "Yeah, it's a little beat-up, but I'm sure those guys at the Geek Squad could help you out with it," he said.

"I've had about enough with the jokes," my mom said. "I

hated them when we worked together before, and I'm not in the mood for them now."

Kaz spread his hands and said, "Sure."

Then he proceeded to nod intently as my mom unveiled a jaw-dropping laundry list of high-tech bad-guy things. Most of them were too technical for me to understand, but I got the gist of it. Decrypt the hard drive. Get the evidence she needed off it. Give it to her in a nice, easy form. Get Bailey to an air-gapped safe house, so far off the grid it couldn't even *see* the grid, until she got back from where she had to go. And fix us up with something like digital witness protection.

Kaz thought a minute and said he could do that.

"And we'll need three identities," my mom said.

"I'm a mathematical genius, too," Kaz said. "I can count, and there are only two of you."

"For the time being," my mom said, and I loved her more than I ever thought was possible.

Kaz shrugged, like this was the sort of conversation he had every day. Which I guess it probably was. Then he asked when we needed all this by.

"Now's good," my mom said.

Kaz nodded again. Then he waited.

My mom didn't say anything as she dug into her bag, scooped out the diamonds—my lovely, lovely diamonds—and spilled them all over Kaz's keyboard.

The three of us looked at them for a minute. Finally Kaz said, "The Tiffany job."

I didn't know what to say, so I didn't say anything. Which

was apparently the right approach, tough-guy-wise, because my mom also didn't say anything. Just more definitively.

"They're gonna be difficult to unload," Kaz said.

My mom was silent.

"They'll lose forty percent of their value. At *least*," he said.

More silence.

Kaz sighed, pulled a Mylar comic bag out from one of the desk drawers, and swept the diamonds in. A few bounced off the keyboard and rolled under the table. Kaz pointed to a broom and dustpan on the other side of the room. "Go get 'em," he told me. I looked at my mom, who nodded.

For about five seconds there, underneath the desk, I thought about trying to slip a few in my pocket. Then I thought again. Kaz had seemed pretty la-di-da about the whole thing, but that had been mostly in his tone of voice. I'd seen the way he watched the diamonds roll. He was counting every one.

Once I'd crawled back out and handed the diamonds over, Kaz settled himself into his chair and started entering a series of long passwords into his computer. But then he stopped and said, "There's just one last thing."

"Kaz—" my mom began. I knew that tone of voice, too. I did not like that tone of voice. The only thing that made me happy about it was that it was not currently pointed in my direction.

"Just one last thing," he repeated. "About the payment. I want to be able to tell my buyers that there are no loose ends out there from the heist. Nothing traceable. Nothing that might cause a problem. That this is the whole lot," he said. "That's the case. Isn't it?"

Kaz was looking at my mom when he said it. My mom was looking at me. I was looking anywhere else I could. And I was thinking about that old expression about honor among thieves.

An old expression my dad used to use, as it happened. The dad who I was *this close* to seeing again.

So I sort of nodded.

I know. Maybe not the best thinking on my part. But if I *had* told them about Rebecca's bracelet—I was pretty sure Mr. Jones's cut was down a black hole somewhere and wasn't the issue—maybe Kaz wouldn't have taken the diamonds. And then he wouldn't have started decrypting the hard drive to help us track down my dad.

They huddled over a computer screen and started whispering, and my mom shooed me off to a corner to wait patiently. *Don't bother us, kid, the grown-ups are working.*

So I excused myself to use the bathroom.

And that's where I've been. Just catching this up.

I guess I'm out of the action for now. End with a whimper, not a bang.

I better get back there, though. See what's happening.

Okay. Let's do this.

Although I don't know why I'm still doing it. This. This talking. I guess it's just that . . . I mean, I have to tell the end of the story, don't I? See where it was going, all along?

I'd never have guessed here.

You know, it's funny when being trapped in flaming wreckage beneath a collapsing building feels like the preferable situation.

But that's where I am now.

Well, I mean, not where I am physically. Physically, I'm back at my house. Waiting. Waiting for my dad to come home.

And not like waiting-for-the-past-five-years-and-maybe-he'll-turn-up waiting. It's more like he's-supposed-to-arrive-in-two-hours-by-private-helicopter waiting.

But my mom . . .

Let me try to tell this the right way, in the right order. Get my thoughts straight. A lot has happened in the past three hours. Three hours? Is that even possible? Yeah, that's what the phone says. Man.

THREE HOURS AGO

So. Back of the comic book shop.

When I got back from the bathroom, I saw that Kaz had connected the hard drive to one of his computers and I could see he was accessing it. I creeped over to take a peek.

I'd assumed there'd be a lot of furious typing with letters and numbers flashing on the screen superfast. But it was . . . cuter than that.

I guess Kaz had designed a visual interface that looked a lot like a manga. The home screen was like a little map of the world, and as he moved his mouse around, parts got bigger or smaller. All sorts of characters were popping up: rows of impossibly proportioned Valkyries break dancing in skimpy bikinis, for example. A monkey holding an ice cream cone tap dancing on top of the Eiffel Tower. A lightsaber skewering a cheeseburger wearing a tutu.

Kaz looked up for a second and saw me staring. I guess he was happy to have a bigger audience, so he waved me even closer. "To provide an additional level of security, I've transformed most of the data outputs into a series of visual images that will stick in my mind," he said. "For example, 1010 is a picture of the Roger Moore James Bond, while 1001 is the original, great Sean Connery. And since a banana is a different kind of data, say, a file type, Connery holding a banana is a file type coded 1001. But since I'm a genius, it's about a hundred times more complicated than that." He leaned back, twirled around on his chair, scrolling and clicking. "This way no one but me can see what I'm seeing."

Behind him, my mom looked at me and rolled her eyes.

He patted the hard drive. "So what do you need off this thing?" he said.

"Anything that links to Gerry," Mom said. "On the drive itself or down any trail the drive information leads to."

She didn't ask about Mr. Jones's plan. I guess that would have come next.

"Right-a-roonie," Kaz said, and kept typing, no pause, no break.

Pictures of my dad—from the Internet, I guess, or maybe other, more secret places—started flashing on the screen one after another. Pictures of my dad as a kid, wearing overalls and a little cowboy hat. Pictures of my dad and my mom, one onstage in that play, a few in Paris and somewhere else I didn't recognize, one at their wedding . . . they came and went, faster and faster, and just as I thought I was going to lose it, just start bawling or something, the pictures disappeared and were replaced with a bunch of animated mushroom houses with frowny faces on them, like in those old video games.

I'd already gotten the impression Kaz was laid-back. He

didn't actually look like a surfer, but he gave the impression of surferness, if you know what I mean. But something had thrown him. I know because he stopped typing to look at us.

"Where'd you get this hard drive?" he asked. "I don't like where these trails are heading . . ."

"If you're as good as you used to be back in the day—or half as good as you say you are now—it won't matter," my mom told him.

This was the kind of fourth-grade psychology that I would have been legitimately embarrassed to let get to me, but geniuses don't have to be emotionally mature, I guess. He grunted and got back to work.

For about another minute. And then he pulled at his hair and said, "Tell me you didn't do what I think you did to me."

I blinked, because my mom wasn't standing there anymore. It was Mayhem.

She had gotten into the armor fast. I mean, *fast*. Like I didn't think I wasn't looking, but I must have looked away, and there she was. Tall and metal. "YOU'RE IN IT NOW, KAZ," she said. "THERE'S JONES, AND THERE'S ME. AND I'M THE ONE STANDING NEXT TO YOU WITH ROCKET LAUNCHERS."

Kaz started cursing.

"LANGUAGE," Mom said, which was about the most ridiculous thing I'd heard in months. She put a hand on his shoulder, and Kaz yelped. I don't think she turned on the thermals. I hope not. Because that would have been, well, torture, wouldn't it? I don't think she would have done that.

Whatever she did or didn't do, though, it worked. Kaz

started typing faster and faster. "My security protocols are only going to hold so long," I remember him saying, and my mom told him he'd better make sure he was out, and out clean, before they fell.

Even though Kaz had claimed his interface was impossible to crack and all that, I was pretty sure the rows of purple death's heads and mushroom clouds that started marching across the screen two minutes later meant different.

And now I knew it was serious, because the cutesy map interface disappeared, and instead there were those windows with lots of letters and numbers, the ones I'd expected in the first place. He started muttering to himself, things about wiping traces and rapping protocols and other stuff that made no sense to me whatsoever.

And then we saw it.

Him. Dad.

"Live feed," Kaz muttered. "Hope you're happy." And kept typing.

And I was, but also I was torn apart at the same time, you know? Because it was Dad. But it was an older, thinner, sadder Dad, walking around a small room, reading a newspaper—a real, paper newspaper, just like the kind he had always liked to read.

I had expected him to be shouting and screaming, or crying, or catatonic. But I guess you can't keep that up for seven years.

I thought I would feel more, though. When I saw him, I mean. I had gone through all of this, for months, for him. Caroline. Clapham Junction. And even though I started to cry, inside it felt a little . . . smaller, I guess, than I had expected. I remember when I went to my grandmother's funeral, mom's mom, and I was there, at the graveside, and they started shoveling dirt on the coffin, and I could hear that *thunk*, *thunk*, and I thought: *This is it, you know? This is really it*, and I was sad, but it wasn't overwhelming. It felt smaller, almost surreal. Like I was watching the scene on TV.

Which I guess was what was going on here. Maybe that's why it felt so small. Maybe it'll be different when I see him, in—how long now? Just a few minutes. I hope so.

Considering everything. Considering what Mom . . .

The point is. It was him. He was there. Wherever there was.

I looked at my mom. She wasn't crying, and she wasn't smiling. She was firm, set, furious. "GIVE ME A LOCATION," she said. "GIVE ME A LOCATION, KAZ. I'M GOING TO BURN IT ALL DOWN."

But then the screen started dripping blood.

Not actual blood—some kind of computer graphic. But it was bright, and red, and Kaz stepped away from the computer like it was real, and said we had to get out of here, we'd been made, reverse-hacked, his proximity alarms had been time-looped and shunt-delayed—

And that was when there was a massive explosion and machine-gun fire lit up the entire building, getting Kaz in the head and the neck.

It didn't get me, obviously, since I'm telling you this story. No thanks to my reflexes or anything. I was getting better at dodging these sort of things while wearing the suit, but when it's just me, my instincts are to freeze, flail, and scream.

Is it weird that I feel worse about the fact that Kaz died with my mom threatening him than that Mr. Jones killed him? It has to be. But that's how I feel. I want us to be the good guys.

She saved me, of course. Mom. With the Mayhem suit on, she was able to bend over, cover me, and take the brunt of the blast on her back. And then—it must have been within three, four seconds—she ripped out a big chunk of wall and plunked it down between me and the bullets. It was the wall separating Kaz's back room from the comic bookshop, and before it came down and blocked my field of vision I got a good view of the customers running screaming out the front door.

And the four nasty-looking military-grade drones flying above them.

I'll be honest, if I expected anything, it would have been the Bloody Front. Maybe even Assassin himself, itching for payback. But I guess wherever they were hiding out after Clapham Junction, they couldn't get here, not at five hundred miles per hour, anyway.

Now that I'm thinking about it, if Mr. Jones had these drones, why he didn't use them to drop a big old bomb on us from a thousand feet up? Take both us and the hard drive out in one gigantic blow.

It must have been because of Mom. How he felt about her. What he needed. Or hoped for, despite everything. So more precise targeting was necessary.

Or maybe I'm wrong. Maybe he wanted to see us die up

close and personal. Because I could see the red camera lights on the drones, and they were recording.

Anyway. Once I was as safe as possible, Mom went into action.

I didn't see everything. There were wall fragments flying everywhere and it was incredibly loud, so I had to keep closing my eyes and putting my fingers in my ears. But I saw enough. I saw Mom rip apart a drone with her bare hands—well, gauntlets. That was awesome. And then she did this midair maneuver where she fried one drone with a boot rocket while swinging a second one right into a bank of computer equipment, which shorted out.

Which left one final drone. Mom floated there, in midair, looking at it. It looked back at her and chattered out a few bullets, which spanged off Mom like they were nothing. It fired a missile. At such close range, Mom simply caught it and crushed it into a ball, the same way I did with that car. It looked even more awesome when you got to see it with your own eyes, not through the monitor. And then Mom held out her hand, palm up, and the thing crumpled to the floor, done.

The whole fight had taken thirty seconds. Maybe.

Mom touched down and gently, so gently, pulled me up from behind the wall. "Are you all right?" she asked.

I asked her what that last thing was.

"Microwaves," she said. "Fried its insides."

I didn't know the suit could do that.

"Not everything was in the files," she said. "There's so much you don't know."

She stopped and leaned over, and for a minute I thought she was going to give me a hug. But she reached past me and lifted up Kaz. I thought she was going to, I don't know, lay him to rest or something.

But she was just moving him aside. To get what was underneath him.

The hard drive. In a million jillion pieces.

Nobody, absolutely nobody, could have done anything with *that*.

I gave her a big hug, trying to ignore the fact that it felt like putting my arms around a truck. She took her helmet off, and leaned over, and gave me a soft kiss on the head.

And then we both heard it.

That voice, that smooth, calm voice, coming from a computer. No, from all the computers—the ones that weren't fried by the explosion.

"What a beautiful moment," Mr. Jones said.

⌐

It was like a scene from one of those music videos from the eighties, the ones you can find on YouTube. A guy in a Halloween mask—one of those death's head ones this time—showing up on five different screens at once. It was almost silly, except, of course, it wasn't.

Mayhem and Mr. Jones stared at each other for a moment.

Then my mom spoke.

"Come on, Leonard," she said. "I'm not going to talk to you while you're wearing that stupid thing. Take it off."

The mask didn't budge.

I got this feeling that for the first time since I'd met him,

I was sure—absolutely, completely certain—that Mr. Jones, Leonard, didn't know what to do.

I could relate. This was his Rebecca encounter, kind of. I mean, on the one hand, I had never attacked Rebecca with drones. On the other hand, my mom and Mr. Jones had an actual history. . . .

Wait. I'm having this horrible image of Mom and Mr. Jones, you know, together. Make it stop. Make it stop. Make it—okay. It's gone. Mostly. That's . . . I mean . . . I can't. Not ever, but especially not now.

The point is that I'm pretty sure that right then, Mr. Jones—the guy who always, always had a plan—didn't know what he was going to do. I'm sure he had thought through options. I'm sure he'd played out this conversation a hundred times. But this I know from personal experience: when you're in love, or obsessed, or both, all that goes out the window when the actual moment comes.

Maybe he'd told himself something like, *I'm going to keep the mask on. It shows I'm in control. Whatever she says, whatever arguments or threats she makes, it won't matter.*

But if that's what he said, he was right. It didn't matter. Because she said what she said, that one sentence, and he took off the mask.

I guess I wasn't surprised. I'd've done the same thing. In his shoes. Lord knows I'd done worse.

So what did he look like? I probably shouldn't say. I mean, if someone hears this, that means I'm probably already in jail, but there are worse fates than that. . . . The truth is, it doesn't matter. He's not like this frightful supervillain with a burned-up pizza face, or a mysterious set of scars or mystical tattoos. He's just a guy. He looks like a middle-aged guy. That's what he looks like.

"It's good to see you, Barbara," is what he said. "We're really seeing each other, face-to-face, for the first time. In so many years." That's when I noticed that his hands were trembling. And even there, in the middle of a bombed-out store, Kaz's body lying three feet from me, I felt a stab of sudden sympathy—empathy? I can never remember which is which—for the man currently holding my dad hostage. I guess I felt like we had some things in common.

My mom told him, in calm, soothing language that I think would have sounded natural coming from a psychologist—or, now that I think about it, a hostage negotiator—that she wished she could say the same, but they were in a difficult situation. "But maybe that could change," she said. "Maybe we can change that together. Even after all this time, after everything, maybe there's a way out. Especially now that"—and she pointed to me—"now that things are more out in the open."

Let my dad go, she said, and leave us alone, and that would be the end of it. We would walk away. Heal. And then—who knew? Maybe in a while, they could do business again. Maybe even become friends. Probably a long while, but maybe. They'd both been around enough to know those things sometimes happened.

"Or alternatively," she said. "I could destroy you. It's your choice."

My mom is a world-class actor. Liar? Let's say actor. Even though the stuff about them being friends one day was hard to swallow, she really sold it. And she was even able to give off this vibe—it makes me nauseated to say it, but it's true—that one day, there could be more than that. That maybe she'd find that she had changed, Dad had changed, he wasn't what she remembered, she'd been in love with a memory. And that she'd face up to what she hadn't wanted to admit: the strong, decisive genius was who she was supposed to have been with all along. It might take some time, maybe even that long time she was referring to, to put her conscience at ease, but she could see it happening.

She didn't say any of that. She didn't think it, either. At least, I'm almost positive she didn't. But it was there, in her tone and her body language, subtle, subtle. Even the threat part seemed almost . . . regretful. *What a tragedy it would be. To have to blow up a real man like you.*

Which is another way of saying that although Mr. Jones is like a hundred times smarter than me, and I knew what Mom was saying was pure bull, it took him a full ten seconds to respond.

And he smiled when he did. When we saw that smile . . . the best way I can put it is that my mom shrunk a little bit. Because she knew it hadn't worked. She'd put her best shot out there, and it hadn't done the trick.

When he finished smiling, he said, "I have a counteroffer. Here it is. I will kill Gerry in sixty minutes."

✐

Unless.

Unless my mom agreed to take his place.

That was the counteroffer: a trade. My dad would be free

to come back and live with me. And my mom would stay as Mr. Jones's, well, *guest* was the word he used, but who were we kidding.

Oh, and it had to happen right away.

It would be easy enough. All my mom had to do was finish putting on the Mayhem suit, and then disable the override switch. Then Mr. Jones would airlift her to his favorite undisclosed location by remote control. The minute he had control of the suit, he said, he'd let my dad go.

And that was when I spoke up for the first time.

Well, shouted, more than spoke up, really. I said this was insane. I said there was no way we would do it. I said Mom would kick his butt all the way to next Sunday and back again.

No one paid the slightest bit of attention.

There was about five seconds of silence after I finished my tantrum. And then my mom asked Mr. Jones, "What makes you think I'd trust you to keep your word?"

To which he responded, "Once I have what I want, what do I care about anything else?"

He tried to smile big again when he said it, make it a real supervillain thing, but now he didn't have the mask on and I could see the truth of it. The desperation.

Then he added, "Not that you have much in the way of choice. Trusting me is your only option. If you don't, I'll kill Gerry anyway." And then he made a big show out of looking at his watch. "In . . . fifty-seven minutes."

And this time—I'm sure we both noticed—his hands weren't trembling.

My mom took a deep breath, looked Mr. Jones straight in

the eye, and said, "I'll have to call Bailey a cab if I'm not driving him back. It'll take some time."

It was the most ridiculous thing to say—I mean, I actually laughed out loud. And then immediately felt terrible. Terrible and horrified, all at once.

Because this was happening.

She put her hands on my shoulders, and told me she needed me. I stopped her to say no, you've got it wrong, I need *you*, and she interrupted me—I think she knew she had to get through it, before she couldn't, and there wasn't a lot of time to waste—and she said she needed me at home, transmitting proof of life.

She could see in my face that I didn't get it. She turned back to the screens. "Leonard," she said, "let me be clear here. I understand that you are probably clinging to some twisted fantasy about Stockholm syndrome." Which I looked up, by the way, on the way home. It means prisoners falling in love with their jailers. "This is not going to happen." But with that same . . . tone, that slight hesitation, letting him hang on to the chance that maybe she couldn't say it, to him or even to herself, but that maybe, just maybe, given time and circumstance, it just possibly could.

It was just a strategy. I'm sure it was.

But she kept talking. "I can tell you this: be smart. It's going to happen *even less* if Bailey doesn't send me proof of Gerry's safe return."

We waited. It was impossible to tell what Mr. Jones was thinking. At least for me it was. The only thing I knew for sure was that the seconds were ticking away.

Finally, "Deal," he said. "Five minutes after you're in the air, Gerry's on his way. Any time in the next fifty-four minutes is fine."

"Deal," my mom replied. And then she screamed.

It was a long, loud scream, accompanied by gunfire.

Hers.

And by the time she was done, every computer in the room that had shown Mr. Jones's smug, smiling face was in tiny pieces.

NOW. SATURDAY. 5:17 P.M.

Hold on. I think I hear a knock. I hear something, anyway.

Maybe it's Dad.

Maybe it isn't.

Wouldn't Dad still have his own key?

It's stopped. Unless it wasn't there to begin with. Unless it was just my imagination.

Unless . . .

I'm just freaking myself out here. Sit tight. Keep going.

TWO HOURS AGO

There wasn't much to say before she went.

I mean, of course there was. But what are the things you say when you know that, in a little over forty-five minutes, you're never going to see your mom again?

I spent a lot of that time in her arms. As in, cradled by Mayhem in midair, like I was a baby. We'd had to get out of the comic shop fast, before the SWAT teams arrived, and so she flew me back to a ravine, a mile or two away from the hatch, from home. That's where we had our final conversation.

I told her I was going to find a way to get her back. She told me—crying, but insisting—that that was something I could never do. For my own safety, and for Dad's, I had to promise her: I would *never* try to track her down, or Mr. Jones. I would never go to the police or the government. I would try to live my life with Dad, to grow up to be the happiest and best person I could be, and to forget everything about these past few months—everything except that she would always, always, *always* love us.

We were both bawling through this. I mean, snotting

crying. But when I really lost it—I couldn't even see—was when she told me I was the one who was going to have to tell Dad it was okay if he wanted to get married again. "You need a mom," she said, and that was—I mean that was it.

I'm sorry. I have to stop here for a second.

Okay. There were other things, too. She asked me if I wanted her recipe for tuna noodle casserole. And although I did, otherwise I'd never eat it again, I didn't want to spend our time together talking about celery or parmesan cheese or whatever. Then she tried to give me advice on how to be a good man—but it felt too much like something from a death-bed, and I just couldn't.

So we spent most of the time holding each other and hugging.

I mean, that's what you do, right? In a situation like that?

I don't think it was a bad way to spend the time. I'll live with that.

And then, precisely fifty-nine minutes and forty-six seconds after Mr. Jones had made his counteroffer, my mom sealed herself into the Mayhem suit. I couldn't see her flip the override switch, of course, but she must have. Since all of a sudden the suit rocketed away.

And Mr. Jones must have frozen the arms and the vocal circuits, too. Because she didn't say goodbye. Or even wave.

So now here I am, sitting on my bed. In my room. Waiting.

He'll come in. We'll hug. We'll take the picture right away, and—

I just realized something. No one told me what to do with the picture once I take it.

I mean, it's not like I have Mr. Jones's e-mail address . . . and I've never been able to text him. I can't text to a number with no area code. It's always been one-way.

Was he assuming that since he has access to my phone he'll just find the photo there?

Or did he never intend to show it to her?

But he has to, right? I mean, that's the whole *proof* part of *proof of life.*

I just had another thought. This one's worse.

Mr. Jones is an evil mastermind. It wouldn't be too hard for him to make a fake photo or video, would it? I mean, people on YouTube do it all the time. And if he did that . . . then he wouldn't have to let my dad go in the first place.

And when you think about it: Why would he? My dad may

not be a genius supervillain like my mom—at least, I don't think he is—but he's dangerous for Mr. Jones to have walking around. I mean, my dad knows who he is. He's seen his face.

And so have I.

And I don't have the Mayhem suit anymore.

Listen to me, talking to myself like this. I'm freaking myself out here. It's Dad at the door. It's got to be. It's not going to be, I don't know, Assassin and two of his Bloody Front buddies looking for revenge. Right?

More knocking.

Maybe Dad's just trying to be sensitive. He knows this is going to be tough. He's not going to burst in on me. He'll let me come to the door. Take my own time.

The problem is that I have no idea if that's the kind of thing Dad would do. It's been a long time.

The knocking's stopped. I wonder if that's a good thing or a bad thing.

Who's there?

NOW. SATURDAY. 10:14 P.M.

Yes!

Yes yes yes yes yes yes!

I can't believe that worked!!!!

So. Here's the first thing. I was right.

Mr. Jones was not, in fact, planning to arrange a happy—okay, semi-happy, given the circumstances—reunion. He was planning a double-cross the entire time. I bet he was on the phone to Assassin the minute my mom took off, giving him my home address.

It's just that by the time they got to my house, I wasn't there.

I was approximately one thousand feet away.

Which is not a lot, it's true.

It just seems like more when the distance is vertical.

Maybe I should explain. Now that we're back home.

I thought maybe the Bloody Front would have planted a bomb or poison gas when it made a big mess of the place looking for me. But as soon as we got in, Mom swept it with every piece of technology she has. She swears it's clean. So I have a little more time now.

As soon as I'm done with this, we're going to sit down and have dinner.

All three of us.

And Mr. Jones, if you're listening in, you might enjoy hearing the story of how you got absolutely, positively hosed.

What do I mean, saying *if*. I know you're listening.

In fact, we were counting on it.

THIS AFTERNOON

TAKE TWO

Mom had figured it out right away. The double-cross. I mean, even *I'd* suspected it, and I'm not 1 percent the genius she is. But she didn't say anything about it. Not until we were alone. Not until she had shot out the computers and, along with them, your method of spying on us, Mr. Jones.

I imagine that to you it looked like she had lost it. Let me tell you something, Leonard. Mom never loses control. Mom is in *charge*.

I thought I'd understood that. But until I saw her lower the guns, still smoking, bullet casings clattering on the floor, and then heard her say, "Come on, Bailey, we have a lot to do," I don't think I had any idea.

You see, Mr. Jones, you did her a bit of a favor, arranging your final battle—what you thought was your final battle—in Computer Hacker Central. Mom knows electronics inside and out. She built the Mayhem suit, after all. And now she was surrounded by them. Some of it blown up and shot to pieces, yeah, but there was enough in working order—she had kept enough in working order; she'd aimed *very* carefully—for her to do what she needed to do.

You've probably figured out what that was by now, wherever you're hiding. I wonder where that could be. A super-secret invisible submarine? A private island? I don't care, really. As long as you stay there . . .

Three things she needed to do.

One: Fix my phone.

Maybe you thought there was only five minutes' worth of conversation in almost an hour because we spent the rest of the time crying and comforting each other. That's what it sounded like, right?

Well, we did do that. For about thirty seconds. And then Mom chopped and looped and slowed the digital stream so that those thirty seconds took up about forty-five minutes. If you were listening in—and we knew you were—you thought you were eavesdropping on what was going on.

But you weren't. Leonard.

Time elapsed for number one: about, I don't know, three or four minutes. Mom was working fast.

Two: She'd already messed with time. Now it was space's turn. You're not the only person who can play with GPS results, it turns out. The phone showed us spending most of the hour in the ravine near our house. But we were not. We were in the May-cave, working hard.

You were on the lookout for us to mess with our phones, see. But you didn't expect us to mess with the local cell towers. The ones that report phones' locations. The ones that Mom had hacked a month ago. And hadn't done anything with until now.

Time elapsed for number two: less than a minute.

Most of our time was spent on thing number three.

A homing device. Putting that together with stuff liberated from Kaz's computers was pretty straightforward. For my mom, I mean, not for me. The hard part was the plastic coating.

Plastic coating, of course, so that she could swallow it.

The only way to make sure she could get it into your secret hideout undiscovered.

I can't believe I'm using those words unironically, but that's what it is, right? You hid out for years there, in secret . . . so secret hideout it is.

Well, *was*, anyway. Now it's charcoal.

Back to my tale of triumph.

Before we wrapped up, we checked, double-checked, and triple-checked that the device signal was working. It showed up loud and clear on my receiver.

The one inside the second suit of armor.

⬩

I know, right? *Whaaat?* I mean, *second suit of armor*, what's that about?

Sorry . . . I'm a little punchy. Kicking some major Mr. Jones butt tends to do that to you.

The point is—*Leonard*—you didn't know about the second Mayhem suit. To be fair, *I* didn't know about the second Mayhem suit. But I should have realized a lot earlier that the

I'm-just-working-my-contacts business Mom was giving me after I found out she was Mayhem was too . . . passive for someone like her.

I mean, this is someone who used to rob banks with you. She doesn't twiddle her thumbs.

She was building another Mayhem suit. And as soon as she was finished with it, she was going to use it. On you.

But things were more difficult the second time around since she knew you were watching her every move. She assumed you had her credit cards monitored, her movements tracked. She was being constantly watched by covert drones. It wasn't like she could go out and buy thousands of dollars' worth of electronics equipment to build Mayhem Jr.

Which means it took forever.

Even now, after everything that's happened, I'm only beginning to understand what you put her through. I knew she was depressed after the disappearance. But now I don't know how she avoided going insane.

Somehow she stayed sane, and she built the suit. Day by day, week by week, month by month, she did a thousand little bits of soldering and programming. And under cover of darkness, she built it. *She persisted*, that's how the saying goes, right? She definitely did. And she built it.

At least, mostly. I mean, you've seen it close up, Leonard. I wouldn't exactly call it a finished product. In our Shakespeare unit this year we read *Hamlet*, and there's this description that stuck with me where Hamlet calls his uncle a king of shreds and patches. And that's what this second suit is. A thing of shreds and patches.

It looks like it was put together inside a junkyard. There are pieces that stick out, and I'm not going to lie, it's a pain to put on. It's not made of whatever the real Mayhem suit is, so it doesn't armorize. You have to climb into it. And when I did, there are these snaggy pieces that gave me scratches up and down my left calf, and I think the way the missile strut supports are uneven has given me a neck crick that might have me needing a chiropractor.

But you have to admit, it got the job done.

My mom had had no intention of letting me know about it. Two Mayhem suits meant two Mayhems, and as far as she was concerned that was one Mayhem too many. She had been walking on knives, last night, trying to decide if she should use the suit to rescue me. Knowing that if she had to, she would, but that it would mean I would insist on using it myself. And so that was how it was going to stay—her in Mayhem Classic, the second suit in mothballs, and me packed off to some black-hat babysitting service—until you made that impossible, with what you did to Kaz, and with your so-called deal.

Ironically, this plan let me be the one to beat you in the end. I almost feel grateful. Almost.

But, you may ask, why didn't I find the suit before? All that time I spent in the May-cave? Well, it wasn't in the May-cave, at least not after my first visit—and I was, um, kind of distracted that first time. Mom moved it after she knew I'd found the lab. To a perfect hiding place, the one area of our house she knew no teenage boy would ever go of his own free will.

The laundry room.

It wasn't even hidden that well. Or maybe a better way to put it is that it was hidden really well, but in plain sight. It was camouflaged as piled-up junk in the back corner. I had seen it, in fact, when I'd searched the house, but figured it was some rusty junk from the garage. And it had a unique repeller field on it. Not a high-tech one: I'd just been afraid that if I asked about it, Mom would assign me some chore like taking it to the recycling center. So I paid as little attention to it as possible, which was, of course, exactly Mom's plan.

It's sad when you think you're so clever, but it turns out other people can read you like a book.

Maybe you know what I mean.

Anyway, when Mom shook the suit out, and the magnetic fields locked on, and the pieces came flying and clacking together—not quite as cool as armorizing, but pretty freaking incredible—I told her I was ready for anything. Any plan. Any mission.

And I could see from the look on her face that she wasn't entirely sure that was true.

She saw me seeing her, and tried something like, *It's not that I don't trust you, it's the armor I'm worried about,* but she could tell I wasn't buying it, and she changed tack.

"I'm sorry," she said. "It's just that . . . you're my little boy, you know? And no matter what, I'm always going to see you that way. . . . Sometimes that means I don't give you enough credit for what you've accomplished."

I knew that with seventeen minutes left before our deadline, it wasn't the time or place for family therapy, but I have to confess: It did feel good to hear that. I could have done with a bit more—there had been a few years without much in the way of positive reinforcement—but General Mom, having seen she'd rallied her troops, moved on.

She told me you were coming for me. Not in person, since you'd be too busy gloating and celebrating your triumph, or, maybe, practicing your explanation to Mom about how Dad had suffered a tragic accident on his way home. You'd send someone. Within a few minutes of her taking flight.

Someone to take care of loose ends.

"I hate putting you in this position," she said. "All I want to do is keep you safe. But we're beyond that now. This is the only way to be safe. For you, first and foremost, and for all of us."

You know, thinking about it now, it's not clear that that was true. Wouldn't it have been safer for me if Mom had told you to go pound sand? It would have sacrificed Dad, but she would have been around to protect me. . . . I mean, it worked out—obviously—but it wasn't what you'd call the safe play.

Or was there no safe play? If she had done that, wouldn't we have spent our lives looking over our shoulders, waiting for the next time you came back? I don't know. All I know for sure is that Mom isn't the type of parent I grew up thinking she was. Safe, regular.

I guess I know one other thing. None of that matters. Because there was absolutely no way I was not doing this. To save my dad, and now, my mom. But it was more than that. It was for Caroline, and what you did to her.

And for me. For the lying, and the manipulation. For what you did to me.

I was not to engage.

That's what Mom said. No matter what.

Yes, it would have been the easiest thing in the world for me to put on the suit—well, not the easiest, because like I said that thing scratched like you wouldn't believe—and to blast whatever welcoming party you were sending me into the stratosphere. Since Mom had designed this suit on her own, there was no back door, no remote control. Neither you, nor anyone you sent, had any idea this was coming.

A point which I think has been made more than clear by now.

But there was a chance that at least one of your henchmen would report it before I took them out. I mean, there was no guarantee you wouldn't be watching the whole operation on helmet cameras. And that would have ruined the big show.

So it had to look like I was just a kid on the run. Like I had gotten spooked, and bolted, and they had just missed me.

They went into the ravine, didn't they, Leonard? I bet that's what they did. They figured I'd slipped into the May-cave, then went out the back. That was what we thought might happen. Hoped, anyway. It's a long ravine, with lots of places for a person my size to hide. Even with thermal sensors and night-vision binoculars and whatever other gadgets they were packing, it probably would've taken them fifteen, twenty minutes—*after* they finished searching the house—to check and clear it. I was long gone.

By the way, the next time you talk to them, tell them I don't appreciate what they did to my room.

Or maybe I'll get the chance to tell them myself.

The hardest part of the plan—at least for me—was the lying.

It's true. I'd gotten better at lying over the past few months. Not as good as you, of course. I'd lied to my mom, to Rebecca, to—to Caroline, and, let's not forget, to myself. But most of those lies were . . . *natural* is the best word I can think of. They spilled out, one after another, and they sort of . . . gained momentum.

Doing it *intentionally*—recording the story we'd rehearsed about how I was sitting at home waiting for Dad—that was harder. In reality, I was strapping on the backplates, configuring the visor settings, adjusting the boot jets. Thinking of everything. Remembering the order Mom and I had agreed on. Keeping my breath steady and even, trying not to repeat my takeoff checklist under my breath.

You didn't notice, did you, Mr. Jones? I'll take that as a compliment.

You know what? I wonder whether you even listened at all, once Mom was on her way. You probably just . . . turned me off, stopped listening, since I didn't matter anymore.

Well, I bet you're listening now.

It took forever to do all that. Mom had gone through it with me half a dozen times. When I told her I'd gotten it, she made me tell her how to do it backward, then every second step, then every fourth. I actually thought at one point that if this did end up being our last hour together, my last memories of her would be really annoying.

But it worked. Even while I was fake pouring out my heart

on the recording—and, yeah, once or twice, having some genuine emotional moments—even while I was keeping an eye on the video feeds Mom had installed on our front door, I was assembling, checking, and rechecking the suit, making sure it was ready to go.

And that it was fully armed.

So the moment the screens showed a gas and electricity truck driving up to our house, and the monitor's magnification control spotted the scars running down one of the workmen's cheeks, I was out of there.

All that *I think I hear a knock* and *Wouldn't Dad still have his own key?* routine was delivered straight to you from high in the sky. I mean, I had cloud cover by the time they hit our living room.

And I was on the hunt, following Mom's homing device to wherever you were taking her.

Our big X-factor—the variables in the plan we had no way of accounting for—were speed and distance. The device was telling me that you were flying Mom somewhere at approximately two hundred miles an hour. Not even close to the real Mayhem suit's top speed. But still too fast. Mom was basically encased inside a fighter jet. And I very much wasn't.

The suit gave me some protection, but I could feel the wind punching me, smacking me around, threatening to tear my head right off my neck. At least that's what it felt like. I couldn't go half as fast as she was going, plus she had had a massive head start.

Luckily, you didn't take her very far.

I guess it's not shocking that you wanted to be near us—near her, I mean. It's the one thing that's kept you going all these years, right, Leonard? And distances are tricky things. It's like when someone you know from camp lives twenty miles away and goes to a different school, and you never see him during the school year. You could have been thirty miles away from our town and we'd still never have run into you.

Especially, you know, since you were hiding inside a mountain.

The same mountain where I dropped off the money after my first robbery, it turns out.

I remember being confused about how you got there, since there weren't any roads anywhere nearby. Well, I guess— how did you put it in those training sessions of ours?—I had to stop thinking so two-dimensionally. What I should have said was that there weren't any roads on the *exterior* of the mountain. Inside it was another matter.

Here's one thing I've wondered: Don't a lot of your projects need construction crews? And for someone who's all about supersecrecy, isn't that a big problem? I mean, I only got a quick look as I was busy destroying everything I could on my way into the center of the mountain, but it did seem like the kind of place that took a long time to build.

I'd say I'm sorry about the mess, but, you know, I'm not.

My guess is, Leonard, that you didn't build it. You don't do things you can get other people to do for you, and with your government contacts, maybe . . . maybe it was one of those abandoned Cold War places, like where the top brass were supposed to hide if the Russians started bombing. And since you're a comic-book guy, the idea of a secret underground mountain lair was too tempting to pass up. Am I getting warm? And then—this feels like you, too—you somehow arranged to have it disappear from the government's records.

Or, on the other hand, maybe they know exactly where it is. They're just too scared of you to do anything about it.

Dad? Is that you?

That was Dad calling me.

Dad. Calling me. From down the hall.

Just saying those words . . .

He was letting me know we were going to have dinner soon. It's later than we usually eat, but you can look at it another way—we're already six years late for family dinner.

We're ordering in, obviously. I don't think anyone's in emotional shape to cook. Even figuring out where to order from—the fact that we're juggling three voices, three opinions, rather than two—that in itself made Mom sniffle and Dad's voice get all hoarse and throaty.

Sushi. We haven't had it since the night Dad disappeared. Symbolic or something.

Apparently, it's my dad's favorite. I never knew.

I'll have time to get to know him again, I guess.

I can't wait.

But I made them promise that I could finish this first, before we ate.

I earned it.

So. Mr. Jones. In case you haven't yet been able to review your security footage, here's what happened.

I should have known better than to doubt Mom. But when the homing signal brought me to the side of a mountain in the middle of nowhere . . . I have to admit, I started having dark thoughts. Had something gone wrong with the electronics? Had you found the device—I didn't even want to think about how—and sent me off on a wild goose chase?

It almost worked, by the way. The camouflage. Mom was at least twenty minutes ahead of me, and I kept hearing this voice in my head: *She's getting farther away, she could be anywhere, anywhere at all.*

And then I saw it. Or the thermal scanners did. I don't think it was visible to the naked eye. That tiny bit of metal, warm metal, poking up out of the mountain.

It could have been an exhaust vent, or a wireless antenna, or just a mistake in construction. But I knew it meant that something was there, underneath. And then I realized that the mountain looked . . . familiar. From our earlier encounter. And that was all I needed.

Had you just been so eager to get your hands on the loot from that first robbery that you arranged to meet close to home? Or were you so confident I wouldn't suspect anything that you didn't care? I think probably it was the second. Which was understandable since you had been leading me around by the nose the whole time, and I hadn't suspected a thing. Well, that's not true. I had some suspicions, you have to give me credit for those.

Not that I need you to give me credit for anything. I don't care what you think. . . .

The point is, you would have been right, if it wasn't for the homing signal. And the suit's instruments. And then, a minute later, the antiaircraft missile launchers and machine-gun embankments that popped out of the ground.

Those were good indicators I was on the right track, too.

We had prepared for this, Mom and I. Or at least talked through the possibility. You were confident, we knew, but also paranoid. Wherever you were stationed was going to be stocked with sensors and crammed with defenses. But what you didn't have was the Mayhem technology. Without my mom, you'd never been able to get it right.

But Mayhem was never yours. It was Mom's. And now mine.

Still, for all your lies, there was at least one thing you told me that was true. Something you said at the beginning. This rescue-mission thing—it couldn't be done with a drone. It needed a person. An alert, experienced, committed person.

Funny how that came back to bite you, huh?

I understand I may sound like I'm bragging here. But you know what? I don't care. Because after mess-ups and mistakes and losing someone I loved, I. Rocked. This.

I fried the antiaircraft missiles before they could get anywhere near me. Well, I fried their targeting circuitry, which meant they spiraled and fritzed all over the place and then exploded against the side of the mountain. Which, on the one hand, looked enormously cool. On the other hand, it started a fire. As someone who cares about the environment, I felt bad about that, seeing the trees and brush smolder and go up. But it made your getaway a lot, lot harder, I'm sure. Which helps, more than a little.

It was the missile explosions that knocked out the machine guns. Which looks like genius on my part, but I have to admit it was a coincidence. Either way, those big explosions opened up the small machine-gun ports, turning them into medium-size jagged holes. With a little bit of Mayhem-ing, they got ripped open into big jagged holes. Big enough to crawl in through.

I burned myself against the still-cooling metal on the way in. Not seriously, I'm sure you'll be disappointed to hear, but enough to remind me that this wasn't the real Mayhem suit. I was significantly more vulnerable.

Which had been the last thing Mom had said, before she got into the real suit. And it hadn't just been about the suit. It was about getting overconfident. Being cocky.

Which she was right about, I guess. I mean, I almost took care of you for good, didn't I? If it wasn't for that one stupid mistake. . . .

But I'm not going to focus on that now. This is a good night. We *won*. Thanks to good decisions I made. And I'm just a kid, right?

Forget I said that. I'm not asking you for approval. That's ridiculous.

Let me get back to the story of how I saved Mom and Dad and set your plan, whatever it is, back years. At least.

The maintenance tunnel servicing the machine guns connected to a slightly larger hallway, and that hallway led to the main access corridor. I knew I had to hurry. You were clearly on red alert, and even if the fires and explosions had knocked out any external cameras—and there was no way I was going to bet on that—I could see other cameras, up and down the halls, swiveling in my direction as I passed. You knew I was coming.

So I didn't take the scenic route. I bashed as direct a line as possible from my entry point to the location of the homing signal, according to the map my suit was drawing for me on the monitors. Wherever the direct line didn't involve a door, I made one. With fists and grenades.

I was keeping an eye out for goons and henchmen to disarm—remember, no killing—but there weren't any. In fact, there wasn't *anyone*. Miles of rooms, it seemed like, and just you and your prisoners. Is that who you are? Is that how you live?

I don't pity you. Considering everything you put my family through. Everything you've done to the world, to innocent people. But I imagine you, month after month, year after year, wandering the halls there . . .

Sympathy for the devil. Huh. None of that.

Then it was time for the next trick up my mechanical sleeve. *Distraction*, my mom had told me. *Once you've lost the element of surprise, keep him off-balance.*

You don't get the rumble and roar with Mayhem Jr. that you get with the original, but there's an impressive amplification. I'm pretty sure you heard me, not just through the screens, not just through the speakers, but through the walls. *I'm coming for you, Mr. Jones.* In the unlikely case that you missed that, I know you heard what came next: a personal, curated Bailey playlist of pure 100 percent rock and roll, guaranteed to raise . . . well, maybe not a smile, like Sgt. Pepper and the band, but hopefully something.

Especially since I was playing it at earsplitting volume.

You get some awfully good acoustics inside a mountain. Lots of echoes. I was hoping that the music, along with the feedback distortion from computers in rooms up and down the halls, would make it hard for anyone not inside an armored suit—like, say, you—to think rationally.

And so maybe you'd even try to turn off the computers.

Because—don't ask me the details—as computers cycle down, they're more susceptible to the virus Mom had created. The one my suit was broadcasting in every direction as I flew through the halls. Crunching through any server I could find, gobbling up your data, transmitting it back to the drives Mom had hooked up in the May-cave . . .

Yeah, the scientist's precious hard drive got cooked by the drones at Kaz's place. But that doesn't matter anymore. We've got it all. Petabytes of it. Everything you had, we sucked it dry. Whatever your plans are, we'll know. And we'll figure out how to stop them.

Did you realize that? I think you did. Judging from how freaked out you were when I finally found you.

I mean, I get it. A good chunk of your hideout was on fire. There was music blasting all over the place. And that tablet you always carried around was probably flashing zillions of warnings about data loss and security breaches and who knows what else.

I should have been happy, seeing that. Triumphant. I should have said something like, *Who's the boss, now?* The Mayhem Jr. suit doesn't have the volume of the original, but it would have been pretty epic.

But I didn't have time to gloat. I didn't even think about it, then.

Seeing someone holding a gun to your father's head drives those snappy comments right out of your mind.

It took me a second to register what was happening.

The door I'd smashed through was disintegrating around me, and even though I knew the suit's visor would block out wooden splinters or pieces of shrapnel, I had the bad habit of closing my eyes as I went through something solid.

But then I blinked, and the dust settled, and what I saw . . .

Well, the first thing I saw, actually, was the pizza.

Boxes and boxes of it, open along a long table. Every topping combination imaginable, even—gross—Hawaiian. You could have fed two dozen people, easily.

But that's not what you were doing. I recognized the boxes.

They were from Strombolini's, this place Mom talked about loving when she was in college. When the two of you knew each other.

You know, a long time ago, when I was a kid and saw snow—in our part of the country, it doesn't snow often, so it was cool to see it—Mom used to tell me this story about college. At midnight the night of the first snowfall of the school year, she would go with a friend of hers to Strombolini's and share a whole pizza. Each year meant different toppings, and they had to be kind of bizarre. The first year was pepperoni and anchovies, the next was, I don't remember, something cheesy, but with, maybe, salad dressing. And senior year was Hawaiian. I remember that.

Was that friend you, Mr. Jones? Yuck.

I guess this was your psycho way of having a special romantic moment.

Look. I don't know much about women. But here's something I can teach you, Leonard. If you literally have to nail the woman you're interested in to the floor by armorizing her giant robot boots so that they weigh hundreds of pounds, and then refuse to let her control them, pizza is not going to do the trick. Especially when you are holding a gun to the head of her husband.

I understand that was not originally part of the pizza plan. Still.

Maybe I sound calm about this now. Maybe. But that's because I know how it ends. And if I wasn't trying, with every bit of me, to stay calm—to tell this straight, and cool—I would be shouting and screaming and cursing all over the place. Like, I mean, you actually *held a gun to my dad's head*. And then what? You would have shot him? In front of me? YOU WOULD HAVE—

All right. It's over now. It's over.

Back to me winning. And you losing.

It looked like Mom had been trying to talk to you when I burst in. It also looked like she hadn't been having much success. You were holding the gun to Dad's head with one hand and tapping at your tablet with the other.

I'm guessing that had something to do with the drones that came up behind me. No big deal—radar, auto-targeting, and thermal bursts took them down as quickly as they came. Which was good. Because I was not concentrating, in that moment. I had lost focus.

I was seeing my dad.

I was seeing him look at me, and look so happy. There was a bullet about six inches from his brain and it did not seem to concern him in the least.

But no one was going to die. Nobody.

My mom looked at the two of us and she smiled, and she said loudly, "I love you both so much. Forever and ever."

And it worked.

I mean, it's not that she didn't mean it. But it was also a calculated move. She was thinking that hearing that, on top of everything else, might make you . . . sloppy. Send you over the edge.

And it did.

I'd never seen it before, but I guess they call it pistol-whipping. You took the gun, and you cold-cocked my dad on the head, just *whapped* him. It was . . .

I thought I hated you before. But I could almost see my hatred at that point, streaming out of me. It was clear and cold and green and I wanted to take it and strangle you with it. To forget about everything else and fly for your throat.

I think it must have been reflex for you. Right? After all those years of not being able to kill my dad. Knowing that no matter how much you wanted to, that was the one thing you couldn't do, because you needed him alive to get Mom.

Or maybe you were so obsessed with your idea of being a supervillain, right out of a comic, that you felt, somewhere, subconsciously, that as the bad guy, no matter how much of a genius you are, you're supposed to make a stupid mistake at the end.

I don't know. But one thing's for sure. It was a stupid mistake.

Because as my dad slumped to the floor, bleeding from his scalp, unconscious, you gave me a clear shot.

Which I should have taken. But I didn't.

I'd like to tell you it was because I'm better than you. Because I had made this deal with myself—no killing—and no matter how much someone might deserve it, I was going to live up to my promise. I should probably say that.

But I guess maybe I'm not talking to you after all. I'm talking to myself, too, and I have to be honest. Honestly? I'd've been fine blowing your head off. And it would have been easy, too. Flexing one finger, that was it.

The real truth, the honest truth, is that I just didn't think of it.

I wanted to hit you. Plain and pure and simple. And as I'm sure you remember, that is exactly what I did.

I flew across the room and smashed into you with a tackle that would have made Logan proud. I felt your ribs break, and that made me happy. I yanked you clear of my dad. Turned your gun into scrap metal. And then I held you high in the air and flipped up Mayhem Jr.'s visor and looked you right in the face. Eye to eye.

And it was terrible.

I mean, it should have been a moment of triumph, right? The big heroic thing to do? But you were so angry, and hateful, and in pain, too, all sorts, that I couldn't do the regular comic-book thing. I couldn't just toss off some clever line, even if I'd been able to think of one. I couldn't say something moral and righteous and good guy–ish.

I mean, given everything, I didn't have the right, did I?

So instead I threw you across the room.

I saw you bounce off the wall and land in a heap, and I think I might have heard something crack, but I wasn't paying much attention. I was picking up my dad.

He was unconscious—you had hit him hard—so I scooped him up the same way I would grab the neighbor's toddler, back when I used to babysit, when it was time to take her to the changing table and she didn't want to go.

I looked down at him in my arms, bearded and thin, and all I wanted to do was give him a kiss.

So I did.

And then I dropped him.

When Mayhem practically took the back of my head off.

⟋

Overconfident.

Overconfident, overconfident, overconfident.

I should have checked that you were unconscious. I should have tied you up. I *definitely* should have smashed your tablet.

But I didn't do any of those things. And while I was having a mini-reunion with my unconscious father, you had scrambled back to the tablet—like the insect you are—and activated your final weapon. The Mayhem suit, which was still under your control.

With Mom in it.

You must have felt so, so clever. You had finally figured out that the override control was in the helmet.

Which meant that I could see Mom's face, horrified, furious, as her body and arms went after me and Dad.

I flipped around, hunched over Dad, protecting him, and took the first barrage of gunfire on the backplate, but I knew I was in trouble right away. The Mayhem suit—the real one—was faster, stronger, better in every way than the one I was wearing.

You weren't nearly as experienced with it as I was, though, Leonard. That was my one advantage.

I turned over the table, scattering pizza boxes and slices everywhere, and dumped Dad behind it. That wouldn't save him from, say, a missile, but I was hoping you would get too invested in the spectacle of a Mayhem vs. Mayhem cage match to focus on finishing him off. I didn't have a lot of options—I had to focus on Mom, who was now trying to fricassee me with the thermal generators.

"Shift defenses to full, Bailey!" she shouted. Her mouth and her brain were still her own, of course. And without the helmet, you couldn't block her voice from coming through the speakers. I could hear her.

But I couldn't listen. If I did what she said, I'd be playing defense until the battery drained. And then I'd be toast. I had to go on offense.

I flew in toward Mom, and I heard you laugh. It was more of a gasp than a laugh, I suppose. Those ribs must have hurt. Am I right? And then you said something about doing this low-tech, and I had less than a second to wonder what that meant before Mom's arm slammed into my side.

I knew from personal experience what it was like to hit something as Mayhem, but I'd never been on the other side. I can't recommend it. Mom's technology held, and my suit kept my ribs from vaporizing, but I'm going to have bruises for weeks.

On both sides, since you followed it up with her other arm. And then again. And again. She had gotten in close, and we were like boxers at the end of a fight, huddling against each other.

Right when our faces were almost touching, when you couldn't hear us over the banging and clanging and the sound of your own smug ego, Mom whispered, "Put your arms around me. Give me a hug."

I looked at her, confused.

And then she whispered, "And fly backward. Then magic ride."

And I got it.

When I was little, long before Dad disap—I mean, before you kidnapped him—Mom insisted I go to gymnastics. Which I bitterly objected to at the time, but the truth is, I kind of liked it. I was terrible, but I kind of liked it. The thing I was the worst at was somersaults. Clearly, I did not get very far. But mom tried to work with me on them. She did this thing that she called a *two-person forward roll* but I insisted on calling a *magic ride*. I was terrible at it then, and I'm terrible at it now. And to do it in midair . . .

We didn't need to land pretty, though. In fact, that was kind of the point.

This is probably what you remember. Me, jetting backward toward you at top speed, bringing Mayhem with me. You, doing the smart thing under the circumstances, which was to try to fly Mayhem in the opposite direction. But I grabbed hold of Mom even harder, and then I started our magic ride.

I don't know what it looked like coming toward you. A wheel of fate? Something symbolic like that? Probably just a big, messy whirl of metal and flame moving fast and out of control.

You tried to run, but I had managed to aim us well enough to crush the tablet against the wall. Unfortunately, you were holding on to it at the time.

I heard you scream as your hand, well, *went*, along with your control over Mom's suit.

But then you got away.

I mean, we let you go. We had to. When you told us about the self-destruct sequence . . .

Not in the mountain. That would have been too corny, even for you. You're not a go-down-with-the-ship kind of guy. No, you looked us straight in the eye and told us that the destruction of the tablet had triggered a countdown that would lead to the self-destruction of seven of your facilities storing nuclear and biological material. Each of them located within fifteen miles of a major urban center. If you weren't at one of your safe houses within sixty minutes to deactivate the sequence, then, well, *boom*.

My mom said you were bluffing. You said she was welcome to find out, but that there was something she should know: each of those cities had been carefully selected because they held the highest concentration of her friends and associates.

And then here was the funny thing. You named names. And I hadn't heard of any of the people that you mentioned. Not one.

But they were important to Mom, based on her reaction.

Does that mean you know her better than I do? So what if it does, right?

She thought about it for ten seconds. Which is a long time, if you're standing there, in the middle of a battle zone that is also on fire, facing someone who has recently tried to kill you and your family. And then she punched you in the stomach. Not hard enough to disable you—she was always calculating, and she knew you'd need to be able to get to your escape pod or whatever—but *hard*. And then she told you to get the hell out of there. Which you did.

And then so did we.

◢

Flying is nice, as I've said before. It's particularly nice when you do it as a family. And since Mom's instruments didn't indicate any nearby threats, we took our time.

About halfway home, Dad woke up. Mom was carrying him like a child in her metal arms, and he looked up at her, and then he looked at me, and said, "Is this a dream?"

"NO," Mom said with a smile. And then she dearmorized her visor, just the visor—I didn't know you could do that . . . I guess I still have a lot to learn about the suit—and repeated, "No."

And Dad said, "That's good," and fell asleep again. I was worried about a concussion, but Mom said he was fine. I wonder if she's a doctor in addition to the other stuff.

Nothing would surprise me anymore.

Time to go. Sushi's here. And the story's done.

It's just . . .

There's something left to say. Something I need to tell them. Mom. And Dad. And I need to tell them right now.

Caroline.

Now that it's all over, now that the adrenaline's wearing off, this is what's left. And it's burning the back of my throat and clawing at my guts—and that's when I'm not actually paying attention. When I really think about it, it gets hard to breathe.

I left my best friend lying there—

I chickened out. I didn't tell Mom before. I should have, but I didn't. It was in the middle of everything and I had just found out she was Mayhem and my mind was blown and overwhelmed and I couldn't, but that's no excuse. That was . . . weakness.

But I can do it now. I can be strong. I can go down the hall and sit down and say, *Mom, Dad, this is what happened*, and just tell them.

And Mom will tell me that there was nothing I could have done and that it was a tragedy, but it was unavoidable, and Dad will say—well, I don't know what he'll say, but he'll say something—and it won't make me feel better. But I need to do it. It's the first step. To what exactly, I don't know, but it is.

And maybe they can help me figure out what to say to Caroline's parents. Because I have to tell them. Tell them what, I don't know, but I have to tell them *something*.

I owe her that—

Hold it. What's that sound?

It's coming from my laptop.

My chat program is pinging.

It's Rebecca. And . . . it looks like she's tried me ten times, maybe more, already.

Oh, man.

So much has happened in the last twenty-four hours, I haven't focused on the fact that I *stood up the love of my life for the winter formal dance*.

Not that that's even close to the most important thing that's happened in that time. Getting Dad back. Finding out about Mom. Caroline. It's not even in the same *universe*.

But . . .

It's still pinging.

Ten times. She must be furious. Which I get, but to be honest, I assume she'll go back to never having anything to do with me again. It's not like I can give her much of an explanation.

She's asking for video. Why not just text me? She wants to curse me out to my face?

I'll talk to her after dinner. I'll call her back.

But what if . . .

All right. I'm going to answer.

I'm going to.

I'm answering.

"Rebecca?"

"Bailey! Are you all right? What happened to you? I tried to text, a lot, but it says your phone's out of service or something!"

The SIM card, I forgot about the SIM card out the window!

"What?"

"Uh, nothing. Yeah, my phone broke. Listen, Rebecca, I'm—"

"Bailey, we have to talk."

"I know, and I'm so, so sorry, but can we—"

"Right *now*, Bailey. You know what it's about."

"I know, and I can explain—"

"The bracelet, Bailey. You have to tell me about the diamond bracelet."

"The—what?"

"I knew there had to be a story, but—Bailey. The FBI just left my house. And they wanted to know where I got it."

Was this you?

"What?"

"No, Rebecca, sorry. I wasn't talking to you."

"You weren't—"

"Did you tell them? Where you got it?"

"I told them I needed to talk to a lawyer. But Bailey, my parents told them. They're on their way."

"Your parents?"

"The FBI, Bailey. They left about ten minutes ago."

"Rebecca, I have to go."

"Bail—"

Someone's knocking at the door now.

I'd better delete this.

And go downstairs and tell my parents that it's probably not over.

Not yet.

ACKNOWLEDGMENTS

This is not a comic book. But *in* the comic books, there was a well-known character with a big red S on his chest who could squeeze a lump of coal and, through unremitting effort, turn it into a diamond. Sally Morgridge is just such a superhero: an editor who can take a manuscript and give it facets undreamed of by its originator, along with a high shine. I can't thank her enough for her tireless work and her brilliant suggestions.

My gratitude to Sally is only matched by my thankfulness to my agent, Alec Shane, who took a chance on a new writer of fiction. Alec is a remarkable reader, thinker, and advocate, and I am extraordinarily lucky to be able to benefit from his sage advice and good humor. Whatever else I am or may be, from now on, I am also a novelist, and for that, I cannot thank *him* enough.

I am also grateful to the prodigiously talented team who has worked on the book's production: Levente Szabo, for somehow sneaking into my dreams and bringing Mayhem to life with his beautiful cover art, and Chandra Wohleber, for her rigorous and yet simultaneously sensitive copyediting.

My wife, Miri, is nothing like Bailey's mom, except for her genius. And her strength. And her devotion to her children and family. Well, she doesn't have a robot suit hidden away in a secret basement. At least, I don't think she does. It is one of the great gifts of my life that we get to make our lives together.

And our family: Eli, Ezra, and Talia are all a little too young to read this book now, but they are a part of it—from asking if I "worked on the robot book today" to trying to type the manuscript for me. (Sally edited those parts out. Probably for the best.) I love them more than anything.

My brothers, sisters-in-law, and in-laws are as warm and caring as anyone could possibly wish for, and I'm grateful to them—Noah, Andrew, Sara, Rachel, Bob, and Sherry—for all their support. To my nieces and nephews—Boaz, Jordana, Moses, and Delilah—you'll get your copies soon: try not to stay up too late reading, your parents will kill me.

Finally: Mom and Dad.

This book will come out right around your fiftieth anniversary. An awe-inspiring achievement by any measure, but the way the two of you have spent that half century—in love with each other, in dedication to family, in friendship, and in community, working hard to care for others in so many ways, and having so much fun and adventure doing it—evokes something like pure delight on the part of your children, and your grandchildren, who love you so much and wish you every happiness for so many years to come. This book—which, it should be noted for those still reading, is not autobiographical in any way—is for you.